STAR TREK 56:
SANCTUARY

STAR TREK NOVELS

STAR TREK GIANT NOVELS

A *STAR TREK*®
NOVEL

SANCTUARY
JOHN VORNHOLT

TITAN BOOKS
LONDON

STAR TREK 56: SANCTUARY
ISBN 1 85286 428 1

Published by
Titan Books Ltd
19 Valentine Place
London SE1 8QH

First Titan Edition September 1992
10 9 8 7 6 5 4 3 2 1

Printed and bound in Great Britain by Cox and Wyman Ltd, Reading,
Berkshire.

To Jean Reich, who's been our
sanctuary in so many ways.

Historian's Note

This adventure takes place during the original five-year mission of the USS *Enterprise*.

Foreword

I never met Gene Roddenberry, but his effect on my life has been extremely far-reaching. I might have struggled several more years to become a published (not to mention best-selling) novelist had he and Pocket Books not created the Next Generation book series. G.R. personally approved the outline for the book you are holding in your hands, and for that I am extremely grateful. I could go on and talk about how much Star Trek means to me as a whole, but I think you can judge that for yourself from this book and my Next Generation novels. Suffice to say, I miss you, Mr. Roddenberry. Thanks a lot.

Now, prepare yourself for a blitz of thank-yous. My feeble memory needed a lot of help to complete a book taking place during the original five-year mission. First of all, to those who read it and offered comments along the way: Andrea and Kevin Quitt and the toughest critic of all, my wife, Nancy. Then to Judy and Garfield Reeves-Stevens, who loaned me their long-out-of-print *Concordance* and offered me plenty of moral support. Thanks to that fount of Star Trek knowledge, Jim Shaun Lyon, and my creature researchers: Priscilla J. Ball, Cory Sims, Marte Brengle, Jon Woolf, Carolyn Kinkead, Jim Singleton, Anne Davenport, and Matthew G. Mitchell. Actually, they're all human, but they know a lot about things that aren't.

Special kudos to Kevin Ryan, my editor, who believed in *Sanctuary* and persevered to get it approved. Thanks to friends and colleagues who helped me in various invaluable ways: Ashley Grayson, Caroline Meskell, Eric Baldwin, Phyllis Hirsen, Steve Robertson, Barbara Beck, Susan Williams, Marilyn Dennis, Jane Emaus, and Linda Johnston.

One theme of this book is that space travel is a privilege that can be taken away. In many respects, it's already been taken away from us after the great hope that was inspired by the Apollo moon flight more than twenty years ago. I don't wish to belittle the space shuttle program, but I expected more from space travel than the Pentagon plopping a spy satellite in orbit every now and then. The proposed orbital space station has been compromised to death, and NASA is on the ropes financially and morale-wise. The once-proud Russian space program is apparently gone forever.

Thanks to visionaries like Gene Roddenberry, space travel exists in our imaginations and popular culture, but that's not good enough. It's time for the private sector to pick up the fallen banner. I speak principally of Japanese companies and huge multinationals that haven't got anything better to do with their money than buy expensive trophies like country clubs and movie studios. It's time for the Sonys and General Electrics of the world to return to us the wonder of space travel. They have the money, resources, and technology to do it. What about joint ventures? What secrets does NASA have anymore? But I suppose our government will continue to be xenophobic and continue to guard technology that we no longer have the will to use. It's sad that space travel has been taken away from us, and there is no one who wants to give it back.

John Vornholt

Chapter One

CAPTAIN KIRK leaned over his helmsman's shoulder and stared at a tiny dot on the viewscreen. It was barely distinguishable from the stars around it, but the stars were moving in relation to the *Enterprise*. The blip wasn't.

"Are we gaining on him at all, Mr. Sulu?" asked the captain.

"Negative, sir," answered the veteran officer, blinking away the heaviness from his eyes. This chase had started twelve hours ago, and it was beginning to take its toll on everyone. "His top speed matches our top speed warp for warp."

"How is that possible, Keptin?" asked Chekov with frustration. "That ship must be one-tenth the size of the *Enterprise*."

"Approximately one twenty-second the size of the *Enterprise*," responded a voice behind them. First Officer Spock straightened up from his science station. "However, size has nothing to do with warp capability, especially on a ship with low mass and a small crew. With minimal life-support needs, ninety percent of a ship's energy can be devoted to its propulsion system. It would also appear that the designers of Auk-rex's ship were able to avail themselves of the latest Starfleet technology."

"And why shouldn't they?" muttered Kirk. "They've been plundering our trading vessels for five years now. Blast that pirate! I thought we had him."

"Begging the Keptin's pardon," said Chekov, "but in thirty-eight minutes, we will enter a sector of space that has never been charted or explored by Starfleet. Do you wish to continue pursuit?"

"Absolutely," Kirk replied. "Auk-rex has attacked three freighters in the last month, and Starfleet wants an end to it." He turned to his trusted first officer. "Spock, you've got to figure out where he's going. Chart his course."

The Vulcan raised an eyebrow. "That will be difficult, Captain, since we have no firsthand knowledge of this sector. But I shall try."

Kirk rubbed his eyes and said, "Lieutenant Uhura, radio our position to Starfleet and tell them of our intentions."

"Aye, Captain," answered the communications officer as her hands moved over her console.

Kirk strode toward the double doors of the turbolift, and they whooshed open at his approach. "You can reach me in sickbay," he announced to no one in particular. "Maybe McCoy has some ideas."

Dr. McCoy smiled slyly over a snifter of brandy. "So, Jim, he slipped through your fingers. The trap wasn't good enough?"

"Nothing wrong with the trap," Kirk answered testily. Perhaps the most irritating thing about McCoy, he decided, was that Bones liked to see people

2

act human. And to err was human. "It was a good idea," he insisted. "But somehow, that thief sensed the freighter was a dummy. He got close to the bait, but he didn't nibble."

"That's why he's been around for so long." The doctor shrugged. "I know he's been a real pain in the cahoot, but you've got to admire Auk-rex a little bit. It's not easy being a pirate these days, with so many treaties and regulations. As I understand it, he never takes life wantonly."

Kirk scowled. "No, he just cripples a ship and takes its most valuable cargo. He figures out what it's carrying by tapping directly into the computer, then he beams it off before they know what hit them."

"Hmm. The computer data is worth something too, I bet. What else do we know about him?"

"Not much," Kirk admitted. "He's sophisticated but very mysterious. We don't know if he's human, or Klingon, or what. He never hails a ship by voice or visual, always code. And he sticks to trading routes on the periphery of the Federation. Starfleet has so many questions for him, they don't want him killed, only captured."

The doctor shook his head, clearly amused. "And in order to capture Auk-rex, we are basically seeing how far and how fast the *Enterprise* can go."

"That's about it," answered Kirk. He took a sip of his lukewarm coffee and frowned. "I came here to see if you had any ideas, but it sounds like you're rooting for the pirate."

"Well," said McCoy, smiling, "it's that part of me that always roots for the underdog. Here we are, a big starship, and we can't capture one little puddle-jumper."

"Hardly a puddle-jumper," Kirk said evenly. "That little ship is the equal of anything in Starfleet." The captain mustered a smile. "He's fast, but not fast

3

enough. He can't lose us, and sooner or later he'll have to come out of warp. When he does, we hit him with a tractor beam and it's all over."

The doctor nodded. "But will it be sooner or later?"

"I wish I knew," admitted Kirk.

A high-pitched tone sounded, followed by the voice of Mr. Spock: "Bridge to captain."

The captain crossed to the wall and switched on the comm panel. "Kirk here. What is it, Spock?"

"We are crossing into the uncharted sector now," Spock answered. "No change in status, but I have a theory about where Auk-rex may be headed."

"I'm on my way," answered Kirk, switching off the panel. He turned to his friend and smiled. "So, Bones, do you want to come along and root for your underdog?"

"Wouldn't miss it." The doctor grinned.

When Captain Kirk and Dr. McCoy reached the bridge, everyone but Spock glanced expectantly in their direction. The slim Vulcan stood motionless over his science console, absorbing data that were scrolling by too fast for a human to read. Kirk waited patiently until Spock turned to face them.

"Where do you think he's going?" asked Kirk.

"I can't be certain," Spock admitted, "but long-range scanners indicate that the course of the pirate vessel will take it directly into a solar system with nine planets, one of which may have an atmosphere capable of supporting humanoid life. Although Starfleet has never officially explored this sector, we have compiled a number of reports and rumors."

"Why, Spock," remarked McCoy, feigning astonishment, "it's not like you to traffic in rumors."

"Perhaps not, Doctor," agreed the Vulcan, "but everything we know about this sector is unsubstantiated. Therefore, we have no choice but to traffic in

4

rumors." Spock turned to Kirk. "Have you ever heard of a planet called Sanctuary?"

"Sure," answered McCoy. "It's a mythical planet, a place where fugitives from all over the galaxy can go to escape their persecutors. It's one of those places like El Dorado or Atlantis—sounds good, but there's never been any proof that it exists."

Spock nodded. "It does not exist in any area explored by Starfleet. However, most of the galaxy has *not* been explored by Starfleet. Klingon charts list such a planet in this vicinity, and the sanctuary planet is mentioned in the mythologies of numerous spacefaring worlds. According to legend, Sanctuary accepts all who fear capture or harm, both the justly and unjustly accused. It accepts no appeals from pursuers, and no one who has reached Sanctuary has ever been captured later."

"What are you saying?" asked Kirk, striding to his captain's chair. "That Sanctuary is a real planet, and that's where he's headed?"

"I cannot say whether Sanctuary is real," replied Spock. "But the Klingons believe it exists, and so may Auk-rex."

Kirk nodded, gazing thoughtfully at the tiny dot on the giant viewscreen. "He doesn't have many options, does he?"

"No, Captain."

James T. Kirk straightened up in his chair. "We didn't get much of a look at his ship, but do you think it's capable of atmospheric reentry? Could he land on this planet?"

"His ship is small enough," answered Spock. "It has already proven quite versatile, and atmospheric reentry would help it elude larger ships that must remain in orbit, such as the *Enterprise*. Even if his destination is not the fabled sanctuary planet, landing on a planet's surface would seem to be his only means of escape."

"Mr. Sulu," asked Kirk, "how long before we reach this unnamed solar system?"

"Forty-four minutes," answered the helmsman.

Kirk punched the communicator on the arm of his chair. "Captain Kirk to shuttlebay. Prepare shuttlecraft *Ericksen* for immediate launch."

"Aye, Captain," came the reply. "How many in the party?"

Kirk glanced back at Spock and McCoy. "Three," he answered. He switched off the communicator and smiled slyly. "Bones, would you like to make a bet with me that your pirate won't get away?"

"Sure." The doctor shrugged. "What have you got to wager?"

Spock raised an eyebrow but said nothing.

"If I lose," said Kirk, "I'll take that physical you've been nagging me about. If you lose, you quit nagging me about it."

"All right," agreed the doctor. "But don't you still intend to lasso him with a tractor beam when he comes out of warp drive?"

"I do," said Kirk, nodding with determination. "But he'll come out of warp drive slightly ahead of us, and there may not be enough time. If he makes it into the planet's atmosphere, we'll have to follow him to the surface in the shuttlecraft. Then we'll send his coordinates back here and beam Auk-rex and his pirates off their own ship, just like they beam the loot off the ships they attack."

McCoy observed wryly, "You seem to have thought of everything."

Kirk nodded, the smile fading from his lips. "I hope so."

* * *

They were still a hundred million kilometers away from the planet, but the scanners magnified and stabilized its image until it filled the viewscreen. The aquamarine sphere was wrapped in swirling white mists and tied with darker strips of rain clouds. Where the surface peeked through the clouds, it revealed the turquoise of endless seas or the occasional speck of verdant green.

From this angle, there appeared to be only one good-sized continent, but the seas were speckled with islands, some of them in long chains that resembled broken necklaces. One pole was completely covered with ice, and the system's sun glinted so brightly off its blinding whiteness that it looked like a neon skullcap. No one needed a sensor to know that the shimmering planet brimmed with life. If it was not named Sanctuary, it would surely be one for any traveler weary of the blackness of space.

"A pretty planet it is," observed Montgomery Scott, chief engineer of the *Enterprise.* As third in command after Kirk and Spock, Scotty had joined his comrades on the bridge in case he had to assume the captain's chair. "And I'll be glad to be coming out o' warp drive, I'll tell you. The engines canna take much more."

Captain Kirk smiled at the familiar remark, but his good humor was short-lived.

"The quarry has slowed to warp one," announced Sulu. "We'll overtake him in two-point-five minutes, about the same time we reach the planet."

The captain leaned forward tensely. "Steady as she goes, Mr. Sulu—take us down to warp one. When he goes to impulse power, I want to be only a second behind him."

"Keptin," said Chekov, "we are close enough that I can lock on with phasers."

"That's a last resort," Kirk warned. "Starfleet won't

7

learn much about Auk-rex if we blow him to bits. But we don't want him to know that. Ready tractor beam."

"Aye, sir," answered Chekov in his clipped Russian accent.

"Uhura?" asked Kirk.

The lieutenant swiveled around in her chair. "I'm hailing him on all frequencies," she reported, "but there's still no response."

Kirk nodded. "I doubt if he wants to negotiate, but let's keep trying."

"Captain," said Spock, a trace of curiosity in his voice, "I am receiving odd readings from the planet. Our sensors are not registering as they should—"

"Captain!" exclaimed Sulu, cutting off Spock. "He has stopped completely and is reversing course, heading toward us!"

"He has launched a photon torpedo," Spock announced with no emotion.

Kirk barked, "Shields up!"

Chekov pounded a button on his console, and a second later the *Enterprise* was rocked by an explosion.

"A miss, sir!" proclaimed Chekov. "But a close von."

"He has reversed course again and is headed to the planet," said Spock, who turned away from his instruments and looked at Kirk. "His approach is nonorbital. I would say he is preparing to land."

Kirk pounded the arm of his chair. "Damn him! If he thinks that little stunt will save him, he's wrong. Sulu, take us to impulse power."

"Impulse power," said Sulu, sliding down his trimpot controls. There was a slight whine in the engines as the ship dropped out of warp drive.

"Activate tractor beam," Kirk ordered.

Chekov plied his controls for a moment, then shook

his head, puzzled. "Negative reaction, Keptin," he reported. "Something on the planet is counteracting the effect of the tractor beam. It's like an unusual gravity field."

Captain Kirk bolted from his chair. "Bones, Spock," he ordered, "follow me!"

The captain paused at the turbolift and motioned to his chief engineer. "Scotty, you have the bridge. Take us into standard orbit and have the transporter room stand by for coordinates. Get a security team down there, too. Tell shuttlebay to prepare for launch."

"Aye, Captain," said the Scotsman. He eased himself into the captain's chair as Kirk, Spock, and McCoy rushed out. "Take us in, Mr. Sulu. I'll inform security to prepare a little welcoming party for our visitors."

"Separation successful," Spock relayed into the radio as the shuttlecraft *Ericksen* veered away from the *Enterprise*. Kirk, in the pilot's seat, got his first look at the planet through a cockpit window and not a viewscreen. It appeared even more serene and inviting in its hazy blueness. In every other direction, innumerable stars twinkled with an immediacy not captured by the electronic imaging of the viewscreen.

"We are gaining on Auk-rex's ship," said Spock, studying the copilot's instruments. "It has just entered the outer atmosphere of the planet. Close to the planet's surface, we will have far more maneuverability than they have."

Captain Kirk leaned forward in the pilot's seat, pushing the controls of the small craft to maximum speed. Behind him, he could hear Dr. McCoy shifting uneasily in his seat.

"What's the matter, Bones?" he teased. "I thought you wanted to be right in the thick of things—to root your pirate on."

McCoy shook his head. "I don't know, Jim," he muttered. "Something about this just doesn't seem right. I have a feeling Auk-rex knows more than we do."

"I would have to agree with the doctor," said Spock.

Kirk blinked with surprise at his trusted comrade. "You agree with McCoy about his vague feelings of unease?"

"Not vague feelings," corrected Spock. "But I was unable to complete my scan of the planet, and it possessed some very unusual characteristics."

"It's class-M," said Kirk, "you can see that from here."

"Agreed," said Spock. "However, I would have preferred to complete my examination."

"Can we delay at all," asked Kirk, "and not lose their trail?"

"Negative, Captain," came the reply. "The success probability of our plan is very high, barring unforeseen circumstances."

"My favorite kind," muttered McCoy.

A voice chimed from the intercom: "Scott to shuttlecraft."

Kirk hit the switch. "What is it, Scotty?"

"I don't want to alarm you, sir," came the response, "but there appear to be at least six ships orbiting the planet. Three of them are leaving orbit in order to intercept the pirate ship, or us, I can't tell."

"What!" exclaimed Kirk. "What kind of ships?"

"Unable to verify at this time," Scotty replied. "They were stationed on the other side of the planet when we approached. This seems to be a very busy place. . . ." His voice was obliterated by waves of static.

"Entering atmosphere," Spock announced. "Please brace yourselves."

Kirk manipulated the controls as the shuttlecraft

was jostled slightly upon entering the upper atmosphere of the aquamarine planet. The invaded air roared in their ears, and speech seemed like the most pointless of efforts. Heat rose inside the tiny cabin as their view was obliterated by streaks of ionized flame. Whatever was happening above the planet faded in importance as they gradually entered the ecosystem of the living astral body.

When they emerged below the clouds a few minutes later, Kirk noted that it was as if they had embarked on an ocean cruise. For countless kilometers in every direction, nothing was visible but the clearest aqua seas, so clear that clumps of seaweed could be seen waving to them from the depths.

The ship skimmed over the dancing waves for several seconds. "We should have Auk-rex's ship in view in a matter of moments," Spock reported.

Kirk had other things on his mind. "Scotty? Scotty?" he repeated, trying to raise the *Enterprise.* There was no answer, even when Kirk tried again on his personal communicator.

"What's going on here?" he complained. "That entry shouldn't have knocked out our communicators."

"Visual contact with the quarry," said Spock. Although Kirk and McCoy peered relentlessly into the dimpled horizon, they could see nothing but sloshing sea. But Kirk's eyes caught movement in the clumps of sargassolike weeds beckoning from the bottom.

He jammed the controls hard to port as a thick brown tentacle lashed at them from a cresting wave. The shuttlecraft banked around the sinewy appendage, and they swiveled in their seats to see a gigantic mollusk lumber to the surface and roll lazily in the sun. Its purplish body blotted the turquoise sea like an ink spill.

"Nice welcoming committee," said the captain,

leveling off the small craft at an altitude that no longer skimmed the waves. "We're not as close to the water as we appear."

"We're close enough for my taste!" snapped McCoy. "Isn't there any *land* on this planet?"

"Yes, there is," Spock replied. "And we are approaching it rather rapidly."

Kirk pointed excitedly at a dot of activity on the hazy horizon. "I see him!" he exclaimed. "To starboard. I think I also see land."

"Quite correct, Captain," Spock agreed. "We will be passing over what might be considered a large island, or a small continent. If we were here for any length of time, I would prefer to study the marine life, which I am sure is more varied and abundant than the terrestrial life."

McCoy scowled. "Get us out of here in one piece, and I'll buy you a ticket back."

Captain Kirk tried his communicator again. "Kirk to *Enterprise*. Uhura, do you hear me?" He waited for an answer that never came, then tried the shuttlecraft's comm panel—with the same results.

"The communicators are still out," he grumbled. "Spock, how are the other shuttlecraft systems?"

"Other systems are operating efficiently," the Vulcan replied, shifting his gaze from the cockpit window to his instrument panel. "Auk-rex is headed toward a mountain range. Do you wish to pursue?"

"We've come this far," Kirk said gravely, "let's get him."

Lieutenant Uhura swiveled around in her chair, not hiding the concern in her voice. "Mr. Scott," she called, "still no word from the captain. And we're being hailed by one of the ships in orbit. A *Klingon* ship."

Scotty stiffened in the captain's chair. "Has he armed his weapons?"

"No, sir," she answered.

"Shields are still up," said Chekov. "We can go to red alert on your order."

"Put his ship on the screen," ordered Scotty.

At once, the threatening figure of a Klingon warship popped onto the viewscreen. Its predatory visage was softened by the bluish outline of the planet behind it, and it kept a respectful distance in its own orbit.

"And the other five ships?" asked Scotty.

Sulu shook his head. "One of them fired some shots at both the shuttlecraft and the pirate. But the atmosphere, or something, deflected them. I can't place the origins of the other ships—they all seem of different types. I'll put the computer on it."

"Fine," said Scotty, not really thinking that any of this was fine. His captain, first officer, and ship's doctor were out of contact, and he was sharing orbit with a Klingon and God-knows-what-all.

"Put the Klingon commander on the viewscreen," he said disgruntledly.

The image of a Klingon officer appeared on the screen. He was an older Klingon, with bumps that undulated down his forehead and gray hair that hung to his shoulders in a haphazard tangle. His face looked thin and wiry and was graced with a slim patrician nose. But beneath his short-sleeved leather armor, huge biceps bulged and forearms rippled with tough sinew.

He pounded the console in front of him. "Earth Captain," he growled, "I salute your bravery!"

Scotty blinked in surprise. "Bravery? What do ye mean by that, sir?"

Magnanimously, the Klingon flung his arms open. "I have always heard that humans are cowardly," he replied, "but this was a magnificent act! I have orbited this planet for many years—I have no idea how many in your reckoning—and I have never seen such devotion to duty. I salute those brave warriors who pursued the fugitives to the surface of the planet. May they live to catch them and disembowel them in the public square!"

"Aye," said Scotty uncertainly. "We will give them your regards, when they return to the ship."

"Return to the ship?" asked the Klingon, puzzled. "What ship?"

"The one I'm sitting on."

The Klingon roared with a laughter so fierce he dissolved into tears. "That is a rich jest," he finally sputtered. "Surely you do not expect to see them again? That's what is so brave about their action—to know they will never return!"

"Never return?" asked Scotty. He could hear Uhura, Chekov, and Sulu echoing the same words.

"Of course," said the Klingon. "You know there is an impenetrable shield around the planet. Ships can go in, but they can't come out. Or else we would all go in and disembowel our fugitives."

"I see," Scotty replied, leaning forward intently. "Tell me about this place. Is this the sanctuary planet?"

"Yes, this is Sanctuary. Where did you think you were? The other scum about here are bounty hunters, so we two are the only representatives of imperial powers. My orders are to intercept and prevent Klingon fugitives from reaching Sanctuary, so I will choose to ignore the hostilities between us for the moment. Will you station yourselves here to intercept other fugitives?"

"We are awaiting orders," Scotty answered, trying not to betray any more of his ignorance than he

14

already had. "We are investigating. In your experience, nobody ever gets off the planet?"

"Nobody," answered the Klingon sympathetically. "That is why I hope your landing party is successful, to teach that riffraff down there a lesson. Or else you have lost your men in vain."

Chapter Two

CAPTAIN KIRK leaned forward in his seat, adrenaline pumping, as he watched a disclike vessel weave between green foothills and towering spires in a desperate attempt to elude them. He heard a loud gulp and glanced back to see McCoy covering his eyes with his hands. Kirk's own knuckles were tightly clenched on the controls. Although they had chased the pirate vessel over thousands of light-years of space, none of that compared with this harrowing pursuit over a few kilometers of rugged terrain.

As Spock had predicted, the sleek pirate vessel was clumsy and unwieldy compared to the shuttlecraft. "We could easily pull alongside Auk-rex's ship," said Spock, "but he is flying too erratically to risk getting closer."

"We can see him fine from here," agreed McCoy. "What are we going to do, with the communicators out? We can't send his coordinates back to the *Enterprise.*"

"He's right," said Kirk. "We need a new plan. Any ideas, Spock?"

"He will undoubtedly run out of fuel before we do," answered the Vulcan. "Flying a warp-class vessel this close to the surface is very fuel-inefficient."

McCoy growled in reply, "That's not a plan—that's just waiting him out. What's the matter with that idiot? Doesn't he know he's beaten?"

Kirk smiled. "Why, Bones, I thought you were rooting for Auk-rex. The last of the rugged individualists."

"That was before the communicators went out," grumped McCoy, "and before we found out this planet is ringed with ships. I knew there was something fishy about this place."

"All right," said Kirk, "if he doesn't land soon, or we don't reestablish contact with the ship, we'll abandon our pursuit and go back. We can send a larger search party later."

"Now, *that's* a plan," said McCoy.

"Mountains ahead," remarked Spock.

Kirk turned his attention back to the horizon. "Mountains ahead" was the kind of understatement only Spock was capable of making, the captain thought. Anyone else would have said, "Awesome towering peaks that reach into the clouds."

Like the smaller spires that graced the foothills, these giant spires appeared to have been carved by the erosion of millennia. Unlike the graceful slopes of Earth, they were angular and twisted; lush green shrubbery did little to soften their rugged appearance. Probably this entire landmass had been covered in water not so long ago, thought Kirk, and the tips of these majestic fingers had once been islands, the first grip of land on this watery world. Now the mountains poked their way through the dense clouds as if they were trying to grab the heavens.

And Auk-rex's ship was headed straight for the tallest summit.

"What's that idiot doing now?" McCoy asked, anticipating Kirk's own thoughts.

Spock answered, "I would say, Doctor, that he is leading us into the mountain range, hoping we will not be foolish enough to follow."

"He'll crash!" Kirk exclaimed, leaning forward intently.

"Quite likely," Spock agreed. "His ship does not have the maneuverability necessary to avoid the mountains."

"He'd rather die than be captured," McCoy said in amazement.

Kirk flipped open his communicator. "Kirk to *Enterprise!* Come in, *Enterprise!*" he begged. There was no response. He hit another button. "Shuttlecraft to Auk-rex!" he shouted. "Come in, Auk-rex!" The silence was as still as the jagged peaks that loomed ever closer.

The pirate vessel no longer weaved back and forth; it blazed toward the highest mountain on an inevitable path to self-destruction. Kirk pulled back on his controls, allowing their quarry more room, but its course remained true. The deadly fingers of rock drew steadily closer, and the captain was forced to gain altitude, brushing against the dense cloud cover. No one breathed in the tiny cabin as destruction towered all around them.

The peaks of the tallest mountains were totally obscured, and the peaks of the smaller ones were all too visible. But more horrifying was the sight of the gleaming pirate ship, hurtling toward a cloud-enshrouded mountaintop.

"Pull up!" urged McCoy. "For God's sake, pull up!"

It was unclear to Kirk whether McCoy was talking to Auk-rex or to him. He increased speed, and the shuttlecraft bore down on its quarry as if it had talons and could pluck the ship from destruction at the last moment.

Kirk watched in horror as the pirate ship was obliterated in a fiery crash that pulverized the mountainside. The captain pulled up on his controls just in time to avoid the same fate.

"Merciful heavens," breathed McCoy, slumping back in his seat.

Kirk pitched the shuttlecraft into a deep bank and circled the mountain to cruise past the crash site. They watched in morbid fascination as a rock slide carried the flaming wreckage into a deep gorge. Seconds later, it was as if nothing had happened to disturb the cloud-enshrouded stillness of the mountains.

Kirk again cruised past the crash site.

"Jim," said McCoy, "if you're looking for survivors, I think you can forget it."

"On the contrary, Doctor," said the Vulcan, "I think there is a fair possibility that there are survivors. Seconds before the crash, two people ejected."

"What?" said Kirk, peering out the window. "I didn't see them."

"You were undoubtedly watching the crash," answered Spock, "whereas I was trying to track the path of the ejection pods. I am afraid that in this rough terrain, it is uncertain whether they could survive ejection. Also, the shuttlecraft sensors have stopped functioning."

"Great," muttered McCoy. "How are we going to find them?"

Spock suggested, "We could land and search for them on foot. I believe I know their approximate location, and there is some terrain in the vicinity that is level enough for a landing."

Kirk strained to look out the window. "Do you

really think there's a chance two people are alive down there?"

"A fair chance," answered Spock. "They may very well be injured."

"We should land," McCoy said forcefully. "We can't abandon two people who need help—this is a medical emergency. Besides," he added, grinning at Kirk, "you're going to lose your bet if we stop now."

The captain nodded. "We've come this far—we might as well see it through. We'll look for them until dusk, then we'll return to the ship and do a complete scan. I hope Scotty is making friends up there."

On the bridge, Scott paced as Sulu rattled off a litany of hull types and ship standards, gazing at his computer screen.

"In addition to the Klingon," he summarized, "there is a Saurian ship, an Orion ship, two more that could best be described as mongrel, and one that defies any description. All are armed, but none appear aggressive. Like the Klingon, they seem to have accepted us as just another bounty hunter."

"Bounty hunters," said Scotty distastefully. "So this is what we've been reduced to, begging help from bounty hunters." He motioned to the beautiful aquamarine sphere that filled the viewscreen. "All because of that accursed planet. Any word from them or the captain?"

"I've hailed the planet on every frequency," answered Uhura. "There's no response. Shall I hail the Klingon again?"

"No," Scotty said, sighing, "try one of the others. Try the Orion ship. They're semicivilized."

A few seconds passed as Uhura sent standard greetings over several frequencies. Scott watched her grip her headset and frown intently as she listened to the Universal Translator. Finally, the lieutenant turned disgustedly to the chief engineer and reported:

"The Orion captain is very busy and can't talk unless we have some prisoners of value on board. If we do, he is willing to trade slave women for them."

Scotty shook his head with dismay. "Heaven help us. And heaven help the captain, the doctor, and Mr. Spock."

Captain Kirk piloted the shuttlecraft between the mountains in a series of lazy circles that brought them into a narrow valley. They landed in a dry rainwash that was the flattest and least overgrown terrain in the lush basin. The plants and trees had a distinctly bladderlike appearance, with leaves that were like thick pods and branches covered with green globules. Orange flowers dotted the tops of the larger pods, and thick vines snaked along the floor of the arroyo.

The door of the shuttlecraft rose, and Spock leaped out, followed by Captain Kirk and Dr. McCoy. Spock pointed his tricorder at the nearest vegetation and twisted its dials. After a moment, he closed the tricorder and clipped it to his waist.

"My tricorder is inoperative," he said.

"Mine, too," added McCoy, following suit. "What is it about this place?"

"Whatever it is," said Kirk, "it's consistent. All our equipment has been affected." He took a few steps and filled his lungs. "Nothing wrong with the air here, though. You can smell those flowers from ten meters away. And the temperature is comfortable. This part of the planet is certainly habitable."

"Well," said McCoy, "there must be some reason all those ships are in orbit."

"Sanctuary," answered Spock. "Their reasons are probably no different than ours. May I suggest we

21

follow the wash to the north? It will take us into the approximate area of the crash, and the walking will be easier."

"Lead on," said Kirk. "Watch out for sinkholes and quicksand. I think it rains fairly often here."

Watchfully, the three explorers walked along the floor of the valley, which was shrouded in perpetual shade by the immense peaks surrounding it. Twice they stopped to watch herds of pale fishlike creatures crawl laboriously across the gully on pseudo-legs that looked like fins. Spock suggested that they were an evolving species that probably moved from pond to pond as the water dried up. McCoy got a start when several fist-sized rocks he was standing near suddenly sprouted legs and scurried away. The largest animal they saw was a winged creature that leaped from a fissure in the mountainside and sailed like a glider after a herd of the ambulatory fish, snatching one up in its reptilian jaws and sailing away to the opposite side of the basin.

As the day wore on, the clouds over their heads dissipated, and they found themselves craning their necks to study the majestic peaks. The mountains rose in profusion like stalagmites, one outdoing another in spindly splendor, but none of them bore signs of life other than native species. They walked until the shadows deepened from one end of the gully to the other, accenting the stark crevices and fissures in the moss-covered rocks. Kirk wondered at the strange calls, neither fully birdlike nor animallike, that echoed in the rugged canyon.

Finally, Spock stopped abruptly. "Captain," he said, "without tricorders or scanners, we could search this terrain for weeks before locating something as small as an escape pod. They could have fallen into a crevice, or they could be in those thickets twenty meters away. We have effectively exhausted the small chance we have of finding them under these circumstances."

Kirk nodded and turned to McCoy. "What do you say, Bones? Are you ready to turn back?"

The doctor heaved a sigh. "I suppose so, Jim. I hate to leave anyone who might be injured, but there are worse places to be stranded than this."

"If we pick up our pace," said the captain, "we'll get back to the shuttle before it's completely dark. Let's go."

As the shadows lengthened, the strange howls and cries increased, as if there was a different set of denizens who made their appearance at nightfall. This caused the three searchers to pick up their pace considerably, even as they took turns trying to raise the *Enterprise* on their communicators. They were almost running along the arroyo when Spock stopped suddenly, twisting his head in every direction.

"What is it, Spock?" asked Kirk.

"Don't you recognize this place?" asked the Vulcan.

"Come on, Spock," said McCoy, "we haven't got time for sight-seeing. Let's get back to the shuttlecraft."

"Precisely," answered Spock. "We *are* at the site of the shuttlecraft. This is where we left it."

"What?" barked Kirk, scanning the dark walls of the canyon. "Where is it?"

Spock bent down and placed his hand in a slight depression in the sandy soil. "The forward strut touched down here. As to where the vessel is, I cannot answer."

Determinedly, Kirk cupped his hands around his mouth and bellowed at the top of his lungs, *"Who's there? Is anybody out there?"*

"No need to shout," said a mellifluous voice.

The trio whirled around to find a slim, white-robed humanoid standing in a spot they had just passed. In the fading light, Kirk could see a pleasant, unlined face and a welcoming smile, but he couldn't determine the sex of the creature. Its demure manner and slight build suggested it might be female, but the timbre of its voice and its substantial height led him to consider the male sex. Its head was shaven bare, and the white robe reached from neck to ground, revealing no trace of breasts or sexual organs.

"I am Zicree," said the figure with a polite bow. "I am a Senite; we are the keepers of Sanctuary. You will see us wherever you journey on this fair planet, so let me explain a bit of our history.

"As you may have surmised," Zicree continued, "we are androgynous. We were bred to be sexless by a religious order that was the first to seek sanctuary on this planet many centuries ago. The original mission of the Senites has been lost in antiquity, and now the order serves to greet new arrivals and welcome them to Sanctuary. If you like, I will transport you to one of our villages."

"What we would like," said Kirk bluntly, "is to have our shuttlecraft back."

Zicree bowed slightly and maintained its pleasant smile. "You will have no need of your shuttlecraft," explained the Senite. "We will afford you all the creature comforts you desire. Please, come with me to the village, and you will see for yourselves."

"We don't intend to stay here," Kirk insisted. "We pursued a craft to the surface of this planet, but it crashed. Now we intend to leave."

The face was pleasant no more. In fact, it recoiled in phrorror. "You are *persecutors!*" gasped the Senite.

"Let me explain," said Kirk. "We didn't know—"

"Foul persecutors!" Zicree hissed. Then, as if ashamed of its anger, the humanoid collected itself and rose to an imposing height. "You have invaded

24

our planet to harm the persecuted, but Sanctuary accepts all. Someday, may you be worthy."

Zicree waved its hand in a deliberate gesture and disappeared.

"That's a fine how-d'ya-do!" snapped Dr. McCoy. "He . . . she . . . it steals our shuttlecraft, then accuses *us* of being foul persecutors."

Mr. Spock raised an eyebrow and looked at the captain. "This is a serious matter," he intoned. "We are totally without supplies, communications, and the ability to leave this planet."

"You don't need to tell me," answered Kirk, flipping open his communicator. "Kirk to *Enterprise*. Come in, *Enterprise*. Come in, *Enterprise!*"

The captain waited a few seconds for a reply that never came, then snapped his communicator shut. "We're going to find a way off this planet," he vowed. "From this moment on, everything else becomes secondary."

Spock suggested, "We may want to find shelter for the night."

As if to accentuate his statement, several eerie howls erupted from the mountains overhead and echoed throughout the darkening valley.

McCoy snapped his fingers and pointed to the spot the Senite had occupied a few seconds before. "Zicree mentioned some villages," he said hopefully. "Maybe there's one not too far from here. Which way should we go to find it?"

"We flew in from the east," answered Spock, "and we passed nothing that looked like a settlement. This mountain range extends to the north, and we may assume that a village would be built in the lowlands, or near the coast. Therefore, I suggest we proceed to the west or the south."

The captain looked doubtfully at the sky. "Does this planet have any moons?"

25

"Two moons," answered Spock.

"There's one of them now," said McCoy, pointing overhead. A pinkish disc was peeking around the side of the tallest mountain, the one where Auk-rex's ship had crashed.

"Let's get going, then," said the captain. "We should have enough light to see by. We'll follow this creekbed south, assuming it must run eventually into the sea."

Kirk knew that there was nothing else to be said or done, so the three off-worlders followed the gully in the opposite direction to the one they had explored earlier. In the darkening gloom, they tripped over the vines that crisscrossed the dry gravel, but that was preferable to trying to negotiate the jungle of bladder plants on either side of them.

The strange howls increased in intensity at one point, and a swarm of flying creatures swooped overhead. But Kirk shouted back at them, and they kept their distance.

The night wore on, and McCoy couldn't remember a time when he had seen the captain angrier, or more determined. They had been stranded on planets before, but he couldn't recall anyone ever stealing the captain's shuttlecraft before. Despite the affront, McCoy hoped his old friend would be more tactful the next time they met a Senite. It seemed the Senites held all the cards in this situation. It was their planet, and if they wished to glorify criminals and belittle authority, that was their business.

McCoy only wished he hadn't been so cynical about Sanctuary being a real planet. It was all too real. If they had thought the myths were true, they might have been more careful in their headlong chase.

The doctor didn't worry much about the *Enterprise*, knowing Scotty was a prudent and cautious man who loved the ship more than anyone and would never endanger it. But McCoy could see the worry in Kirk's furrowed brow and determined stride, and he knew it wasn't entirely due to their predicament on the planet.

Jim worried about the ship all the time, more so when he wasn't on it. This dichotomy never failed to amaze McCoy: Here was a man who loved and fretted over his ship like a jealous husband, yet he was always the first in line to lead a landing party. Well, thought McCoy, a little compulsion never hurt anybody, especially a starship captain.

The second moon made an appearance; even in midcrescent, it was a large white beacon that made their journey easier. The doctor watched as Spock stopped to try an experiment with one of the bladder plants that grew in profusion. He plucked a fist-sized bladder from a healthy-looking specimen and made an incision in it with his fingernail. Then he cautiously sucked some of the liquid that was stored within.

When the Vulcan didn't keel over, McCoy tried some of the juice. It tasted a bit oily and alkaline, but he supposed it wouldn't kill him—at least, not right away. While they stopped to drink, Kirk surged ahead, unmindful of thirst or rest. Spock and McCoy had to run to catch up.

"If the Senites are androgynous," said the doctor, trying to make small talk and break the monotony, "how do you suppose they reproduce?"

Spock cocked his head thoughtfully. "Zicree said they were *bred* to be sexless, which rules out natural evolution. That would indicate genetic engineering with an origin in traditional male and female parentage. How they could exist for centuries as an androgynous species, I do not know, unless they have a large store of frozen embryos that they incubate at given intervals."

McCoy nodded approvingly. "I knew you could figure it out, Spock."

Spock cocked his head at the doctor, wondering whether that was a compliment or not.

"I only know they're thieves," grumbled Kirk. "This whole planet would seem to be nothing but thieves. The sooner we get off, the better."

The words had no sooner left his mouth than a rock came sailing out of the gloom, striking the captain hard in the shoulder. Kirk grunted in pain and dropped to his knees.

The doctor and Spock barely had time to react before a fusillade of rocks pummeled them; they scrambled along the ground, trying to find cover among the bladder plants. One rock struck McCoy in the back, knocking the wind out of him, and he felt Spock drag him out of the line of fire.

Through half-closed eyes, McCoy saw Kirk draw his phaser and aim it in the direction of the attack. Nothing happened when the captain pressed the trigger, and a new hail of rocks forced him to scramble for his life.

Kirk crouched beside the others. "No phasers," he breathed.

At once, Spock gripped one of the thick vines that covered the dry creekbed and ripped it from the gravel with a burst of inhuman strength. As McCoy gasped for air, Spock broke the root into club-sized sections and handed one to the captain.

"The doctor is injured," he whispered. "We must arm ourselves as best we can."

No amount of weapons could have prepared them for the blood-chilling screams that rent the night air. They were screams of rage and attack, intended to terrify. Several large figures rushed out of the darkness, and Kirk jumped to his feet to meet them. Spock was a second behind him, and McCoy could do little more than observe the fight amidst excruciating efforts to catch his breath.

The captain swung his club and smashed it over the head of a burly creature, which promptly crumpled to the ground. His club in splinters, Kirk was easy prey for two attackers who wrestled him off his feet and rolled with him into the gully. Spock fared better, jamming his club into one attacker's stomach and applying the Vulcan nerve pinch to another. He stepped over the two unconscious bodies and was about to aid the captain when a bololike weapon came whipping out of the darkness and wrapped around his neck. Spock was too stunned to resist a second wave of monstrous figures who leaped upon him with horrid cries.

Still racked with pain, McCoy picked up one of Spock's makeshift clubs and staggered to his feet. Determined to do something, he swung his club at the nearest figure, a reptilian creature of solid muscle. It looked back at him almost pityingly, then snarled and smashed him in the face with a massive fist. McCoy tasted his own blood streaming from his nose and wondered if he was going to die. He tried to swing the club again, but arms wrapped around him from behind and yanked him off his feet.

The last thing he remembered seeing was a metal wrench, glimpsed out of the corner of his eye and swerving toward the center of his face.

Chapter Three

PAIN—and a splash of water in his face—brought McCoy to his senses. The pain was no longer localized in his rib cage but stretched the entire length of his body, from his face to his tightly bound arms and legs. The water that revived him also washed flakes of dried blood into his mouth, and he wondered if his nose was broken. The mere act of opening his eyes brought a blast of pain from a wound on his forehead.

When McCoy saw the monstrous apparition of a bipedal lizard staring down at him, growling with laughter, he didn't particularly want to keep his eyes open. But he wanted to know what had become of his comrades, so he twisted around as much as his bindings would allow. He saw Kirk and Spock behind him, getting similar dashes of cold water in their faces. His relief at seeing them alive was tempered by the fact that they were bound as he was—seated on the ground with their arms behind them and their legs tied in front. Their tunics were torn and dirty, and their faces were covered by various welts and lumps.

Captain Kirk looked far worse than Spock, with nasty abrasions on his arms and chest, but that didn't stop him from glaring at his captors. Spock sat in almost peaceful repose, his expression its usual combination of calm and alertness, despite the streak of dried blood that stretched from his hairline down his angular cheekbone to his chin. Early rays of dawn were creeping into the valley, which afforded McCoy a good look at the motley crew that had ambushed and seized them. Judging from the size and grizzled appearance of the gang members, who numbered eight, they were lucky to be alive.

The giant reptilian creature was obviously a Gorn, or some kind of closely related species. There were two Klingons with long hair and unkempt beards, and they glowered at the captives with pure hatred. One of the Klingons kept twisting a crude knife in his belt as if he was anxious to use it. A green-skinned Orion was a member of the party, but he paid scarcely any attention to the captives, being far more interested in ransacking their utility belts and studying their phasers and tricorders.

There was also a burly Tellarite, with his distinctive snoutlike nose. The other three members of the band looked mostly human, but none of them would win prizes as prime specimens of humanity. One of them wore a crude eyepatch and a deep scar that obliterated half his nose. The other two sported long beards and the craggy appearance of mountain men, as McCoy remembered them from Earth history. All eight were male and were wearing clothes that could only be described as rags.

After his cursory examination of the odd tribe, McCoy turned his attention to their camp. It appeared to be a more-or-less permanent encampment, with several ramshackle huts made from dried bladder plants stitched together. Larger leaves formed the roofs. A stream about two meters wide meandered down the center of the clearing, and there was a large fire pit full of smoldering embers. Three strange animals that looked like a cross between rodents and goats were tied to stakes in a makeshift corral, and fish bones were littered all over the camp. Several unappetizing strips of meat hung drying on a line.

McCoy looked back at Kirk, who, despite his anger, was not going to give his captors any cause to further abuse them. They were hog-tied and hornswoggled, as McCoy's daddy used to say, and there wasn't any point in being belligerent.

The Klingons, however, did not feel the same way. "I don't like the looks of those uniforms," muttered the one with the knife. "I say we kill them."

"What *are* those uniforms?" asked the Gorn in a guttural voice.

"They are definitely of the Federation," answered the Tellarite in stentorian tones. "Although what they are doing here, I cannot say."

"The same thing you are," Kirk answered quickly, "trying to get away from the Federation."

The Gorn moved menacingly toward the captured human. "You speak when we tell you," he ordered.

The human with the eyepatch stared curiously at Spock with his good eye. "Is that a Romulan?" he asked.

"No Romulans in the Federation," answered the Tellarite, blinking his pinkish beady eyes. "He must be a Vulcan."

"We *stole* these uniforms," McCoy found himself growling, trying to sound as tough as he could. He expected a swift blow to the head, but instead he got everyone's attention. Apparently, this bunch was bored enough living in isolation to listen to a tall tale.

"We're pirates," said McCoy. "You ever heard of Auk-rex?"

The green-skinned Orion stood up, a phaser in his hand. "I've heard of Auk-rex," he said.

"So have I," said a grizzled human. "I tried to sign up with him on Rigel II, but he had just left."

"Well, you can sign up with me now," snapped McCoy, "if you untie these ropes. But I'm afraid I haven't got a ship anymore."

A Klingon stared suspiciously at McCoy and twisted the knife in his belt. "Tell us what happened."

"They laid a trap for us near Capella IV," began McCoy, "Starfleet, I mean. Sent out a dummy freighter and had a big starship lying in wait for us. We got wind of it just in time to make a break for it. We knew about Sanctuary, so we headed here, but that damn *Enterprise* chased us all the way. . . ."

"Enterprise!" hissed the Klingon. "Captain James T. Kirk." He said the name as if it were one of the vilest curses in the galaxy.

"Indeed, a scoundrel," added the Tellarite.

"Scourge of the galaxy," McCoy agreed. "Anyway, we've been looting Federation ships for so long, we have a whole collection of their uniforms. We knew we couldn't outrun them, so we changed into these uniforms and beamed ourselves aboard the *Enterprise* just before it destroyed our ship. Once on board, we killed the transporter operator and had the run of the place. They thought Auk-rex was dead and had no idea we were walking around the *Enterprise* like we owned it. It was a piece of cake to put a phaser on overload, blow up the engine room, and steal a shuttlecraft during the confusion. So here we are!"

The Gorn gave them a crocodilian smile. "That's smart thinking," he growled. "Can you prove it?"

"We're here, aren't we?" asked Kirk. "If we were really Starfleet officers, what would we be doing on Sanctuary?"

None of them had an answer for that.

"You might end up wishing you had stayed on the *Enterprise,*" grumbled one of the humans. "Sanctuary may look like paradise, but it's not."

For the first time, Spock spoke: "We would appreciate it more if we weren't tied up."

The Gorn turned and surveyed his comrades. "What do you say?"

"I believe one thing," answered the Orion, "they just arrived on Sanctuary. All their equipment is new. The electronic stuff is worthless, of course." He gave McCoy a terrible start by turning a phaser on him and pressing the button. Fortunately, he was right—it was worthless.

"That I don't understand," said Kirk. "Why won't any of the equipment work?"

The Tellarite shook his furry head. "Those blasted Senites!" he cursed. "Who knows what they are up to, or what they want? They have a means to disable everything electronic, except what is theirs, of course. The one thing that unites our little group is that none of us trust the Senites."

A bearded human stared suspiciously at Spock. "I don't suppose the Senites sent you to find us, did they?"

Spock shook his head and replied, "The one Senite we have met refused to return our shuttlecraft and proved somewhat disagreeable."

"You'll never see that shuttlecraft again," said the talkative Tellarite. "I say we let these three go. What harm can they do us?"

When no one could provide an answer, the Gorn growled, "Cut them loose."

Reluctantly, the Klingon drew his knife and sliced the bindings around their arms and legs. "Don't make me regret this," he whispered to Kirk.

The captain, Spock, and McCoy stood stiffly and massaged their aching limbs. Kirk and McCoy staggered to the stream to get a drink and wash the blood from their faces. Spock stood stoically, but McCoy knew the watchful Vulcan was poised for action, should the need arise.

His face dripping wet, McCoy looked up from the stream and pointed to the medikit on his utility belt, which the Orion held in his green hand. "Could I have that back?"

The Orion narrowed his eyes. "I thought you said you were a pirate, not a doctor."

"You beat us up so badly," grumbled the doctor, "that we need first aid."

"No," grunted the Gorn. "We keep everything."

The Tellarite smiled. "Consider it a payment for passing through our camp. We might be able to trade them for something."

Kirk hid his disappointment, but he felt surreptitiously under his tunic and was reassured to find his communicator. "In exchange for the equipment," he said, "maybe you can give us some information. Is there any way to get off Sanctuary?"

The Tellarite snorted a laugh, his piggish nostrils flaring. There were several guffaws, and a Klingon sneered, "You can die."

The laughter died quickly, and a pall fell over the camp, despite the magnificent sunrise that was bathing the mountaintops in a golden light. Kirk's simple question and the Klingon's blunt answer had apparently uncovered a truth that was seldom spoken, and even harder to accept.

"Flying days are over," said the Gorn with melancholy, lifting its reptilian face toward the golden sky. The Gorn didn't look like it could cry, but McCoy saw its heavy eyelids blink several times.

More to change the subject than anything else, the doctor asked, "Are there many camps like this one?"

"There are more survivalists," answered the one-eyed human, "but most people live in the villages. We don't like the villages—they're all run by the Senites."

"What is your specific dislike of the Senites?" asked Spock.

"We don't trust them," hissed a Klingon, "like we don't trust you."

The Tellarite shrugged. "It is mostly a general dislike of being dependent upon the Senites for everything we eat, drink, and own in the world. Like Red says, we are survivalists and prefer to live by our own rules and wits. Plus, we've heard rumors."

"About what?" asked Kirk.

A Klingon snarled, "Why don't you go to the village and find out?"

"Perhaps we should do that," Spock offered.

The Tellarite pointed down the stream, which wandered through lush hills and disappeared in a golden mist on the horizon. "Just follow the stream," he said. "It connects to a river that flows to the sea. At the sea is a village—Dohama, I believe."

Sheepishly, one of the mountain men stepped forward and said, "If you see any women, tell them it's not so bad up here."

Kirk smiled. "We will."

After a brief farewell, Kirk, Spock, and McCoy were on their own again, hiking along the bank of the stream. McCoy noticed the two Klingons following them from a distance, and he wondered if they might attack. He warned Kirk and Spock, but the Klingons turned back after a few kilometers, apparently satisfied that the strangers were leaving their valley.

Spock lowered his voice to ask, "Captain, considering the Prime Directive, should we have left our phasers and tricorders with them?"

"I don't see that we had much choice," Kirk muttered. "And this planet is already an amalgam of useless technology. At least we still have our communicators. Believe me, I'll be happy to explain to Starfleet how we lost our equipment—if I get the chance."

"Ow!" groaned McCoy, massaging his still tender nose. "I wish I could have gotten my medikit back."

"Perhaps," Spock suggested, "the Senites will repair our wounds."

"I don't know," said McCoy doubtfully. "We were told not to trust the Senites."

"Doctor," replied the Vulcan, "we can surmise that all of the people we met in that camp were antisocial criminals before arriving on Sanctuary. They can hardly be expected to like authority."

In spite of their predicament, Kirk grinned. "That was some story you told them, Bones."

"Not bad, huh?" The doctor nodded, quite pleased with himself.

"But highly inaccurate," Spock added. "The computer would alert us if three intruders beamed aboard the *Enterprise,* and the shuttlebay would be sealed if there was an explosion in the engine room. Plus—"

"It was fiction!" snapped the doctor.

"And it served its purpose," agreed the captain. "Now, if we could just talk our way off this planet. Spock, do you think we should trust the Senites?"

Spock replied, "They have not sufficiently demonstrated their trustworthiness. However, their position of authority cannot be disputed."

The captain nodded grimly. "You're right about that. We'll have to find a way to get them to help us."

With that final thought, the three walked wordlessly beside the pristine stream that flowed from the mountains of Sanctuary.

Montgomery Scott paced the bridge of the *Enterprise,* pounding his fist into his palm repeatedly. Uhura glanced back at him from her communications console. She wished there were something she could say to ease the acting captain's worry, but there had been no contact with Captain Kirk, Mr. Spock, and Dr. McCoy for more than thirteen hours. Countless attempts to contact anyone on the planet had failed, and the other ships in orbit were more of a threat than a solution.

Uhura was waiting for Scotty to turn to her and ask her to send a message to Starfleet. The message would report the disappearance of three of Starfleet's finest officers, but it would report the *Enterprise* as being safe. She knew what the consequences would be: Starfleet would be alarmed, but they would realize that the *Enterprise* was more important than any three officers, no matter how skilled and experienced. As a precaution, they might order the *Enterprise* to evacuate orbit immediately. Even if they listened to Scotty's impassioned plea to stay, they would soon realize he could not risk searching the planet. Eventually, in a day or a month, there would be urgent business for the *Enterprise* elsewhere, and Scotty would be ordered to leave. Uhura knew she would be the conduit for this disturbing series of messages, and the prospect filled her with dread and sorrow.

"Commander Scott," she said softly, "I can try to contact the planet again, and beg them to respond on humanitarian grounds."

Scotty stopped his pacing and stood at attention. "Let us try contacting our Klingon friend," he said, not hiding the irony in his voice. To think that a Klingon was perhaps the most civilized of their partners in this futile orbit was hardly reassuring.

Scotty then turned to Chekov. "Ensign," he ordered, "ready another probe."

"But, sir," Chekov said politely, "we have already launched eleven probes, and not one has reported back."

"Make it an even dozen," Scotty replied.

"I have the Klingon commander," Uhura reported. "Shall I put him on the screen?"

"On screen." The engineer nodded.

The gray-haired Klingon appeared on the viewscreen, his rough-hewn features softened by what almost looked like a smile. How boring it must be, orbiting this planet year after year, thought Uhura. She could hardly imagine feeling sympathy for a Klingon, but she did for this one, a dutiful officer at the end of his career, stuck in the most dead-end of assignments.

The Klingon rubbed the back of his neck with a towel. "You must excuse me for being winded," he said. "I have just come from my exercise period. It is my only pleasure."

Judging by his physique and the impressive size of his biceps, Uhura figured he must have plenty of time to indulge his pleasure.

Scotty bowed his head cordially. "We didna exchange names, so permit me to introduce myself. I am Lieutenant Commander Scott of the USS *Enterprise.*"

The Klingon nodded. "I am Commander Garvak of the cruiser *Rak'hon,* from the Klingon Empire. I suppose you are calling to say you are leaving."

"On the contrary," Scotty lied, "we've been ordered to try to retrieve our men from the planet. Do ye have any idea how we might accomplish that?"

Garvak shook his head, not bothering to hide his disbelief. "You earthlings will lose my respect with such foolish schemes. Perhaps what I've heard is correct—you are an inferior species. I have told you, no one leaves Sanctuary. The best we can hope to accomplish is to prevent other fugitives from reaching the planet."

Scotty took a deep breath, and Uhura knew he was trying to keep a cordial tone to his voice. "I understand that," he replied, "but Sanctuary must have guardians, someone who maintains the shield and makes the rules. Is there any way to contact them?"

"The guardians you refer to are called Senites," answered the Klingon. "Communication with the Senites happens very rarely, at their convenience. Some time ago, we succeeded in destroying a ship before it reached their protective shield, and the Senites contacted me. They offered a considerable reward for me to leave orbit forever. I refused and have not heard from them since."

"Is there anything you can tell us about their shield?" Scotty asked.

The Klingon nodded. "It extends approximately thirty kilometers from the surface. They have spot deflectors that they use to stop phasers and other weapons farther out in orbit. That is why most attempts to stop fugitives are unsuccessful. In fact, if I tried to open fire on you right now, it would probably do me little good. The Senites have learned a great deal from all the technology they have amassed."

"If their defenses are so good," asked Scotty, "how do ye know so much?"

Garvak shrugged. "We attacked Sanctuary with an entire fleet. We were unsuccessful, but we did learn the extent of their protective devices. Since then, I have been stationed here, guarding and watching. If I have sufficient warning, I can leave orbit and destroy a ship that is trying to elude Klingon justice. Otherwise, I am powerless. As you are."

Uhura wished the Klingon didn't have to be so blunt—or so right. "Powerless" was the only word to describe their situation.

Scotty cleared his throat and said, "Thank you for the information, Commander Garvak. I won't detain you any longer."

Even the Klingon looked melancholy when he replied, "It was not an inconvenience, Commander Scott."

The screen went blank for a moment, then was filled with the aquamarine planet, looking so serene yet so inscrutable.

Glumly, Chekov asked, "Shall I launch the probe?"

Scotty shook his head and slumped into the captain's chair. "Lieutenant Uhura," he sighed, "we have ta prepare a message for Starfleet."

Despite the cloud cover that flowed and ebbed with a persistent breeze, Captain Kirk was unprepared for the fury of their first rainstorm on Sanctuary. It drenched them in a matter of seconds, making a search for cover futile. But the shower was over in a few minutes. Spock took to calling the landmass they inhabited an island, saying the weather patterns were typical, and Kirk found no reason to disagree.

The stream they had been following had widened to approximately ten meters across and was rushing along at a considerable pace. Kirk stopped in midstride along the well-worn path, knelt, and watched the rapid flow of water. Because he was in the lead, Spock and McCoy stopped, too.

"Are you all right, Captain?" asked Spock.

"I'm not tired, mind you," answered Kirk, "but if we built a raft, we could *float* along this stream. It's gotten substantially wider since it joined up with that underground stream."

"It's also gotten faster," McCoy pointed out. "It's really moving, in case you hadn't noticed."

Kirk countered, "We could reach the village in a few hours, instead of a few days."

"Captain," Spock replied, "may I remind you that we do not know where this stream leads, into rapids or other bodies of water. We would have to go wherever the river took us."

"True," said Kirk stubbornly, "but we wouldn't have to walk. And we would travel ten times faster— unless you really want to do this for the next couple of weeks."

"We would travel considerably faster," Spock agreed, "at a certain amount of risk."

"I'm willing to take it, because the one thing we can't waste is time," said Kirk. "We can't be sure how long the *Enterprise* will stay in orbit, so we have to find our way back quickly. The Senites are the key to escape, so we must get to their village."

Spock nodded. "Very well. I believe we can lash vines together. It will be crude, and we will get wet."

Kirk pinched his damp uniform and shrugged. "I'm already wet."

"Well," muttered Dr. McCoy, "I never thought I'd make a good Huck Finn, but let's try it."

"Let me try this first," sighed the captain, reaching for his communicator. He performed the ritual that was by now so familiar, with the same result—they remained out of contact with the *Enterprise*.

Kirk took the lead in gathering the same kind of vines they had employed as weapons during the attack. Because the creekbed wasn't dry anymore, they had to search through thickets of bladder plants before finding vines that were dry enough to uproot from the ground and break into sections.

Kirk ordered McCoy to look for something that could be used to lash the sections together, and the doctor discovered a sort of creeping parasitic plant with long shoots that intertwined with the bladder plants. By stripping away the thorns and braiding the shoots, they found they could make a natural twine with a fair amount of tensile strength. McCoy's deft fingers set to braiding, while Spock and Kirk uprooted their building material.

Despite the wealth of materials, they were hampered by their lack of tools. They worked the better part of the afternoon and didn't finish the crude vessel until dusk. Captain Kirk had no desire to navigate strange waterways in the dark, so he commanded his tiny crew to look for food and try to get some rest. Spock had turned himself into a guinea pig, stopping often to taste new varieties of bladder plants as he discovered them. Spock had suffered no ill effects from any of his taste tests, but Kirk knew that his Vulcan physiology was unusually hardy; so he and McCoy ate only the mildest varieties. The only alternative was if they chanced upon a herd of ambulatory fish, which didn't seem likely this close to water. They couldn't risk stuffing themselves with strange greenery, so they ate just enough to keep the gnawing in their stomachs to a dull roar.

A strong wind favored them, blowing away the clouds and granting them a dry, starry sky to sleep under. Taking the second watch, Kirk was awake during the deepest part of the night, and he watched the moons of Sanctuary jockeying for prominence. First came the pinkish moon, rising swiftly from the mountains and climbing to an apex that commanded the whole valley. Kirk decided its strange color and fuzzy appearance might be caused by dust and debris that were caught in the moon's own gravity. Perhaps it had begun its career as a captured comet, he surmised, which could explain the shifting tides and sudden regression of oceans on the planet. The second moon appeared later, but its neon brightness took over the night, leading Kirk to believe that it was considerably larger than the pink moon.

With no ground lights visible in any direction, the stars glittered like spilt sugar on a black tabletop. But they looked far away to Captain Kirk. When you were among them, he recalled, they streaked by at warp speed, or glowed like the lights of a familiar city. From solid ground, the stars appeared nebulous, indeterminate.

Was this what it was like on Earth, Kirk wondered, before they perfected space travel? How did they deal with the realization that spaceflight was possible, but beyond their capabilities? How did they fight the longing, the thirst to explore, the need to see what was behind those twinkling lights? The vast new land under his feet was not without a certain allure, but to be shut off from the stars was unbearable.

Kirk still seethed with anger at the thought of the Senites stealing his shuttlecraft. Sanctuary was protection with a price. It welcomed fugitives from the farthest reaches of the galaxy, but it clipped their wings and made them exiles from space. The thought made Captain Kirk shiver more than the constant wind at his back and his damp clothes.

Chapter Four

THEY EASED the raft into the swift current and hung on, unable to climb aboard. The bundle of hollow roots was about two meters long and a meter wide and would have allowed three men to sit comfortably, but the rushing water wouldn't allow it. The current spun the little craft around and around until all they could do was cling. Luckily, the water was only waist-deep, and by concerted effort they were finally able to find footing and hold the raft still. McCoy climbed on in front, Spock in the middle, and Kirk leaped on at the last, and they rode the lumpy conveyance as one would a log. They still spun around out of control, only now they were seated and hanging on.

Keeping their balance was a major effort, and keeping dry had been forgotten after the first second, but they were moving briskly. The banks were nothing but a blur, and Kirk found he had to concentrate on the far-off horizon to gain any perspective. The spinning and speed were so disorienting that he finally watched only the raft in front of him and the backs of his comrades. Spock had been right—they were going wherever the river took them.

They were buffeted the hardest where other tributaries joined the river, but each new influx widened it and made the center of the river smoother. To avoid rocks and debris, they learned to paddle with their hands to stay in the center, about twenty meters from either shore. The water tasted good, and enough sloshed in their faces for them to get plenty to drink, but there was no time to relax. It was a grueling struggle to keep their grip on the sodden vines, while kicking and paddling the raft away from trouble. McCoy, in particular, had to muster most of his strength for hanging on. For long intervals, they spun aimlessly in the center of the waterway.

During an out-of-control period, they suddenly hit white water and were bounced and jostled along at a much greater speed. The water roared in their ears and made talking impossible, and it took all their efforts just to stay afloat. McCoy nearly slipped into the frothing water once, but Spock's strong arm was there to slam him back onto the raft and hold him in place until he found a grip. They were moving too swiftly to take any sort of bearings, and Kirk merely watched and waited for whatever would happen.

The roaring abruptly grew louder, and they were catapulted into midair. A waterfall! thought Kirk. Now the raft was over his head; he groped for it, but it floated just out of reach. He heard McCoy yelling as they dropped several meters through the misty air, but the weightless experience was not unpleasant. It ended abruptly with a collision against very cold water. Kirk sank many meters toward the bottom and had to swim with all his might to break out of the downward current. Gasping for air, he broke to the surface, and then he had to swim furiously to escape the plummeting waterfall.

Several meters away he saw McCoy clinging to the raft, and he smiled. The time it really counted, the doctor had held on. Spock, however, was nowhere in sight, even after Kirk stroked his way to McCoy's side.

"Are you all right, Bones?" he panted.

"Okay."

"Where's Spock?"

McCoy looked around, puzzled. "I thought I saw him. . . ."

Captain Kirk gazed across the smooth surface of the water. They had been dumped unceremoniously into the most beautiful lake he had ever seen. Pristine water the color of amethyst was surrounded by gently drooping trees whose tentaclelike branches seemed to be drinking from the lake. The closest bank looked like an easy swim.

But where was Spock?

The Vulcan rocketed to the surface a few meters away. "Get on the raft!" he barked hoarsely.

Kirk grinned. "Spock, we made it through! We're all right."

"On the raft, immediately," the Vulcan reiterated. "No time to explain."

McCoy wasn't waiting for an explanation, and he clambered from the chilly but peaceful water onto the shaky bed of roots. Spock wasn't far behind him, and Kirk could see that the Vulcan was as serious as he sounded. It wasn't until all three sat astride the raft that the captain noticed a gash on Spock's calf and a substantial stream of green blood.

"Spock, what happened to you?" Kirk demanded.

"I was bitten," Spock replied simply. "I stayed down there in order to find out what did it."

"And what did it?" asked McCoy.

The Vulcan nodded toward the surface of the water.

"I believe, Doctor, that if you watch the water, you will shortly see. We would be wise to keep hands and feet aboard."

That was easier said than done, and Kirk didn't pull his feet out of the water until he began to see languid silvery shapes streaming back and forth directly under them. The creatures snaked their way to the surface, as if they preferred the cold bottom where the amethyst turned black. He drew every limb toward the center of the raft as the eellike fish swam closer and he saw their ferocious jaws, the equal of any pike's or barracuda's. Their long, silvery bodies looked like women's belts, but they were many times larger and full of teeth and sinew. Two of them broke the surface with ribbonlike dorsal fins that were two meters long, stretched across sleek spines. The fish had the vapid eyes and lazy attitude of bottom dwellers who were slumming by feeding at the surface.

Kirk gulped. "Swimming to shore is out."

Spock observed, "This lake probably empties over another fall on the other side, if we can reach it. This is probably the crater of an inactive volcano."

"Smoke!" said McCoy, pointing furiously. "There's smoke!" The doctor gestured toward a wisp of gray smoke that rose over the drooping trees only to be swept away by the wind.

"A settlement," breathed Kirk. "Could that be Dohama?"

"Unlikely," answered Spock. "The survivalists said Dohama was on the ocean, not a lake."

Kirk peered intently at the far-off bank. "I see something more useful than smoke," he said. "Someone is watching us from the bank."

The captain began to wave his arms as much as he could without rocking the raft. "Hey! Hey!" he called. "Throw us a line. A rope. We're surrounded by these fish. Throw us a rope!"

Upon being directly addressed, two naked children with stark white hair stepped out from the cover of one of the tentacle trees. They stared with frank curiosity at the unfortunate rafters, not sure what they should do. It was obvious neither one of them had a rope to throw. The smaller child said something to her playmate, and they both laughed. No matter what Kirk said or how hard he waved, the children were content to watch.

This could have gone on for several hours, but an adult female with a similar shock of white hair appeared on the bank of the lake. She promptly grabbed both children by their arms and made off with them. This prompted even more frantic yelling from both Kirk and McCoy, and McCoy let his foot slip into the lake. At once, he yelped and pulled his foot out of the water with a hideous fish attached. It tried to sink its teeth deeper into his boot, whipping its long body in an attempt to pull him off the raft.

Spock smashed the beast with his only available weapon, his fist, and it lashed out with its tail and nearly knocked the Vulcan off his precarious perch. Reaching quickly, Kirk yanked a loose root from the raft and inserted it between the fish's jaws and McCoy's limb. With an effort that brought a scream of pain from the doctor, he pried the jaws loose. Or, rather, the hideous creature finally turned loose and slithered away.

The doctor examined his own foot briefly and found there were only a few scratches, no deep punctures. "Thank God for good leather," he breathed.

They were careful not to make any more rash moves aboard the raft. The white-haired children were gone, along with their overzealous protector, but shortly a man and a woman of different species appeared on the bank. The dark-haired woman carried a rope, which

49

she tied to a fist-sized stone, while the blue-skinned man cupped his hands to shout at them.

"Do not attempt to swim!" he warned. "The lancefish are dangerous!"

"Now he tells us," McCoy said, smiling with relief.

It took several attempts for the woman to throw the weighted rope directly to the raft, but she had obviously been well chosen for such a rescue mission. Each throw was a near miss until at last Spock made a one-handed grab of the stone in midair. They secured it to the bow of the raft and let the man and woman slowly tow them in.

When they got close to shore, the woman sprinted away, allowing them only a fleeting glimpse of her rugged beauty. The blue-skinned humanoid looked like he would be glad to leave, too, but he reluctantly remained to pull them safely to the bank.

Before they could even thank him, he spoke to them brusquely: "Go past Seaside Falls"—he pointed to the far end of the crater-sized lake—"and set your— whatever it is—in the water at the wide part of the channel. I can help you no more than that. We are a closed community."

He turned to leave, and Kirk called desperately after him, "Dohama! The Senites! Where are they?"

"Do as I have said," commanded the man. "But do not follow me to our village. We kill strangers."

It was spoken as a matter of fact, not a warning, and Captain Kirk was not at all inclined to doubt his word. So they didn't investigate the small band of men, women, and children who lived in the forest by the lake. They hefted their soggy raft and trudged around the crater, looking for a place past the Seaside Falls to put it in.

"Lieutenant Scott," said Uhura with urgency, "message coming in."

Scotty twisted around in the captain's chair. "From Starfleet, I'll wager."

"No." Uhura blinked, trying to concentrate on the intermittent syllables. "From one of the ships in orbit, the *Gezary*, she calls it. She says a fugitive ship is about to enter orbit, and that if we score a hit, she will split the reward with us."

"What in blazes?" muttered Scotty. "Put this woman on the viewscreen, and let's see what she's up to."

Uhura shook her head. "She has broken off contact and is leaving orbit."

Scotty sat up in his seat. "Yellow alert," he ordered, "full shields."

"Shields up," Chekov responded.

"If they're going to start shooting," said Scotty, "let's try to stay out of their way. Sulu, be prepared to leave orbit."

"Aye, sir," answered the veteran helmsman.

Chekov broke in, "Two more ships have gone to impulse power and are leaving orbit. And the Klingon ship is readjusting its orbit."

Scotty sat forward. "Can you get a fix on their course?" he asked. "What about the incoming craft?"

Chekov punched buttons and waited for a long moment. "Their courses are converging," he answered. "The *Gezary* is the farthest out, followed by two others, with the Klingon in a new orbit, which puts him closest to the planet." The ensign turned to look quizzically at the acting captain. "It's almost as if they are forming a gauntlet."

"Taking up stations," Scotty surmised. "Each one trying to guess where the ship is going to be when it comes out o' warp drive. I wonder how many times they've been through this drill?"

Sulu added, "I've located the incoming vessel. I can estimate its arrival and put it on the viewscreen."

"Go ahead," Scotty ordered. "In fact, put some

distance between us. Let's watch the whole thing from the back row."

They accelerated briefly. "Shifting to polar orbit," Sulu announced. "Short-range scan on the viewscreen."

Ship's sensors joined forces with the computer to re-create a scene that would have been difficult to see firsthand. Four bounty hunters, some commissioned and others rogue, lined a strip of space that stretched for a thousand kilometers from Sanctuary. The viewscreen showed the farthest ships as silvery blips, but the Klingon bird of prey and the green-hued Orion cruiser loomed much larger. They hung in space like vultures, hovering over the well-used approach path.

A streak entered the gauntlet and slowly materialized into a silvery missile. At once, phaser fire erupted from every corner of the screen, and the blackness of space filled with a blazing crisscross of destruction. As they tracked the fleeing vessel, the colorful rays converged and shattered the starscape with silent explosions. Seconds later, the aftershocks rocked the *Enterprise.*

"Shields holding!" announced Chekov.

Somehow, through it all, the incoming ship spiraled toward the aqua planet. The Klingon ship laid down a pattern of three photon torpedoes, any one of which should have atomized the tiny craft, but the torpedoes veered off at the last moment and fizzled harmlessly in the atmosphere. Scotty blinked, not sure he could believe what he had just seen, but he felt that Garvak knew what would happen and was treating them to an example of the Senites' remote deflectors. Despite the impressive fireworks, the all-out attack consumed only a few seconds; then the renegade ship had disappeared into the planet's atmosphere and the space around Sanctuary was peaceful again.

Scotty turned to Uhura, who was working her console furiously. "Was there any disruption in the shield during all that?"

Uhura shook her head with frustration. "I tried every channel, but there was no response. There *was* a momentary flux in the wave generation field. Maybe if the landing party tried to contact *us* when a ship entered the atmosphere, they might get through. . . . I don't know."

"You tried," Scotty said, mustering an encouraging smile. "We'll be ready for that opportunity when it happens again."

Then the engineer's brow furrowed thoughtfully under his boyish bangs. He rose slowly from the captain's seat and began to pace. "We can be ready if we're warned in advance," he mused. "And we *were* warned in advance."

"By the captain of the *Gezary,*" Uhura reminded him. "I know the frequency they use."

"One second," said Scotty slyly. "Let's play their game a wee bit. Maybe we'll learn more that way. Lieutenant Uhura, please inform the *Gezary* that we apologize for not firing at the fugitive. At future opportunities, we will be happy to cooperate."

Chekov looked back and shook his head, puzzled. "Now *we* are the bounty hunters?"

"You can win more flies with honey than vinegar," answered Scotty. He added, "We need friends. We need all the help we can get."

The Scotsman stopped directly in front of the viewscreen and stared at the majestic orb called Sanctuary. They were flying over her enormous frozen pole, and the planet looked as white and pure as a child's snowball.

"I'll find yer weakness," Scotty vowed to the icy globe. "I'll break you yet."

* * *

Bruised, battered, cold, and hungry, the three raft-ers drifted into a wide channel where the river could finally stretch out and rest. The sun had vacated the sky, leaving a charcoal smear of clouds, but there was enough light to see the endless silhouette of the ocean, and most of that illumination came from a display of colored lights on the eastern half of the bay. The lights swayed on high standards in a stiff breeze and didn't do much to illuminate the cluster of buildings beneath them. The longer you watched, thought Kirk, the more the candy-colored lights seemed to wave in a welcoming fashion. They were paddling in that direc-tion before he could muster enough strength to actual-ly give the order.

Putting thoughts of unusual aquatic life out of their heads, Kirk, Spock, and McCoy abandoned the raft to its own fate as they neared the shore and swam with desperation. At last they scrambled up the bank and collapsed on the gravel. Too tired to speak, the three staggered to their feet and trudged slowly in the direction of the swaying carnival lights.

As they drew closer, the wind shifted, and they caught the tinkle of music and the smell of food on the ocean breeze. It was a greasy, meaty smell, redolent of fat and spices, the kind that sets taste buds to water-ing. Despite his bruised face and painful foot, McCoy grinned foolishly at Kirk and picked up the pace. The captain glanced at what was left of his grimy uniform and wished he could make a better impression, but the growling in his stomach told him to ignore such niceties. Spock marched stoically beside him, but the Vulcan's stride lengthened as they got closer to the tempting sights and sounds.

Laughter mingled with gay flutelike music, and people could be seen lounging by an arched doorway in the low ornamental wall that surrounded the village. There seemed to be no guards and nothing to stop them from entering. The colored lights twinkled and danced on the standards above the wall, beckoning them. Despite their bedraggled appearance, Kirk, Spock, and McCoy were given little more than passing glances as they strolled through the crowd of revelers, each of whom carried a goblet and a shank of grilled meat. It was as if somebody were throwing a party, and everyone was invited.

Inside the wall, the village looked quaint, like something from Earth's Renaissance period, with crooked little two-story houses, a few grander buildings with porches and porticoes, and a village green. From every rooftop were strung the ubiquitous colored lights, but it was another type of light that caught their attention. In the center of the village green, sparks were shooting from huge iron braziers, upon which mammoth chunks of meat were roasting in open flames. A white-robed Senite dutifully manned each barbecue pit, grilling the delicacies to perfection before doling them out to waiting diners. Other Senites were filling goblets with sudsy amber liquid drawn from wooden barrels, and McCoy began drifting toward these libations.

Kirk caught up with McCoy as he was accepting a goblet from a smiling, shaven-headed Senite. "Bones, we don't know anything about this food or drink. Is it safe?"

"It's not safe to do without food and drink," said McCoy, "and that's our only alternative. I'll tell you more about the drink in a second."

The doctor chugged the liquid for several seconds and came up with a sudsy but satisfied grin. "Tastes like the finest Elysian ale," he pronounced. "I say it's fit for consumption, and I intend to test that meat next."

Kirk sighed not too reluctantly and took a goblet proffered by the agreeable Senite. He was tempted to ask the Senite about their shuttlecraft, but the androgynous being was suddenly deluged with requests for more ale. The crowd included Klingons, Saurians, humans, and creatures too bizarre to be called humanoid. The captain hadn't seen so many different races in one place since the time the *Enterprise* had transported dozens of ambassadors to an important conference. Despite the low-life appearance of many of the fugitives and a few drunken shouts, the gathering was peaceful. And why shouldn't it be peaceful, thought Kirk, with all the free drink and food anyone could want?

He took a sip of ale and had to admit that it tasted better than muddy river water. Strains of lively flute music reached his ears, and Kirk looked up at one of the balconies to see a small orchestra composed entirely of Senites. Like the other Senites in attendance, they toiled tirelessly on behalf of the revelers, creating intricate music to which many were dancing a jig or walking with a skip. Under a colorful awning, there were tables set up, and groups were eating, playing dice or cards, and guffawing loudly. If there was a cheerier place than Dohama on this windy night, Kirk never expected to see it.

He turned around and discovered that McCoy had vanished. After a moment's panic, Kirk spotted the doctor standing with Spock beside one of the barbecue pits. The Senite on duty was grilling a portion of meat and several large vegetables split lengthwise.

As Kirk approached, Spock turned to him. "Our host has graciously offered to cook vegetables for me," the Vulcan explained.

"Is there anything they won't do for us?" Kirk asked sarcastically.

"Nothing, sir," the Senite said without a trace of irony, smiling. "After you have finished eating, I will direct you to the inn, where you can bathe and select clean clothes."

"Sounds good to me." McCoy grinned. "How is my chop coming?"

"Done, sir!" the Senite answered pleasantly. The being gripped the meat with tongs and wrapped it in a cloth napkin before handing it to the hungry doctor.

"You know," McCoy said to Spock, "on Earth there was a tribe of people called Eskimos. Their entire diet consisted of nothing but meat and whale blubber, and they lived a long time."

Spock replied, "Longer than the whales, I presume."

Within a few seconds, both his comrades were wolfing down their food, and Kirk could resist no longer. He couldn't remember when he had tasted food as delicious as the thick chop prepared for him by the Senite, and he made a mental note to let everyone on the *Enterprise* have shore leave in the village. Then he remembered that, no matter how inviting Sanctuary seemed, they were not here by choice and could not leave of their own free will.

"Where do the Senites put the shuttlecraft and spaceships they confiscate?" he asked the cook.

"I wouldn't know, sir," the Senite answered, smiling agreeably. "My duty is to serve the persecuted."

"Leave him alone, Jim," McCoy scolded his friend. "At least while he's cooking."

"Technically speaking," said the Senite, "I am not a 'he.'"

"Sorry," said the doctor, wiping sauce off his chin. "Tell me, what's the occasion for this big shindig?"

The Senite shook its head in momentary confusion. "There is no occasion—this is the evening meal."

"Fascinating," said Spock.

McCoy shook his head. "I don't see what those crazy mountain men could have against *this.*"

"Dohama is not for everyone," the Senite replied.

"Yes," said Kirk impatiently, "and we appreciate the food. But who can tell us about our shuttlecraft?"

The Senite pointed toward an older building at the far end of the main street. It had a big portico and lots of iron railings, several cheerfully lit rooms, and enough banners, awnings, and colored lights to attract attention. "Go to the inn," said the Senite. "The important thing is to rest after your long journey."

"Right," muttered Kirk. He felt he was being talked down to, and he didn't like it. The Senites reminded him of a distant aunt who used to talk to him like a child, even when he wasn't one.

"Cheer up, Jim," said McCoy, hefting his goblet. "We should be happy to get off that river. The Senites seem like reasonable people—I'm sure all we have to do is explain what happened."

Kirk murmured, "If we can find somebody to explain *to.*"

Spock finished his meal and wiped his mouth with the thick napkin. "We have very little choice but to confront the Senites," he agreed. "However, in our present condition, I feel rest is a more prudent course of action."

Kirk nodded toward the garish building. "Lead on."

They strolled down a miniature boulevard, which was decorated with impressionistic statues and well-manicured bladder plants sporting crowns of vivid orange flowers. Carnival lights lined the rooftops, and shops on both sides of the street were open. The businesses were as varied as the creatures in them: a tattoo parlor, a sweets shop, a library, a game parlor, a hat store, a museum of oddities—all run by the ubiquitous bald Senites. At one house, which was bathed in green lights, women dressed in frilly night-gowns leaned provocatively from the windows and balconies. They should have looked attractive, but there was something wrong with them, thought Kirk. Their expressions were so cold.

"Senites," said Spock. "They have been decorated as women. Their purple and red hairstyles are obviously wigs. With a shortage of women on the planet—"

"That's quite all right, Spock," said the captain hastily, "I get the picture. All I want from the Senites is a way off this planet."

Despite the wigs and provocative poses on display, very few customers were frequenting the green-lit house. The smoke shop next door was much more popular, judging by the plumes of dingy smoke that billowed from it. Kirk paused and stared through the window; he saw various combustibles being dispensed, but no money changing hands. It seemed incredible, but the Senites apparently gave everything in this town away for free, including themselves.

Outside the smoke shop, a dutiful Senite was sweeping tobacco butts and other litter into a receptacle. Kirk watched the white-robed figure for a moment, wondering what it thought of the menial labor. His question was answered when the Senite looked up and smiled beatifically at him. Like a monk assured of his special relationship with God, the Senite walked on, scooping up the debris of hundreds of unmindful carousers.

Kirk shook his head and stumbled onward. Despite his immense curiosity and lingering anger, exhaustion was taking its toll. Now that the thought of sleep had planted itself in his brain, he could think of little else. He caught up with Spock and McCoy as they stood on the steps leading to the inn.

"Whatever happens in here," said Kirk, "let's stay together."

"Agreed." Spock nodded.

McCoy yawned. "I'm liable to do anything for a bed."

The door swung open in their faces, and a veritable giant of a man stood in their path. He looked mostly human, except for an overabundance of facial hair, and he cast a disdainful eye on the bedraggled strangers.

"Fresh meat," he sneered.

"What do you mean by that?" Kirk bristled.

"I mean you just got here." The giant scowled. "That's the truth, isn't it? You don't look like you've grown fat and happy in Dohama."

"We just arrived." McCoy nodded wearily. "Will they let us spend the night here?"

"Oh, sure," answered the big man, muscling past them. "They'll let you do anything you want. But when you've had your fill of this life, come and see me on the waterfront."

"Bed first," said McCoy, yawning again and heading into the inn.

"Can you get us off the planet?" Kirk asked hopefully.

The behemoth sputtered with laughter. "You *are* fresh meat, aren't you? Come and see Billiwog. We'll work out a deal." He saw someone in the crowd he knew, hollered an unpronounceable name, then swaggered off.

"Dohama does not lack for colorful characters," observed Spock.

"Hey!" they heard the doctor call. McCoy had proceeded ahead, finding himself in the restaurant section of the inn, and Kirk and Spock wearily followed. It was a friendly place; every spare centimeter was decorated with scraps and mementos from

60

hundreds of visitors and their useless technology. From the walls and ceiling hung strange weapons, odd devices, chunks of metal with the names of ships on them, holographic photos, emblems, tattered flags, helmets, hats, blackened circuit boards—a cornucopia of space junk.

"At least we know where some of the stuff goes," said Kirk, staring in awe at the walls.

Senites bustled about, serving food to an appreciative and loud group of diners. The food looked and smelled marginally healthier than the meat cooking in the open air. A rather chubby Senite approached the newcomers.

"My, my," it remarked, frowning, "you boys look a mess. Have you had anything to eat?"

"We've eaten, thanks," said Kirk, reacting cordially to the mother-hen quality of the Senite. "We're looking for a place to sleep."

"Then you've come to the right place." The innkeeper smiled, taking a key from the pocket of its apron and handing it to the captain. "Go up to room six and make yourselves comfortable. You'll find robes and towels in the closet, and I'll send somebody by in the morning with fresh clothes."

"That's very gracious of you," said McCoy, "but we can't afford to pay."

"Pay what?" asked the jovial Senite. "There's no money on Sanctuary. You're safe now from your former life, be it deprivation, persecution, or the pursuit of false idols, such as money. To show that you have discarded your past life, we ask you to contribute something to our collection from all over the galaxy." The being motioned around the festooned walls.

"We haven't got anything," lied the captain, feeling his communicator in his pocket.

"That's not true," countered the Senite. Before Kirk could respond, the androgynous being fingered the insignia on his chest; it was barely hanging on to the tattered cloth. "I've never seen one like this. You don't intend to keep wearing these clothes, do you?"

Kirk shook his head, unable to deal with the prospect of losing his command insignia and, by extension, his identity. "Tomorrow, maybe," he said.

"Ah, yes, tomorrow," replied the Senite, letting the insignia slip from its fingers. "Sleep well, my children." The innkeeper bustled off to greet more new arrivals.

"Fascinating," remarked Spock. "Apparently, the purpose of this society is to make people feel welcome."

"A little too welcome," muttered Kirk. "I haven't got enough energy tonight, but tomorrow I'm going to get some answers."

McCoy dragged himself toward the stairs. "Jim," he said through yet another yawn, "will you quit looking a gift horse in the mouth?"

Kirk glanced around doubtfully as he trudged up the stairs. Behind him, he heard two Klingons growling as they arm-wrestled. No, he wasn't going to look a gift horse in the mouth, not tonight. But he was going to give it a closer inspection in the morning.

The room was clean and functional, and it had a settee, two cushiony beds, and a full bath. Kirk got into bed, put his head on the pillow, and was asleep in the shortest unit of measurable time.

That night over Sanctuary, a large warship was blown up by bounty hunters seconds after coming out of warp drive. But the scanners aboard the *Enterprise* picked up fifteen fugitives beaming to the planet, all but one of them safely. The unlucky crew member was probably the transporter operator, and his molecules were scattered with the ship's. Nevertheless, it proved to Scotty that the mission of the bounty hunters was a futile one. For all the fish they netted, most of them dead, they were powerless to stop the vast majority who sought Sanctuary.

And what of those who found Sanctuary? Unless they had gills, thought Scotty, the inhabitants had precious little of the planet to play with. He gazed at the sparkling aqua globe. It had better be paradise, he decided, because the people who went there were gone as surely as if they'd gone to heaven.

Chapter Five

A GENTLE RAPPING on the door awoke Captain Kirk, and he sat up in the unfamiliar bed to see Spock sitting on the settee across from him, looking quite elegant in a gold-embroidered robe of royal blue. The Vulcan might have been awake for hours, judging by the alertness in his eyes and the sun streaming through the cheery lace curtains. McCoy was still snoring away in the other bed, even after the rapping sounded again.

"Somebody wishes to enter," said Spock.

Kirk reached for his own robe before calling out, "Come in!"

The door swung open, and they saw the plump Senite from the night before, pushing a rack of clothing in a conveyance that took up the entire hallway.

"Come now, no sleeping until noon," scolded the Senite. "We've got to clean this room. Remember, you can only stay here for two nights. After that, you have to see the landlord about getting a house. Now, what size are all of you?"

Kirk was bursting with questions and residual anger, but he recognized the need to have clothing that wasn't ripped to shreds. From what he could see of the offerings on the rack—mainly nondescript windbreakers and trousers—he knew they would be less conspicuous wearing such clothes. They would look like they fit in, which was all right as long as they didn't *feel* like they fit in. Despite the happy hordes milling around Dohama, Captain Kirk had no desire to spend the rest of his days in mindless carousing.

He knotted the robe around his waist and strode to the open door. The rack of clothing stretched for several meters, but Kirk quickly selected brown pants, a flannel shirt, and a blue windbreaker. All seemed well-made and clean, if not exactly new.

The Senite handed him shoes, socks, and underwear. "Just take what you can wear," it directed, smiling. "You can get new whenever you want—just go to any clothing shop."

"What is your name?" asked Kirk.

"Lincree." The Senite bowed politely. "But you don't have to tell me yours."

"I would like to tell you mine," the captain continued. "It is James T. Kirk. I command a Federation starship that is orbiting this planet as we speak. I can appreciate what your order is doing here, but we came to this planet unaware that it was Sanctuary, or what the rules were. As you said last night when you looked at my insignia, it's a very rare one in this sector of space. In fact, no one from Starfleet has ever been here before. All we ask is that you return our shuttlecraft and let us leave. We won't bother you again, and we'll put this planet on our charts, so everyone will know."

Lincree nodded thoughtfully. "James T. Kirk, I've run this inn for many years, and I've met almost

65

everyone who ever came to Sanctuary, and they all wanted to leave after the first day. It's new, it's strange, it's not what they expected. But mostly they're bothered by the fact that they can't leave the planet to return to space."

McCoy was sitting up in bed, too, listening intently. Kirk held his tongue and let the Senite complete what sounded like a well-rehearsed speech.

"This planet works on one basic principle," Lincree went on. "Integrity. We are successful in keeping the persecutors at bay by maintaining the integrity of this planet and our mission. If we were to allow people to come and go, the persecutors would send spies to the planet in order to kidnap refugees, or kill them. Everyone is safe here, knowing they are free from persecution, and everyone enjoys creature comforts and freedom. You know, Dohama is not the only place you can live. There are many other settlements, some much different from this one."

"In your terminology," said Spock, "we would be called persecutors. Is there no special method for dealing with persecutors?"

"No," answered Lincree, still smiling agreeably. "That is the other bulwark of our mission. We don't care what you've done before you came here. We don't judge you by your past—you are a part of Sanctuary now."

Quietly, Spock selected his wardrobe, while Kirk racked his brain for a line of logic that he could employ against the Senite. At the same time, he fought the sinking feeling that the Senites really backed up every one of their claims. From a security standpoint, a one-way ticket to Sanctuary had many benefits, but not for him.

"What can we do to prove to you that we are sincere?" he asked. "We can't stay on Sanctuary, no matter how lovely it is."

66

The innkeeper looked honestly aggrieved as it replied, "If you insist upon that attitude, I'm afraid your stay here will be disappointing."

"Where is our shuttlecraft?" Kirk asked bluntly.

Lincree smiled. "If you came here in it, then it must be on the planet somewhere." The Senite turned to Dr. McCoy. "Your turn, dear boy. We haven't got all day."

After exchanging the remains of their uniforms for clothing that was at least clean and inconspicuous, the newcomers ate a breakfast of rich pastries—all that was offered in the dining room—then took to the streets again. By day, Dohama was not much different than by night, thought Dr. McCoy. The same mindboggling mixture of humanoids wandered through seedy pleasure parlors, lively game establishments, and greasy food emporiums, all lubricated by ale dispensaries. If anything, Dohama looked seedier by daylight, minus the shadows and colored lights. The nearby sea cast an odor about the city that was both pure and alien.

McCoy had been disturbed by Lincree's little speech about everyone feeling hemmed in when they first arrived on Sanctuary, then later adapting. But the more he thought about it, the less he believed it. Some people were looking for a life of ease; others, like the captain and Spock, would never be happy just lazing in the sun. The doctor admitted to himself that the idea had some appeal, but he couldn't envision a life without any challenges. That seemed more of a sacrifice than giving up space travel. He suddenly had a grudging respect for the survivalists they had encountered earlier.

They strolled down one clogged street after another, studying everyone they passed. By the harsh light of day, the motley populace of Dohama did not appear so jovial, and more than a few were hung-over. They growled and grumbled at each other, and there was the occasional unyielding shoulder when passing a stranger at close quarters. Still, most of the denizens of Dohama loped along in a satiated daze. Why bother thinking or stealing when everything was free? thought McCoy. It was the perfect solution to the homogenization of lowlifes and riffraff from all over the galaxy. No wonder so many of them had accepted this life—it was painless.

Spock was trying to appear unobtrusive, but it was impossible. He looked too interested in what was going on, the doctor decided, and he didn't look hung-over enough. It was easy for the doctor to look bedraggled—his nose was swollen, there was a gash in his forehead and a crust of beard on his chin, and he walked with a limp from the lancefish attack. A well broken in but sturdy pair of boots furnished by the Senites was doing some good to cushion his tender foot.

It was inevitable, thought McCoy, that Spock should stare too hard at someone. In this case, it was a lopsided, red-skinned humanoid with arms that dangled to his knees. The thing was bare-chested and covered with black fur, except those parts where naked skin lay exposed in unappetizing folds of flesh, due no doubt to the rich Dohaman diet. He waddled up to Spock.

"Look, here's a Romulan," he slobbered, "or maybe a Vulcan. I get them two confused. What are you?"

"Vulcan," replied Spock.

"Right answer." The creature winked a bloodshot eye. "Bastard sons of the Romulans."

"That is incorrect," answered Spock. "The Romulans are an offshoot of the Vulcan race, not an older race."

Captain Kirk stepped to his friend's side. "It's not

important, is it?" he asked amicably. 'We're all friends."

The red humanoid lisped, "Moguru would like to be friends."

McCoy joined his comrades, taking heart in their strength in numbers. Moguru had approached Spock alone, so it was three against one.

"Three of you, yes," the bulky humanoid said, bobbing a head that had almost no neck to bob from. "That is what they told me. They say you are looking for a shuttlecraft?"

"Yes!" exclaimed Kirk in a whisper. "Do you know where our shuttlecraft is?"

"Well, hmm, maybe," answered Moguru. His rheumy eyes glimmered hopefully. "What would you give to know?"

Kirk shook his head dejectedly. "We don't have anything to give."

"Oh, too bad," slobbered Moguru. "I would give you a shuttlecraft for one thing."

"What's that?" whispered McCoy.

"A woman." Moguru leered. "You go get me a woman on the island of Khyming, okay? Then I take you to shuttlecraft. I'll take any woman, even human. Easy, for a smart Vulcan."

McCoy asked suspiciously, "How do you know there are women on this island . . . Khyming?"

"Where else they go?" Moguru shrugged.

"All right," said the doctor, "suppose we do it. How do we know you're telling the truth? How do we know you can hold up your end of the bargain?"

Moguru looked hurt at the suggestion he might be less than honest. "I have big friends," he boasted. "They know you." He lowered his voice. "You are the persecutors."

That got McCoy's interest, because they hadn't told anyone on Sanctuary about their circumstances—

except for the Senites. Kirk looked like he was making a decision.

"We believe you." The captain nodded. "I don't know how long this quest will take, because I don't know where Khyming is. Will we be able to find you later?"

"Yes-s-s," slavered Moguru. "Price will not change —shuttlecraft for woman." With a precarious rocking motion, the creature ambled away.

McCoy shivered. "No wonder those women on the lake ran away so quickly. They're the only attraction the Senites can't furnish."

"We learned a couple other things in that exchange," said Kirk. "The Senites have been talking about us behind our backs, and there's an island named Khyming."

Spock observed, "Because one Senite has talked to Moguru about us doesn't mean he knows the location of our shuttlecraft."

"True," muttered Kirk. "We don't know who we can trust, or if we can trust anybody. What was the name of that big fellow we ran into last night, in front of the inn?"

"Billiwog," answered Spock. "He resides at the waterfront, I believe."

"Let's see what kind of deal *he* can make," announced the captain, waving his men toward the unmistakable smell of the open sea.

Scotty tugged at the tunic of his gold-brocaded dress uniform, wondering if he had put on a few pounds lately. There had been too much time in the last few days for drinking coffee, eating, and worrying, as the *Enterprise* cruised lazily around Sanctuary. The occasion for the dress uniform was a break in the monotony, however, as the chief engineer was about to beam over to the ship of a lady bounty hunter.

The *Enterprise* had tightened its orbit to cruise beside the *Gezary,* keeping station within transporter range. After testing the transporter with inert samples, they were sure the Senites' interference applied only to weaponry. After all, more than a dozen fugitives had transported to the planet only the night before, although Scotty doubted whether they could transport off the planet so easily. That was his main mission in meeting with the captain of the *Gezary,* to learn everything she knew about the Senites. Scotty was determined to get some respect from the keepers of Sanctuary, and the *Gezary* had been able to warn him in advance about an incoming ship. They must have some sort of inside information, or at least insight, as to how Sanctuary worked.

Scotty pulled at the tight collar of his uniform and positioned himself on a transporter pad. "Do ye have the coordinates they gave us?" he asked the operator.

"Locked in, sir," responded the female ensign.

The engineer took a deep breath and said, "Energize."

His molecules reassembled in what appeared to be a jail cell, with rusty iron bars all around him. At once, Scotty grabbed his communicator and was about to contact the *Enterprise* to make a retreat, when a small viewscreen over his head crackled on, and a beautiful woman with slightly greenish skin and red hair appeared.

"Do not be alarmed," she assured him. "You are not our prisoner. Our line of business often makes it necessary to transport prisoners to and from the ship, so we take the precaution of beaming directly to our holding cell. It is a common procedure, I assure you. If you will be patient, my jailer will meet you and bring you to the dining room." The image winked out.

Scotty took an even deeper breath and wondered if he shouldn't have been more careful. But the captain of the *Gezary* wouldn't consent to coming aboard the *Enterprise,* even though she was the one who'd suggested that a face-to-face meeting was the only way to avoid having the Senites eavesdrop on their conversation. He spent several anxious moments waiting, until a hidden door slid open and a large, bearded humanoid walked in. The man, who had extremely pale skin and the outlines of antennae around his ears, was carrying a weapon that looked like a steel coil.

"Commander Scott?" growled the jailer.

Scotty stood at attention and nodded. "I am he."

The jailer reached outside the hidden door and tripped something in the corridor. Scotty's cell door finally creaked open, and he stepped out with relief. He followed the jailer into a dingy corridor that badly needed paint and maintenance—the wall lining was cracked and chipped, lighting fixtures were broken, and exposed wires poked out from a circuit box. This was not a favorable impression to make on the *Enterprise*'s chief engineer, and he began to wonder about the wisdom of dealing with such unsavory characters.

His doubts were reinforced a few moments later when he was ushered into a friendly but equally run-down dining room. Large tapestries hung on the walls, but they were so dusty that it was hard to tell what sorts of scenes they depicted. The overstuffed chairs and dining table looked elegant but old—and badly in need of a vacuuming. Overhead, a light flickered annoyingly, but the worst of the offenses was the musty smell that assaulted his nostrils. The only redeeming quality of the *Gezary*'s dining hall was the presence of the female he had seen on the viewscreen, a lovely green-skinned lass with red hair that tumbled down to her waist.

"Welcome," she greeted him with a smile. "I am Pilenna, captain of the *Gezary.*"

"Commander Scott." He nodded formally. "Montgomery Scott of the USS *Enterprise.*"

"May I call you Montgomery?" she asked. "We don't stand on formality much around here."

Scotty eyed the dirty surroundings with disgust. "That, I can see."

"Oh, you don't like our housekeeping?" remarked Pilenna. "Well, we're shorthanded at the moment, and we don't have the parts to repair our support system. I suppose I could get slaves to do the cleaning, but unlike most Orions, I don't believe in slavery."

Scotty shrugged. "You have to live here, not me. But it wouldna take much to make the *Gezary* shipshape."

"No, I suppose not." Pilenna sighed. "But we've exhausted almost all our resources just staying in orbit. I didn't want to go back to my home port without anything to show for all the time we've spent here, but I might have to."

Scotty asked, "Are you affiliated with the other Orion ship that's in orbit?"

"No!" snapped Pilenna, seething. "Filthy slavers, that's all they are! I should have made myself clear—I am only *half* Orion. I'm an escaped slave myself, and my biggest thrill is to capture slavers who have bounties on their heads. There are a goodly number of both slavers and escaped slaves below on the planet."

"I see," said Scotty. "What else do ye know about Sanctuary?"

"Let's not talk business over an empty table," said Pilenna. She clapped her hands, and a short humanoid who was barely a meter tall brought cups and a carafe into the room.

Captain Pilenna seated herself. "Don't worry, Montgomery," she said with a hint of mockery, "we wash the cups and pitchers. I have only a bit of Regulan wine to offer, but it's quite good."

For the first time, Scotty smiled. "I have a fondness for Regulan wine."

"You see," she replied, "we have much in common. What brings you to Sanctuary, besides the wish to see criminals brought to justice, and their captors amply rewarded?"

"It's not so much what brings us here," answered Scotty, "as what keeps us here. Before we knew much about Sanctuary, we sent a shuttlecraft to the surface of the planet in pursuit of a pirate vessel. Now we're out of contact, and we dunna know how to get our men back." He neglected to mention that one of the missing men was his captain; better to let Pilenna think she was dealing with an equal.

"Hmm." The woman nodded thoughtfully. "That is quite a problem, much greater than our dirty ship. I would say your only hope is to appeal to the Senites, although I doubt that it will do much good."

"How do we get their attention?" asked Scotty with frustration. "We've hailed them on every channel, we've appealed to them on humanitarian grounds—all to no avail."

Pilenna took a sip of wine. "I can arrange for you to talk to the Senites. For some reason, probably because they know I'm an escaped slave, they are willing to answer my hail. I can also tell, from increased gamma ray production, when the Senites are arming their deflectors to protect an incoming ship. That's how I warned you the other day, for all the good it did us."

Scotty sat forward excitedly. "How soon can we contact them?"

Pilenna raised one hand and smiled sweetly. "First we must discuss payment for this small service. How soon can you get a crew over here to clean and repair my ship?"

Scowling, Scotty stared at her for several moments. Finally, he reached for his communicator and flipped it open to accompanying beeps. "Scott to *Enterprise*," he said.

"Bridge here," Uhura answered efficiently.

"Patch me through to engineering and life support," said the chief engineer, glaring suspiciously at the beautiful green-skinned woman sitting across from him.

Kirk, Spock, and McCoy wandered along Dohama's picturesque wharf. It differed from other streets in the village in that there were shops and bars only on one side instead of both. On the other side was a vast blur of choppy water, with a few flying creatures skimming along the whitecapped waves. Farther out at sea, a fog engulfed the horizon, making it appear as if the sea and the sky were one entity. It was a lonely and forbidding sight, and Kirk couldn't banish the memory of the giant mollusk whipping its tentacle at them.

There were shouts and a fight broke out in front of them, as a half dozen strange creatures tumbled out of a bar and began belting each other with goblets, fists, and whatever they could lay hands on. Instantly, an army of Senites seemed to materialize, and the white-robed peacekeepers gathered around the combatants and pushed them en masse off the wharf into the sea, as a throng of onlookers howled with laughter. The brawlers sputtered to the surface and sloshed ashore, all the fight washed out of them.

"Quite efficient," observed Spock.

"And cold-blooded," McCoy added.

"Let's avoid them," said the captain, leading his small party in a circuitous route around the crowd.

At the far end of the wharf, tied to pilings and bobbing in the water, was a collection of rickety sailboats. On the shore was a pile of discarded lumber, and they could see a giant figure sawing away at what looked like a broken light standard. As they drew closer, they could tell that the worker was none other than the hairy humanoid they had met the night before, Billiwog.

He waved as he saw them approach. "What's all the commotion about?" he asked good-naturedly.

"A fistfight." Kirk shrugged. "The Senites pushed them into the water."

"Hmm," said Billiwog, wiping sweat from the only part of his body that wasn't covered with hair, his forehead. "Hope they can swim." He went back to sawing the wooden post.

"What are you doing?" asked Spock.

"Well," answered Billiwog, "these lampposts make good masts for my sailboats. On windy nights like last night, usually one or two of them come down. The Senites won't bother with 'em if they're broken, so I grab 'em."

"You made all these boats?" asked Kirk, impressed.

"Who else?" muttered the builder, not stopping his work. "I'm the only one in this town who does anything useful. So, have you fellows had enough of Dohama?"

"Yes," Kirk and McCoy answered in unison.

Billiwog stopped sawing. "Then you're ready to buy a boat?"

Disappointed, the captain asked, "Is that what you meant by getting away from Dohama?"

"What else?" replied the giant. "You didn't think you could *fly* away, did you?"

"We had hoped we could get our shuttlecraft back," said McCoy.

"Hmm," remarked Billiwog with a smirk, "then you're stupider than those guys in the water. Get a boat from Billiwog, and see something of this planet!"

Kirk lowered his voice and asked, "Have you ever heard of an island named Khyming?"

"Oh, you're interested in *women.*" The shipbuilder winked. "Can't say I blame you, there's precious few of them around here. And a rouged Senite just doesn't cut it."

"Then Khyming does exist," said Spock.

"It sure does, Pointy Ears. And if you're fixing to go there, I've got just the craft for you." Billiwog led them toward the most lopsided, rickety-looking boat in the water. "This one's special, sealed with lunk juice. It'll get you to Khyming, easy, and there's room enough to bring a couple women back!"

The captain sighed. "This isn't really what we had in mind, and we're not interested in kidnapping women. What else is on that island?"

"Lots of stuff," said Billiwog mysteriously. "Maybe what you're looking for. Take a trip and see. There's no point in hanging around here."

Kirk could certainly agree with that, but the choppy sea looked more dangerous and alien than anything they had seen in Dohama. "What else is out there besides Khyming?" he asked.

"Who knows?" Billiwog shrugged. "You could play it safe and sail along the coast. You're sure to find other villages, maybe some that aren't controlled by the Senites."

That wouldn't do them any good, thought the captain. "Thanks anyway," he said. "I don't think we're ready to go seafaring yet."

"Suit yourselves," answered Billiwog, picking up his saw. "But I'm a good judge of character, and I say you'll be back." The shipbuilder went back to cutting a new mast.

As they walked away, the captain turned to his comrades. "I'm at a loss," he admitted. "I don't want to explore this whole planet looking for our shuttlecraft, and kidnapping women is out of the question. So what are we going to do?"

"Captain," said Spock, "I have been formulating a plan. The probability of success, however, is far from certain."

McCoy responded impatiently, "What is it, Spock? Nobody else has any ideas."

"We have explored most of Dohama," the Vulcan explained, "and we have seen how and where the fugitives live. Although there are many Senites in the village, they do not appear to reside here. They must live elsewhere, coming here only to perform their duties."

"I see what you're getting at," Kirk said excitedly. "We know the Senites have the ability to transport themselves—we saw Zicree do it the first day. How can we find their transporter?"

Spock lowered his voice. "My suggestion is to follow a Senite after its work period is over."

"Good thinking," said McCoy, glancing around the busy waterfront. "Let's pick one."

Within a few seconds, a stocky Senite strolled by, sweeping bits of litter into a trash receptacle. It seemed to be headed toward the center of the village, and Kirk quickly nodded his head for his friends to follow.

Thanks to its white robe, there was no difficulty in distinguishing the Senite from the fugitives, even when Kirk, Spock, and McCoy followed at a distance of several meters and spread out to look less conspicuous. In a town where the only real activity was aimless wandering, the captain felt fairly confident that they wouldn't be noticed. The Senite seemed to pay them no attention as it steadfastly performed its menial task. Kirk only hoped that there was an end to the Senite's work shift, that it eventually went somewhere to rest and sleep.

It was midafternoon before the stocky Senite stopped to empty its trash receptacle into a bin set up

78

for that purpose. Kirk and company stopped as well, pretending to study a selection of earrings and jewelry that were free for the taking. The Senite running the jewelry stand suggested that McCoy have his ears pierced, and the doctor politely declined. Their quarry, meanwhile, cleaned its trash receptacle thoroughly and handed it to a fellow Senite. The shift was over, Kirk thought excitedly, and he nudged his comrades to continue the chase.

The Senite moved swiftly now, its hands folded in the billowing sleeves of its white robe. Kirk and his men had to walk briskly to keep up, and the captain was concerned that their pursuit would be noticed. But they had no other recourse, and no other plan. After leading them through numerous side streets, the Senite went down a narrow alley, opened an unmarked door, and stepped inside. The door slammed shut, and stood waiting for Kirk, Spock, and McCoy.

"This is it," said Kirk. "What's behind that door?"

"There is only one means of finding out," answered Spock.

McCoy swallowed hard. "Maybe we don't all have to go. One or two of us could wait here."

"No," answered the captain. "The last thing we need is to be separated. With our communicators not working, we might never find each other."

"Agreed," said Spock. "With your permission, Captain, I will lead the way."

The captain nodded. The Vulcan strode toward the unmarked door, with Kirk and McCoy following close behind. To their disappointment, they entered what appeared to be nothing more than a large broom closet. Trash receptacles, bins, and cleaning materials neatly lined one wall; empty clothing hooks and shelves lined another. There were no other doors, no windows, and no sign of the stocky Senite they had followed.

Kirk slapped his thigh and muttered, "Dead end."

"Perhaps not," said Spock. Meticulously, the Vulcan began to feel along the walls, rapping them with his fist to see if there were hollow spots.

McCoy shook his head. "Something tells me they've thought of everything."

Suddenly, the door to the alley opened, and Lincree, the chubby Senite from the inn, stood blocking the sunlight. The Senite they had followed stood behind Lincree, and there were more Senites visible in the alley. Gone was the cheerful expression that Lincree had exhibited earlier in the day.

"You are becoming rather tiresome," said the Senite. "Why can't you simply accept Sanctuary the way it is? As so many others do."

"Because we want to leave!" snapped Kirk. "We came here by mistake, and now you're holding us against our will. If you won't give us back our shuttlecraft, at least let us contact our ship. Or transport us there yourselves. To us, this isn't sanctuary, it's a *prison.*"

"Persecutors!" sneered the stocky Senite behind Lincree. "They are a disruptive influence."

"I agree," said Lincree. "It is rare for us to refuse anyone sanctuary, but this is a crucial time in Dohama. We cannot afford dissension."

The Senite reached into the folds of its robe and brought forth an object that looked suspiciously like a weapon. Kirk didn't wait to see what it was; leaping forward, he smashed into the Senite's chest and gripped its hand, just as a blue beam shot from the weapon and seared a black streak along the wall. The androgynous creature was surprisingly strong, almost his equal, but Kirk fought with the strength of a man who feared for his life. Luckily, their position in the doorway prevented any other Senites from aiding Lincree, and Spock was soon at his side. He applied the Vulcan nerve pinch and Lincree sank to the floor, leaving Kirk in command of the weapon.

Kirk aimed the weapon from one Senite to another until they stood well back from the door, allowing him and his comrades to exit into the alley and move toward the street. They heard raucous laughter from the streets nearby, reminding the captain that they were three among many. There was no doubt in his mind that many of the contented lowlifes of Dohama would side with the Senites against them, if given the chance.

"Will you help us?" he asked again. "We mean you no harm."

"You will not be able to use that," a Senite warned, stepping toward him.

Kirk glanced at the silver object in his hand. It bore more resemblance to a lopsided piccolo than a weapon, and he could find no trigger mechanism. When he looked up, the pack of Senites was advancing, and none of them wore their usual beatific smiles.

"Retreat would seem to be in order," said Spock.

"Let's go, Jim!" McCoy urged.

Kirk nodded, and the three ran from the alley into the street.

Chapter Six

Scotty suppressed a cough and held his breath as a cloud of dust spewed from the *Gezary*'s air filtration system. He motioned to a masked assistant, who stepped forward and removed an air filter that should have been removed years earlier.

"Replace all the filters," Scotty ordered. "I believe our N-4 filters should do the job. Whatever ye put in there, it will undoubtedly be an improvement."

"Aye, sir," said the assistant. "I'll send over to the ship for them."

Scotty nodded and stepped away from the billows of dirt. "I'll be supervising the repairs in the engineering department."

He strode into the main corridor of the *Gezary* and took a breath of relatively clean air. Scotty had twenty-six *Enterprise* personnel slaving away on the *Gezary* merely to make it presentable. In all his years of cruising the galaxy, he had never seen a spacefaring vessel that was so dirty and in such ill repair. Of course, he thought with some charity, Pilenna was not affiliated with an organization like Starfleet, which maintained numerous starbases for the purpose of sustaining its fleet. She was reliant solely upon her crew and her own wits; spare parts had to be begged or, in this case, bartered.

Under normal circumstances, he would never have committed the *Enterprise*'s crew to such a clean-up effort, but, like everyone in orbit around this infernal planet, he faced the problem of combating boredom and low morale. Every member of his crew was well aware that the captain, the doctor, and Mr. Spock were lost, and there was precious little they could do about it. He could only hope that the charity effort aboard the *Gezary* would, in small part, take their minds off the terrible loss they were facing.

His communicator beeped, and Scotty flipped it open. "Scott here."

"Lieutenant Uhura," came the response. "I just received a reply from Starfleet concerning our message."

Scotty's stomach did a wrenching turn. This was the moment he had dreaded. He had been totally frank in his appraisal of the situation to Starfleet, and he could well imagine their reaction. What he couldn't imagine —and didn't want to imagine—were the needs that had arisen in the meantime, needs that required the presence of the *Enterprise* in some other far-flung sector of space.

"What did they say?" he breathed.

"They express their concern," Uhura summarized, keeping her voice as unemotional as possible, "and they want reassurance that the *Enterprise* isn't in any danger. They also remind us that the *Enterprise* is due to take part in maneuvers near the Neutral Zone in seventy-two hours."

"Seventy-two hours." Scotty sighed. "They like ta stick ta their schedules, Starfleet does."

"Should I acknowledge receipt of their message?" asked Uhura.

"No," said Scotty. "Ask them to resend it. Tell them . . . there was interference."

"Yes, sir," Uhura replied. Scotty thought he detected a note of relief in her voice.

"Scott out," he said, snapping his communicator shut.

The work was far from done aboard the *Gezary*, Scotty knew, but it was time to demand his half of the bargain. If Pilenna wouldn't help him contact the Senites immediately, he would simply leave her ship in a shambles. With determination, Scotty strode down the corridor toward the private quarters of the bounty huntress.

Kirk, Spock, and McCoy dashed through the crowded streets of Dohama until they realized the Senites were not following them. Only then did they stop to catch their breath and consider their limited options. Kirk stuffed the useless weapon into the pocket of his drab jacket.

"What now?" he asked, disheartened.

"Captain," said Spock, "I apologize for the failure of my plan."

"It wasn't your fault," McCoy pointed out. "It's obvious we're not going to get any favors out of the Senites."

A Senite running an ale dispensary on the corner gave them a curious look, and Kirk motioned his men to keep walking. There was no sign of the pack of Senites who had cornered them. And why should the Senites make a spectacle of themselves running through the streets? he thought. They had eyes and ears everywhere; Dohama was their turf. They could afford to wait for the three troublemakers to go to sleep or otherwise let down their guard.

"We've got to get out of Dohama," Kirk said finally. "There's no point staying here and some very good reasons to leave. But we can't spend days walking somewhere else. I think it's time to find out more about that other island."

Billiwog smiled and waved when he saw them coming. The hirsute humanoid was sitting on his pile of lumber, grilling a fish over an open fire. "I knew you'd be back," he said simply.

"Why are you cooking your own food?" asked McCoy. "Senite cooking isn't good enough for you?"

He smiled. "Let's just say I like a change of pace."

"We want your best boat," said Kirk. "I know a little bit about sailing, enough to know a good boat when I see one, and that one you offered us wasn't a good one."

Billiwog's face darkened, and he rose to his full, impressive height. "What boat you get depends on what you have to trade."

Kirk frowned, considering. Then he reached into his pocket and pulled out the mysterious Senite weapon. "How about this?" he asked. "We took it from the Senites when they tried to use it on us. It's some kind of weapon."

"Oooh!" exclaimed Billiwog, his eyes beaming with delight. Gingerly, he took the silver object and held it up to the sun. "For this, you get any boat you want. I'll even throw in a couple oars. Do you know how to make it work?"

"No," answered Kirk. "I'd be careful with it, though."

Spock was already walking along the wharf, studying the collection of crude vessels. He stopped in front of the one with the highest mast and began to inspect the workmanship of its hull. He climbed into the boat, checking the inside for dampness.

"Ol' Pointy Ears knows what he's doing," said Billiwog, nodding in Spock's direction. "That's the best boat I have. I traded for it—didn't build it myself. If you're not sure what you're doing, you might be better off sailing up the coast."

"Be straight with us," said McCoy. "What exactly is on Khyming?"

"Women," answered Billiwog, "and political refugees. It's common knowledge that a better class of people gets sent to live on Khyming. One time I was there, I saw what you might call a seminary, where they train the Senites. I can't tell you that you'll find what you're looking for, but I can tell you that you won't find anything in Dohama but a hangover."

Spock rejoined the group. "I have selected a vessel," he reported. "I can find no leaks in the hull or holes in the sail. The mast, rudder, and tiller appear to be sturdy."

Billiwog licked his finger and stuck it into the air. "You're in luck," he announced. "There's a southerly wind that should take you right there—with a full sail. If you leave now, you might make it before dark."

"Which way?" asked Kirk, peering gloomily at the sea and the fog bank beyond.

"Straight into the fog," said Billiwog. "You would probably be able to see Khyming from here if it weren't fogbound. Just don't sail past it. And look out for the lunks."

"Lunks?" asked McCoy.

Billiwog smiled. "Giant sea creatures."

Pilenna slowly buttoned her low-cut tunic, obviously enjoying Scotty's embarrassment. But she had admitted him into her quarters while in a partial state

86

of undress, and he was not going to be dissuaded from his task by a bit of Orion teasing. Except for her flesh being green, it wasn't anything he hadn't seen before.

"Why do you want to contact the Senites now?" she asked with mild disapproval. "You haven't finished your end of the bargain yet."

"Because, I've just received word that I may have to leave Sanctuary very soon. Please, it's a matter o' life and death."

"Isn't everything?" The bounty huntress reached for a brush and began combing her lustrous red tresses. "It would be a shame to see you leave so soon. We were just getting to know each other."

"Were this another time and another place," Scotty murmured, "I would be pleased to get to know you better."

Pilenna smiled. "I once heard a human say, 'There is no time like the present.' But he did not have your sense of duty."

She sat down at her purple vanity and swiveled a small viewscreen into place. "I generally call them from here. It's more private." Pilenna waved her hand over a colored panel, which flickered on. The screen did likewise.

"This is Pilenna of the *Gezary*," she said, "calling the keepers of Sanctuary. May I please speak with the hallowed order of Senites?"

There was a substantial wait, but Pilenna did not repeat her request. She smiled at Scotty, who fidgeted nervously. "They will reply," she explained, "in their own good time."

Finally, a serene face below a bald pale appeared on the viewscreen and a lilting voice replied, "I am Felcree of Sanctuary. How may I help our sister in the sky?"

"I am humbly in your debt," she acknowledged. "With me is the captain of another vessel that orbits your peaceful planet. He is confused and wishes to speak with you."

"So be it," said the Senite, not looking very enthusiastic about the prospect.

Pilenna rose and let Scotty take a seat in front of the viewscreen. "I am Lieutenant Commander Scott of the Federation starship *Enterprise*. Until three days ago, we had no idea Sanctuary existed. This sector of space is unfamiliar to us—in error, we sent a shuttlecraft with three crew members to the surface of your planet. They are na' fugitives, and no one was pursuing them. We havena been in contact with them since they entered your atmosphere, and we hope ye will help us locate them and return them to our ship."

"Impossible," answered the Senite. "As you have no doubt learned, we offer sanctuary to all who seek it, and we cannot determine in advance their motives or worthiness. We safeguard the persecuted by refusing to permit anyone to come to the planet and leave again. This simple security system has discouraged persecutors for hundreds of years, and we see no reason to change it."

Scotty struggled to keep his voice calm and reasonable. "Ye can speak to them yerselves," he suggested. "I'm sure they will tell you they want to leave. Surely you must be able to rectify mistakes like this."

The Senite shook its head and replied sternly, "All who come to Sanctuary do so of their own free will. You must not fear for the safety and well-being of your friends. All who come to Sanctuary are afforded dignity, respect, and creature comforts." The image flickered off.

Desperately, Scotty waved his hand over the panel and begged, "Come back! Come back! You dunna understand!"

He felt tender hands on the back of his neck. "They

understand all too well," sighed Pilenna. "They simply don't care."

Scotty slammed his fist down, shaking the purple table down to the deck. "I'd like ta blow that planet out o' the sky!"

"But you won't," breathed the Orion, her deft fingers massaging the knots of anger from his shoulders. "I've never known the Senites to lie about anything. Your friends probably *are* enjoying dignity, respect, and creature comforts." She cooed in his ear, "There's nothing wrong with creature comforts."

The Scotsman closed his eyes, feeling too numb and helpless to do anything. He let Pilenna's skilled hands play across his chest for a moment. Then, with an effort, he roused himself and stood.

"Madam," he said, bowing politely, "I have too much to do to enjoy yer company at the moment."

"I'm not going anywhere," she answered, smiling. "And, perhaps, neither are you."

A giant wave slammed the tiny boat, as sheeting rain and wind ripped the sail from the mast. Spock tried heroically to wrap the sail around the boom to save it, but he lost his footing as the boat tipped, and the sail tore from his hands and vanished. McCoy hung on to the tiller as if it would do some good, but the boat spun in the maelstrom, out of control. Captain Kirk gripped the two oars tightly, knowing they were probably their only hope of salvation.

The squall had struck suddenly when they were barely out of sight of the shore, just after they reached the fog bank. Before then, their spirits had been as buoyant as the tiny craft, as the sail billowed and they skimmed along the waves en route to a new destination. Kirk remembered quite a bit from the sailing he'd done as a boy, and Spock knew the rudiments.

They let McCoy steer as they manipulated the sail, the ropes, and the boom; managing a boat with a single sail had proved relatively easy, as long as they kept the wind leeward, at their backs. Even entering the fog hadn't dampened their spirits, because they knew it meant they were closing on Khyming.

Unfortunately, the fog had masked the pending storm, and they didn't know enough about the sea to realize that the choppy waves meant a squall was brewing. Before they knew it, they were in the squall. Now there was nothing to do but ride it out— somehow.

"Keep low!" yelled Kirk. "Keep to the center of the boat!" His greatest fear was that one, or all, of them would go overboard.

Like three men riding a giant bucking bronco, they lurched up and down over the waves. The howl of the wind was horrific, thunder shattered their senses, and lightning punched the sky with jagged rays. With the sail gone, Spock set to bailing water with a small can Billiwog had tossed into the boat at the last moment. Incredibly, he held onto the boom with his other hand and kept it from sweeping back and forth, taking their heads off. Kirk longed to pull out his communicator and make a desperate attempt to contact the *Enterprise,* but he didn't dare let go of the oars, not for a second. McCoy huddled in the stern of the boat, wrestling with the tiller.

This nightmare made their day riding the river seem like a walk in the recreation room, thought Kirk. He was drenched and so sick of water that he vowed never to take a shower again. The sky was getting darker, and not just because of the storm. What would they do if they were driven way off course, past Khyming? The captain squinted his eyes against the spray and tried not to think about it.

Finally, mercifully, the wind began to abate. The rain was still coming down in sheets, but it brought only discomfort, not a terrifying ride at the mercy of a frenzied sea. One by one, Kirk, Spock, and McCoy lifted their heads. The waves continued to jostle the boat, but they weren't as fearsome as a few moments earlier. Except for the relentless rain, the storm seemed to be losing force.

Kirk finally loosened his grip on the oars and handed one to Spock. "You take the port side," he ordered, "I'll take starboard."

"Which direction are we going?" asked McCoy. "I had a compass in my pack, but those damn survivalists took it."

Kirk smiled. Relief that they were still alive washed over him like the warm rain. "Well," he remarked, "we have to make a guess. In one direction should lie the island, in another Dohama, and in a third, more of the coast. If we guess wrong and row in the fourth direction, we'll row ourselves farther out to sea."

Spock furrowed an eyebrow and said, "I beg to disagree, Captain. We do not have to guess. The storm was accompanied by a one-hundred-eighty-degree change in wind direction. Therefore, rowing into the wind should take us south, toward Khyming. There are two unknown factors, however—that we were blown off course, and that the wind will change again."

"So," the doctor concluded, sighing, *"your* guess is we should row into the wind?"

Spock nodded. "I would categorize it more as a theory than a guess, Doctor, but I do believe the windward direction will take us near our destination."

"Sounds good to me," said Kirk, plunging his oar into a peaking wave. "Let's put our backs into it!"

Spock stroked his oar through the turbulent sea, trying to stay in unison with his captain, while McCoy laid into the tiller, maintaining a course straight into the ragged wind. With muscles straining, they began a slow pull toward an unseen shore.

Scotty strode onto the bridge and took the captain's seat with a vigor that surprised Uhura, watching from her communications console. He stared at the aquamarine planet on the viewscreen, as if making up his mind about something.

"How did repairs on the *Gezary* go?" she asked conversationally.

Scotty cleared his throat and straightened in his seat. "Very well," he answered. "Although I think the captain of the *Gezary* wasn't completely satisfied."

"Were you successful in contacting the Senites?" she asked.

Scotty's shoulders drooped slightly, and he gazed around at the expectant faces of Chekov, Sulu, and the other bridge personnel. "I talked to them, all right." He frowned. "But they refuse to change their rules for anything or anyone. They maintain that all who come to Sanctuary do so of their own choice, and their greatest protection is that no one can leave. Short of mounting a full-scale attack on the planet, I dunna know what we can do ta change their minds."

The acting captain stared at the planet and set his jaw firmly. "I've reached the conclusion that we must depend upon Captain Kirk, Mr. Spock, and Dr. McCoy to arrange their own escape, however they can. We must be ready to help them at a moment's notice. That means listening, watching, monitoring, and being aware of everything that happens below on the planet. We know there are fluctuations in radio and gamma waves when the Senites are forced to use their deflectors, so we must be aware of any minute changes."

Scotty took a deep breath and concluded, "If anyone can escape from that heathen planet, it's those three. We just have to stay here as long as Starfleet will let us, then be ready to help them."

Chapter Seven

CONSTANT RAIN CHILLED Captain Kirk to the marrow of his exhausted bones, but every pull of the oar brought them closer to the island, he hoped. Beside him, Spock strained in unison against his oar, while McCoy wrestled with the tiller to keep them on a course into the wind. One result of the rain was that the fog had been washed away, and Kirk could see the pink moon creeping over the horizon directly behind the boat, casting a strange salmon glow over the rippling waves.

Kirk peered into the drizzle, hoping Khyming would have its share of lights. Otherwise, they could row right past the island in the thickening darkness. At least the sight of Sanctuary's first moon gave Kirk some indication that Spock had been right; they were still heading south. He vividly remembered the pink moon rising over the northern mountains on their first night on Sanctuary.

The *Enterprise,* the shuttlecraft, the chase and horrendous crash of Auk-rex's ship—it all seemed eons ago, in another lifetime. Kirk would never admit defeat, but he had to admit that time was running out for them. Every day they spent on Sanctuary, every day out of contact, was a day closer to the moment when the *Enterprise* would be summoned elsewhere. Perhaps the ship had already been called to an emergency, Kirk thought glumly. Of all people, her captain knew the value of the *Enterprise* to the Federation, and it far outweighed the lives of any three crew members. Unless there was an emergency, Scotty could jockey for a certain amount of time, but what else could he do? The captain could only hope that Scotty hadn't risked sending anyone else to the planet in search of them.

The sun was setting on their fourth day on Sanctuary, and they were no closer to discovering where their shuttlecraft had been taken. Kirk knew why, of course. The Senites' logic was so sound that even Spock had found no reason to quarrel with it—they kept the fugitives safe by separating them from their persecutors forever. Everyone was forgiven his crimes, even those persecutors foolish enough to chase their quarry to the planet.

Kirk had never given real thought to the concept of sanctuary before. This version, he mused, denied everyone what they sought: The persecutors lost their prisoners; the prisoners lost their freedom; and the saviors were turned into jailers. Kirk didn't know whether to hate the Senites or feel sorry for them.

"Captain," queried Spock, "can you verify whether that is a light I see to starboard?"

Kirk leaned eagerly over the right side and peered into the gloomy distance. Rain pelted his face, making it difficult to stare, but he did think he saw something shining in the distance—a star on the water.

"McCoy!" he barked. "Make for that light."

"Where? Where?" rasped the doctor, squinting into

the rain. He couldn't see the light immediately, so he aimed the boat in the direction Kirk was leaning.

Spock and Kirk took up their oars in earnest. Ignoring bodies that were shaking with exhaustion and cold, they drove the tiny craft through cresting waves. Finally spying the solitary light, McCoy set an unyielding course. Kirk began to imagine he saw a faint silhouette of land to go along with it. No matter where they landed on Sanctuary, the captain vowed to himself, he was not going to take any more journeys by water.

As they neared the light and saw that it was no mirage, Kirk began to worry about rocks. All they could see was a simple white light, like a lantern, where a searchlight would have been much preferred. For all he knew, the light might be perched on deadly boulders, where they could be sucked in and pulverized without warning.

As if in answer to an unspoken prayer, Sanctuary's huge white moon gleamed through rents in the racing clouds as it slowly rose from the east, fitfully lighting the way through a small harbor dotted with reefs, made more dangerous by low tide. At the sluggish pace at which they were rowing, they had no difficulty avoiding those accumulated remains of billions of microscopic animals, but Kirk wondered what might have happened if they had scudded into the harbor with a full sail and the wind at their backs. They might be swimming at this point, he decided, or sprawled across a reef with their boat.

The island itself was barely visible as a dark and forbidding outline. There was apparently nothing on shore but a simple adobe hut, where the light hung swinging on the porch. No one seemed to be around; the darkness had taken hold, broken only by flashes of moonlight, and rain continued to pelt them.

96

"I see a beach," Kirk called, pumping the oar through the water. "Do you see it, Bones?"

"Yes, yes!" the doctor called. "I'll make for it."

But the closer they got, the stronger the offshore current became, dragging the boat away from the elusive light. Kirk and Spock rowed like whipped slaves, but they couldn't make any headway in the tumultuous surf.

"Stop! Stop!" Kirk gasped, his body spent and his muscles quivering. "We're not, getting, closer."

"I volunteer to swim," said Spock, taking off his boots.

"No, no!" protested Kirk. "I will—"

"Jim," said the Vulcan, "I am weary, but I am not as close to exhaustion as you. Please, tie the end of this rope to the boat and feed me the line as I swim."

Every passing wave buffeted them in a new direction, and McCoy had a difficult time trying to keep the tiller pointed in the right direction. "Listen, you two," he shouted, "let me go. I haven't been pulling an oar."

But Spock had stripped off his jacket, shirt, and boots, and had one end of the rope tied around his waist. He stood poised to jump into the water. "With your permission, Captain?"

Kirk was busy wrapping the rope around a spar, then his own waist. "We don't want to lose you, Spock!" he shouted over the slathering surf. "If you feel yourself weaken, pull on the rope a few times, and we'll pull you back. That beach must have a steep drop-off to create such a strong current, so watch your step."

"I will heed your advice," Spock replied. A second later, he dove gracefully off the side of the boat and was soon slicing his way efficiently through the waves.

Spock had only one plan, and that was to get beyond the breakers where the offshore current wasn't so fierce. As long as he swam on the surface, it couldn't impede him too much, and he felt the incoming waves giving him impetus. But if he slowed for an instant or let his legs dangle in the water, a whiplash effect threatened to hurl him backward. So he kept his arms and legs moving—despite utter exhaustion—trying to ride the waves to aid his progress.

The beach was getting deceptively closer, but Spock knew from the strength of the undertow that he must still be over the drop-off. The sand lay just a few meters away, and he could see their beacon—an electric light bulb or lantern, he realized—swinging jauntily in the wind. Obeying a very human impulse, he put his foot down to see if he could touch bottom.

Almost immediately, Spock realized that what he'd touched was not the bottom, but something *lying* on top of it. His foot struck what felt like cold jelly, or an ice pack. It clung to him gently at first, then more insistently, as flaps of sticky coldness wrapped around his foot and consumed his ankle. Spock didn't waste a precious moment; he instantly pulled on his rope to signal the captain.

His sudden motions intrigued the beast, and he felt it ooze up en masse from the sodden sand and wrap around his entire leg. Spock began to kick with his other leg and paddle his arms with all his might. But the creature clung and he could feel a thousand little suckers begin to explore his flesh. He pulled on the rope as hard as he could and bellowed, "I am in need of assistance!"

In the boat, Kirk and McCoy tugged on the rope for all they were worth, and they quickly pulled in the slack that trailed after Spock. Spock felt the rope tighten around his waist, and he knew his friends had heard him. But when they began to wrench him away from the slimy entity at the bottom of the drop-off, they began a tug-of-war contest. The thing retreated deeper into the sand, trying to take Spock with it.

For the first time, the Vulcan was yanked underwater. Fortunately, he had taken a breath and used that moment to give his captured appendage a firm yank. He didn't completely free himself from the cold stickers, but he got part of his leg free, and he kicked at the tentacles with the other, bobbing to the surface long enough to gulp air before the creature regained its slimy grip and dragged him deeper.

In the moment before the water closed again over his head, Spock saw Kirk and McCoy reeling in rope, getting closer to him at a fast rate. He went under just as the boat picked up an incoming wave and began rushing toward the beach. Kirk staggered to his feet and grabbed an oar, ready to do battle or make a rescue, whichever came first.

Spock's breath was nearly running out, and he tried to control his strength as he swam steadily toward the surface. The thing still gripped his foot—but leisurely, as if it no longer felt threatened. The tug-of-war was over for the moment, and Spock felt the rope scratch his shoulder and head in the other direction. With powerful strokes, he reached the surface and took a deep breath before the mollusk pulled him under again.

A wave dumped the boat on the shore, smashing it into pieces. Kirk and McCoy scrambled to untangle themselves from the mess and claim a foothold in the sand. Suddenly, the rope around Kirk's waist yanked taut, dragging him across the wreckage, and he grabbed his oar. As a wave crashed over his head, he felt McCoy gripping him under his arms and halting his slide back into the water. Kirk scrambled to his feet and helped McCoy get to his, and they dug their heels into the sand as their opponent renewed its claim on Spock.

The rope pulled tight, yanking them off their feet and smashing them into an incoming wave. Sputtering, Kirk struggled to his feet, and he knew the thing was winning. Then suddenly he heard gasping and splashing, and he realized that Spock was alive and only a few meters away. He redoubled his efforts, pulling in the rope hand-over-hand. Spock was unsure why the thing had retreated, but it no longer held his leg. He clung gratefully to the lifeline until he felt himself tumbling into Kirk and McCoy.

They hauled the bedraggled Vulcan ashore, far from the breaking waves, and all collapsed on the sand. Panting, Kirk looked up—and saw the slim Senite standing by the house. Even with the hood over its head, the being was recognizable as Zicree, the first Senite they'd met—the one who knew the most about their missing shuttlecraft. Zicree held a small blue instrument in its hand.

Kirk stared at Zicree for a moment, then turned to check on his friend. Spock was kneeling on all fours, spitting out water and trying to fill his lungs with air instead.

"He'll live," McCoy reported, "but that was awfully close. What *was* that, Spock?"

"A giant . . . mollusk," the Vulcan rasped. "Try to imagine . . . a snail that is as large . . . as the bridge of the *Enterprise.*"

"We call it a lunk," said a voice behind them. Zicree had strolled from the house to the water's edge. "In fact, that lunk is well known to us. We call him Old Hemcree."

"He retreated," panted Spock. "Somehow . . . you drove him away."

"With this," the Senite replied, holding up the blue instrument. "Sound waves. Few humanoids can hear them, but the lunks are repelled."

Kirk stood up and smiled gratefully. "Then you

saved Spock's life. Thank you. I remember you . . . your name is Zicree."

The Senite sighed disgustedly. "I remember you as well. Because it was I who welcomed you to Sanctuary, you are more or less my responsibility."

"Give us back our shuttlecraft," said Kirk, "and we'll be gone."

"You were almost 'gone' a second ago," the Senite replied wryly. "As difficult as this may be to believe, we Senites admire initiative. Therefore, you may stay on Khyming. To live on Khyming is a privilege, and your behavior will determine how long you may stay. You will find clothes and food in the small house that guided you here." The Senite turned and started toward the dark forest beyond the shore.

"Wait!" called Kirk. "We have many questions. We need help."

The Senite turned briefly and replied, "I just helped you, and I wasn't obliged to do so. I want the population of this planet to have drive and initiative, as you three have. Therefore, I will help you if I can. But don't expect to leave Sanctuary. That is beyond my powers, and certainly beyond yours."

The white-robed figure disappeared into the thick foliage that surrounded the spit of beach. With the rain still coming down hard and each man exhausted to the bone, Kirk wasn't about to look another gift horse in the mouth. He motioned his men to follow him to the little hut with the welcoming lantern.

True to Zicree's word, they found clean clothes of the same ilk as they were wearing and a simple but plentiful meal of coarse grains cooked with considerable skill and seasoning. They even had bowls and spoons, Kirk noted. Already, the dietary standards of Khyming seemed to be far different from those of Dohama. They now had warm porridge sitting in their stomachs, dry clothes on their backs, and a sturdy roof over their heads. Kirk watched Spock and McCoy fall asleep and felt himself drifting off into a sleep as heavy, he imagined, as the lunk under the waves.

The captain stepped out of the hut the next morning to find that the rain had stopped and fog had reclaimed the island. The morning mist was so thick that he could hear but not see the waves that pounded the treacherous beach a few strides away. He stepped forward cautiously and found several chunks of the boat that had washed farther ashore. The landing party was tough on watercraft, Kirk thought ruefully.

Then he shuddered at the thought of the creature that had nearly gotten Spock, and perhaps all of them. Of course, the Senites had learned how to control the lunks, just like they controlled so much of their environment. Were there limits to their control? wondered Kirk. Did they ever make a mistake, ever leave the barn door open?

"Captain!" he heard the familiar voice of Mr. Spock calling.

"Over here!" answered the captain. He kept talking so that Spock would find him in the pea soup. "I'm not sure what kind of special privilege it is to live in this fog all the time."

"We haven't seen the rest of the island," Spock observed.

"How do you feel?" Kirk asked. "Any ill effects?"

"Only this." Spock indicated his bare foot, lifting it to show the captain a rash of circular welts that covered his appendage from toe to midcalf.

"Ouch," said Kirk sympathetically. "Does it hurt?"

"I can bear it," replied Spock, "if I do not wear a boot. Actually, I feel quite well."

Kirk stretched his arms and took a deep breath of

cool mist. "I feel good, too. It's amazing what a couple good meals and lots of exercise will do."

"Nearly get you killed!" called a third voice from the fog. Dr. McCoy straggled over to join them. "Are we on our way somewhere else already?"

"Yes," answered the captain, "I believe we are. Unless, Bones, you want to become a beachcomber."

"Oh, I'm all in favor of finding a town or something," countered the doctor. "But I'm all for staying there, too. That is, unless we have a chance to get back to the ship."

Kirk looked around but saw absolutely nothing but dense gray humidity. "The Senites must have transporter rooms, computers, and central controls," he said, "and I have a feeling this may be a base or something. Let's find that seminary Billiwog was talking about. First, we have to answer the usual question—which way?"

"Captain," said Spock, "last night Zicree walked into the forest rather than transported. I believe we should look for the path it took."

They retraced their footprints in the moist sand and found their way back to the hut, where they gathered up whatever they thought they might need in the way of clothing. Their only other possessions were their useless communicators. Kirk tried to contact the *Enterprise* on each of the communicators in turn, but they remained inoperative. Someday they would find a way to make them work again, he vowed to himself, sticking his communications device into his most secure pocket.

At the edge of the forest, the fog broke up enough to show the ghostly shapes of mammoth bladder plants, covered with parasitic vines and muted flowers. The constant rainfall and warming currents of Khyming had apparently created giant plant life that far outshone anything on the larger island. From the forest echoed a variety of calls and shrieks from the lower forms of animal life, and Kirk saw an occasional bladder tree tremble as something moved within its thick branches. He forced himself to look along the ground, where Spock had said they should find the beginnings of a trail. It was McCoy who finally motioned excitedly for them to join him.

What the doctor had found was little more than a faint trail, and Spock surmised that it might be a path frequented by the small mammals they had seen in the survivalists' camp. But it was all they had, so they followed it, ducking under overhanging moss and vines. The deeper they progressed into the jungle, the more the fog seemed to retreat but the less there was to see, except for higher and higher bladder trees with denser things clinging to them.

They nearly ran head-on into a solid wall of rock before they realized they were in a valley. Along the cliffs, they found a pond fed by a small waterfall, which tumbled from such a height that its origin was obscured by fog. The gurgling water tempted them to take long drinks and spend a few moments in contemplation of the majestic forest and its cacophony of sounds.

That was when they heard voices from deeper in the jungle. Kirk put his fingers to his lips and motioned Spock and McCoy to spread out. He was expecting to meet more Senites, and was pleasantly surprised when two young women stepped into the clearing.

The women were clearly not Senites, not in the simple white shifts they were wearing and the unadorned long hair that flowed around their shoulders. Their reactions, however, to seeing three male strangers were entirely different: The fair-haired one smiled amiably, and the dark-haired one bolted for the forest.

"Wait," said Kirk, holding out his hands, "we mean you no harm."

"I appreciate that," said the fair-haired woman. "I don't expect anyone to do me harm on Khyming. Renna!" she called. "These gentlemen say they are harmless."

Cautiously, a lovely young brunette stepped from the mist that clung to the swollen bladder plants. She could be no older than twenty-five Earth years, thought Kirk, but she had a hard wariness about her black eyes that made her seem much older. She also had a clean bandage across her forehead and another on her knee. "You have no weapons?" she asked.

"None," said Kirk.

Spock added, "Even if we had weapons, they would not function."

"You'll have to excuse my friend," the fair-haired lady replied, "but she only arrived on Sanctuary a few days ago, and she isn't quite acclimated. It's okay, Renna," she insisted, "Khyming is closely monitored. These men couldn't be dangerous."

"Permit me to introduce myself," said McCoy with all the southern charm he could muster. "I'm McCoy, this is Jim, and that's Spock. We're new on this island, too—we sailed over from Dohama last night."

"Oh, Dohama," said the fair one distastefully. She took a step away from them.

"We didn't like it there either," Kirk assured them. "We have a friend among the Senites on this island—by the name of Zicree."

"I know Zicree," replied the dark woman. She turned and looked reproachfully at her friend. "Where are you going, Kellen? Now it's your turn to be rude, and you have lived here for many years."

Kellen lowered her head sheepishly. "Renna is correct. I shouldn't judge you because you came from

105

Dohama, but some of the stories we hear about that place . . . never mind. You have seen more of the world than I have, that is certain."

Kirk smiled. "We haven't seen anything of Khyming but the beach and a small hut. Can you show us to the village?"

"Is it permitted?" Renna asked her friend.

"I suppose so," Kellen said reluctantly. "But you and I were going to look all around the island today."

Renna glanced at Kirk, then touched the bandage on her forehead. "Let's return to the village," she declared. "I want to see how my father is doing." With that, the slim brunette turned and marched back into the forest, and everyone hurried to fall into line behind her on the narrow path.

Kirk found himself walking behind the lithe Kellen. "What did she mean about her father?" he asked.

"Her father was tortured before they escaped and came here," explained Kellen. "They were both badly injured, and her father remains in grave condition. She was only released yesterday."

"You have a hospital here?" asked McCoy, having overheard.

"Yes." Kellen shrugged, as if the question were stupid.

Kirk jogged up the path in an attempt to catch the fleet Renna. "Wait a minute!" he called.

She slowed her pace slightly. "I am sorry. I haven't made many friends here, except for Kellen," she explained, "and this is all a little strange for me. If my father recovers, I'll be a lot happier."

"You are political refugees?" asked Kirk.

Renna nodded and dabbed at her eye for a moment. "It was terrible. People can be beasts, you know. All because we opposed the dictator of our country. Many people sacrificed to help us escape, but in the end, this was our only refuge."

"What planet did you come from?" asked Kirk.

"Alloseng," answered Renna.

"Alloseng?" Kirk pondered. "I've never heard of it. And you seem to be human, like McCoy and I."

"I suppose you've been to every planet in the galaxy?" scoffed the young lady.

"No," Kirk said, smiling, "but a fair number."

"Then maybe you won't mind if I query you," said Renna. "Where are *you* from?"

Kirk debated whether to lie to this fellow newcomer or tell the truth. The only advantage to lying was to avoid repulsing her with the knowledge that they were persecutors, somehow related to the beasts who had tortured her father and pursued them to this forgotten garden. Telling her the truth, on the other hand, might allow him to enlist her aid in their predicament.

"You hesitate," observed Renna. "That probably means you are about to tell me a lie. Save it for someone else."

"No," answered Kirk, "I've decided to tell you the truth. My friends and I are persecutors."

Renna jerked her head, startled, then began walking faster. Kirk struggled to catch up, as some kind of creature in the trees mocked him with cawing laughter.

"We're not political persecutors," Kirk insisted, "and we know now we shouldn't have come here. But we made a mistake. We were chasing a criminal, someone who had plundered innocent trading vessels, leaving them crippled in space."

"A murderer?" asked Renna.

"No, not really," the captain admitted. "A pirate."

"Perhaps they only took what they needed," Renna suggested.

Kirk shook his head and lowered his voice to reply, "What brought us here isn't important. What's important is that we're trying to find a way off this planet. Have you seen any sign of the space vessels confiscated by the Senites? A transporter? Anything that might help someone escape?"

Renna slowed her pace again and couldn't disguise the interest in her voice. "Kellen would be horrified if she heard you talking like that. So would the Senites. To them, everything about Sanctuary is perfect. Why would anyone want to leave?"

"You've only seen this one island," answered Kirk. "Believe me, some other parts of Sanctuary are far from perfect. In the mountains, there are people living like animals, barely surviving. But they prefer that to Dohama, and I don't blame them."

They heard light footsteps running up the path behind them. "We'll talk about this later," whispered the dark-haired fugitive.

"Renna!" called Kellen, passing Kirk and taking her friend's arm. "If we take this other path, I can at least show you the wind turbines. They harness the wind's energy and make electricity for us."

Renna smiled politely. "Maybe some other time. I really must see how my father is doing. I have the rest of my life for you to show me around."

"That's right!" Kellen giggled.

The women walked arm-in-arm down the widening path, and Kirk turned to meet Spock and McCoy.

"I want to see that hospital," said McCoy.

"We'll have to move cautiously," answered the captain. "But I told Renna who we are and that we want off Sanctuary."

Spock raised an eyebrow and asked, "Was that wise, Captain? The Senites might consider that unacceptable behavior."

"We haven't got any choice," answered Kirk. "We need help. And I don't think Renna wants to live here the rest of her life either."

"On the other hand," said McCoy, "Kellen told me she was practically born on Sanctuary. She came here with her parents, and this is all she knows."

"Just like the Senites," remarked Kirk, frowning. He motioned with his head, and the three explorers jogged up the path after the women.

The trail began a steady ascent, and the fog lifted to the point where they could just make out the silhouette of a huge mountain that dominated the island. Near the base of the mountain, they glimpsed a ghostly stand of white propellers twirling in the wind. Kirk assumed that the sleek windmills must be many times larger than they appeared at this distance, and he wondered if the Senites had also harnessed the rivers and waterfalls. The peak of the mountain was invisible in the sunken cloud cover, but he imagined it to be a delicate spire, like the mountains to the north.

Their first glimpse of the village of Khyming was of a white pavilion mounted among the bladder trees on the side of a cliff. The expansive open-air deck was obviously positioned to afford a congenial view of the jungle—as much as the fog would allow. There came the tinkling sounds of conversation and silverware dancing on plates, and Kirk could see vague figures moving about on the high pavilion.

"If you are hungry," said Renna, "you should get something to eat. Kellen and I are going to the clinic."

"May I come along?" asked McCoy. "I promise not to get in the way, and I'll leave if you ask me to. I'm a doctor. At least, I was before I came here."

"I have no objection," said Renna. "I'm afraid we won't get to see him for very long."

McCoy glanced hopefully at his captain. "I promise not to be gone long, Jim, and I'll come right back here."

"What are you worried about?" scoffed Kellen. "No

harm can befall you on Khyming. This is the most blessed island on Sanctuary. Only the best people live here."

Kirk cleared his throat and said, "I can imagine that. We'll wait for you here, Bones. Keep your eyes open."

"See you later." Renna smiled, then turned and walked off so briskly that Kellen and McCoy had to run to catch up.

That left Kirk and Spock alone to confront the gleaming pavilion. The wind had changed slightly, and the spicy smell of fresh pastries came wafting through the fog. Kirk spotted a spiral staircase that dropped down through the floor of the giant tree-house, and he motioned Spock to follow him.

They emerged into what could only be called an elegant outdoor café. Aproned Senites bustled back and forth between sedate tables filled with politely chattering diners. No one was dressed as shabbily as the two new arrivals, but no one seemed to pay them much attention as they stood gaping at the plates of food that whizzed by. There were baked bladder plants stuffed with seafood, various greens and tuberlike vegetables, some yellow grain that smelled delicious, and loaves of dark bread piled high at every table.

Looking past the food, the view from the pavilion was indeed magnificent—a blossoming jungle bathed in wisps of fog. Above them stretched the poles and superstructure of an immense awning, which could apparently be rolled out in an instant in case of rain. At the rear of the pavilion, a phalanx of doors opened into what smelled like a flavorful kitchen. Small shops and Senite vendors dotted the walkway that led from the café to other parts of the whitewashed village.

"Two for lunch?" asked a Senite, breaking Kirk's reverie.

"Please," the captain answered. "Does lunch require payment?"

"No, sir," answered the Senite, looking quite shocked.

Spock replied, "That is convenient."

"A table with a view," Kirk added.

"Certainly, sir."

They followed the Senite to a small round table on a balcony overlooking the sumptuous foliage of the jungle. Having spent the last few hours down there, Kirk swiveled in his chair to survey instead the village of Khyming and its denizens. Simple white houses built along the cliffside were connected to similar shops and bungalows perched in the bladder trees by swaying rope bridges. The bridges were linked by intermediate pagodas and pavilions, rising like mushrooms from the floor of the canyon. Creatures of various races strolled the spidery bridges, oblivious to the depths beneath them. Every building in Khyming was painted an unrelenting white, which gave the town a strangely sterile and bland appearance, despite its remarkable design.

"Those bridges look flimsy," he said to Spock, "but they make travel between one level and another very convenient."

"They are adequate in a town where the only mode of transportation is walking," Spock pointed out. "The population appears to be in good physical condition, due, I would say, to constant walking and a healthy diet."

"Healthier than Dohama," Kirk agreed. He shook his head in puzzlement. "Why feed two towns entirely different food? This whole place makes no sense."

Spock cocked his head. "I would disagree, Captain. I think it makes considerable sense from a logistical point of view. In Dohama, the Senites have a large and potentially dangerous population to feed and placate. Ale and fatty food seem to accomplish that task. On Khyming, the aim is apparently to keep the population healthy, which stands to reason if the Senites themselves live here."

Kirk glanced around at the wide variety of humanoid species calmly eating lunch. He saw blue skin, green skin, brown skin, and one creature with black on half of its face and white on the other half, perhaps a native of Cheron who'd fled during the racial wars that decimated that planet.

The ratio of females to males was probably two to one, which meant that the popular wisdom of Dohama was correct—the women got sent to Khyming. That was probably for the Senites' benefit, too, thought Kirk, because it prevented fights over women in Dohama. Nobody dining in the outdoor café seemed to be in any sort of hurry, and many conversations lingered after the dishes had been carted off.

At that moment, two Senites hovered over them, one setting the table and another pouring glasses of water. A third one headed their way with a tray of bread and steaming bowls of food. Kirk wanted to make conversation with them, but he could see that they were busy and had several tables to service. The food looked and smelled delicious, reminding him of Earth delicacies like eggplant and tabouli.

"Fascinating," said Spock, after the efficient servants had padded away. "I have never seen such conformity among non-Vulcans."

"Being all of one sex must help," Kirk grumbled. "All I want to do is get back to my ship. If we could just find a weakness in their security system. . . ."

Spock motioned about the thriving outdoor café and replied, "If the Senites have been functioning in this manner for hundreds of years, with this degree of efficiency, it will be difficult to find a weakness in their security system."

"We can try," Kirk insisted under his breath. "I think this island is the place to look."

"That may be," answered the Vulcan, "but the Senites are accustomed to dealing with strangers. We have been told we are on probation, and we are probably under surveillance as well. We are surely on our own, with no prospect of intervention from the *Enterprise.* Plus, no one has any recollection of anyone ever leaving the planet."

Kirk shook his head and muttered, "There must be something in our favor."

"We are alive," Spock replied, holding an aromatic spoonful of black vegetables under his nose, "and the Senites are good cooks."

Chapter Eight

RENNA, KELLEN, AND MCCOY made their way across a
long rope bridge that spanned the distance between
the base of the cliff and a nondescript two-story
building perched among the trees. The women led the
way with the doctor following uncertainly behind.
The doctor was frowning; he was getting seasick with
all the blasted swaying.

Kellen stopped and mildly reproached him,
"What's the matter, McCoy? Afraid of heights?"

"Not on your life," snapped McCoy. "I'm afraid of
falling. And I like bridges that stand still when I walk
on them."

"These bridges are quite well maintained," replied
the longtime resident. "I think they're beautiful."

"Will you two hurry!" Renna said impatiently,
gripping the rope handrails and climbing determinedly toward the white building.

She was so far ahead that McCoy was in no danger

of catching up, not at the rate he was moving. "Is her father badly injured?" he asked Kellen.

"The Senites are doing all they can," she answered. "If they can't save him, no one can."

They caught up with the dark-haired woman at the door to the clinic. On the door was a blue star, which apparently marked it as a medical facility. A burly young Senite stood guarding the entrance.

"Admittance is impossible at the moment," the Senite told Renna in a high-pitched voice.

"Please," she begged. "You wouldn't let me in this morning either. I must know how my father is doing."

"One moment," said the guard, pushing open the door and disappearing inside.

Renna was clearly distressed, and McCoy's heart went out to her. "Maybe he's resting," suggested the doctor.

"I felt better when I was inside there with him," she said, frowning.

The Senite returned a few seconds later. "You may come in for a brief period," it said, holding the door open for them.

They entered a waiting room that was conspicuously empty, suggesting to McCoy that the population of Khyming was fairly healthy and well adjusted. Another Senite, this one older and more distinguished-looking, stood waiting beside a pair of double doors. Upon its white robe, noticed McCoy, were various stains and smears of blood.

The older Senite nodded in greeting. "We operated on him again this morning," it explained, "but his internal injuries are very severe. He is sedated, but if you wish to see him for a moment . . ."

"I do," Renna insisted.

Kellen shivered. "I'll wait here."

McCoy said nothing, not wanting to offend the

115

Senites and ruin his chance of seeing their facility. The Senite doctor, as McCoy assumed it was, held open the double doors.

McCoy followed Renna into a large and well-equipped recovery room with six beds, each surrounded by monitoring devices that were the equal of those in McCoy's own sickbay, if not better. Through thick glass panels, he could see two operating rooms beyond, and they looked every bit as impressive.

Only two of the beds in the recovery room were occupied, but there were six Senites in attendance. Renna walked directly past the first patient, who appeared to be an elderly Senite, and made her way to the other bed, where a frail, white-bearded man lay sleeping. Suspended from the ceiling over the bed was a silver canopy that bathed the patient in a warm orange glow. Renna stood beside the bed, gazing at the thin man and wringing her hands.

"He is in stasis," said the Senite doctor.

"Stasis?" replied McCoy with concern. "Is his blood pressure that low?"

The Senite gave McCoy a curious glance. "He was dead when he was brought here. We resuscitated him, but his internal organs are crushed, and his hip and both legs are broken. We have not replaced his hip, feeling that it is pointless unless we can stabilize his circulation. He needs heart, liver, and kidney transplants at the very minimum. He has also suffered brain damage."

"If he was tortured that badly," asked McCoy, "how could he even live to get here?"

The Senite raised an eyebrow and replied in its furry voice, "That is a very good question."

Renna was oblivious to their conversation. "Father?" she asked urgently. "Father, can you hear me?"

"He cannot hear you," the Senite doctor said. "If he

were conscious, the pain would be unbearable, no matter what we gave him."

Again, she seemed not to hear them. "Father, father . . ." she breathed, her voice choking.

McCoy lowered his voice. "He's not going to make it, is he?"

The Senite doctor shrugged. "We can keep him alive, of course, but that is not our way. Quality of life is more important than simply life."

"What about artificial organs?" asked McCoy.

"We gave him an artificial heart this morning," answered the Senite, "but arterial damage is extensive. He is more comfortable now, but his prognosis remains unchanged."

Renna began to sob, and McCoy gently took her arm. "Let's go," he whispered.

She didn't fight McCoy as he led her back into the waiting room. Seeing their crestfallen faces, Kellen turned away and rubbed her eyes. Somberly, the three of them stepped out into the hazy sun of the mountain village.

"Well," said McCoy with forced cheerfulness, "the doctor said he's hanging in there."

"That's not what he said," muttered Renna darkly. "If you were his doctor, what would you tell me?"

"To be brave."

"Brave!" she spat contemptuously. "All my life I've been brave—done things no young girl ever ought to do. That man is all I've ever known my entire life. I have followed him, and he has been there to teach me. I've never been alone."

"Don't you have a mother, or other family?" asked McCoy.

Renna shot him a glare. "Not on Sanctuary, I don't."

"You're not alone," said Kellen brightly, "I'll be

117

your friend. Let's not talk about depressing things. Come on, there's still time to see the wind turbines!"

The blond woman took Renna's arm and led her toward one of the three bridges that stretched from the clinic. "Are you coming, McCoy?" she called.

"No, thanks," he answered. "I'm going to find my friends."

Renna looked back plaintively, as if she didn't want to go look at wind turbines with her overly cheerful escort. Then she bowed her head and dutifully followed Kellen down the swaying bridge.

"I tell you, Jim," said McCoy over a glass of very tasty olive-colored wine, "that man could not have gotten those injuries from being tortured. Well, he could have, but he wouldn't have lived to get into a spaceship and come here. They're more like the kinds of injuries you would get in an accident—or a crash."

Spock raised an eyebrow and asked, "Are they the kinds of injuries one might sustain in an escape pod that ejected too close to the ground?"

"Yes." McCoy nodded. "That's exactly the kind of injuries they are."

Captain Kirk stroked his chin and looked over the balcony at the alien terrain of the lush island, stretching beneath him into the misty distance. All afternoon he had spent sitting in an outdoor café, drinking, eating, and talking. That might be a good life for a gigolo on Rigel IV, but it was not the kind of life he had grown accustomed to as a starship captain. He ached to do something to escape from this plush prison, but what?

"Okay," he answered, "maybe that dying man is Auk-rex and Renna is what's left of his crew. What good does it do us? We can't get *ourselves* off this planet, let alone a prisoner."

McCoy looked chastened. "You told me to keep my eyes open. I thought you might be interested."

Kirk smiled and patted his friend's shoulder. "I'm sorry, Bones. Of course I'm interested in what you've found out. I would just be more interested in getting back to the ship."

The doctor shrugged. "Can't help you there. But I do think Renna, whoever she is, feels the same way we do."

"What about her friend?" asked Spock. "Surely Kellen must know her way around this island as well as anyone. She has lived here almost her entire life."

"Hmm," said Kirk thoughtfully. "Maybe we should try to be extra nice to Kellen. Let's go find those two. I can't stand to sit here any longer." He rose decisively to his feet.

"Wait a minute," protested McCoy, "I'm not done with my wine."

"Don't get too relaxed," warned Kirk. "We're not staying here forever."

They strolled the rope bridges and narrow catwalks of the whitewashed village, glancing into the occasional shop or inspecting the wares of a Senite street vendor. In many respects, Kirk decided, Khyming was a high-class variation of Dohama. The food was healthier, but it was still prepared and served exclusively by the Senites, making everyone dependent upon them. There were sedate cafés instead of rowdy bars, but the populace still spent much of the day sitting and drinking.

If one desired new clothes, jewelry, or toilet articles, one simply walked into a store and took them, just like in Dohama. Instead of tattoo and gaming parlors, Khyming had hair salons and tearooms. Instead of rouged and wigged Senites, Khyming had the real thing—women—and several of them smiled flirtatiously at Kirk as he passed them on the narrow walkways. Now and then, a family passed by with children in tow.

A young woman with yellow skin and a pattern of bumps on her forehead brazenly held out her hand and stopped Kirk. With wide purple eyes, she looked appraisingly from him to Spock to McCoy.

"You three are new here," she remarked, smiling. "I know every man in Khyming. Here is my card. If you would like a wife, or even something less long-term, please stop by my salon. I perform an introduction service for many eligible and desirable females, of all races. Many of them are quite willing to share a husband."

Kirk fingered the paper card, which bore an address they had passed earlier. "We'll think about it," he said, smiling back.

"You could have your pick," she added, purple eyes twinkling.

After she sauntered away, Spock raised an eyebrow. "Fascinating," he observed. "Here they have the opposite problem they have in Dohama—not enough men."

"She's like Billiwog," remarked McCoy. "She doesn't have to work, but she's still trying to do something useful."

"That's just it," said Kirk with exasperation. "What kind of life is this, if everything is just handed to you?"

McCoy shrugged. "Some would think that isn't so bad."

"Some isn't me," said Kirk. He glanced around the cliffside retreat, noticing that darkness was starting to filter through the fog. "We had better find a place to stay for the night."

The doctor cleared his throat. "Maybe if we asked that lady who gave you the card . . ."

"You'll end up married," Kirk warned him.

"With three or four wives," McCoy agreed, grinning.

A Senite passed by, scooping bits of litter into a trash receptacle at the end of a long handle. "Excuse me," Kirk asked the androgynous being, "where do new arrivals spend the night?"

"The guesthouse," answered the Senite, pointing to a sprawling structure at the base of the cliff.

Unlike the glorified treehouses, this building looked like a ranch house from Earth's Midwest, thought Kirk, and he eagerly led the way. They trod across a rope bridge to a small pavilion, then wound their way down a spiral staircase to the ground.

McCoy sighed. "Feels good to be on solid ground again."

"Captain," said Spock, pointing in the direction from which they had just come, "I believe that may be the seminary we were told about."

Kirk and McCoy followed the line of his outstretched hand and saw a magnificent white building, perched on the highest visible ledge of the mountain and partially hidden by twisted spires of rock. The encroaching fog made the place look ethereal, like a palace from a childhood fairy tale. From the village itself it would be impossible to see the structure, and Kirk wondered how people got to it. He could see no bridges connecting the palace with the rest of Khyming.

"We've got to get in there," Kirk vowed.

"There you are!" called a familiar voice.

They turned to see the lissome Kellen striding toward them from the guesthouse. "You've got to help Renna," she said. "I can't seem to do anything to cheer her up. If her father dies, I don't know what will happen to her."

Captain Kirk bestowed his most charming smile

upon the young woman. "We were just looking for you. Tell me, what is that building up there?"

"The seminary. It's where the Senites live."

"What a magnificent building," he mused. "Can you take us to it?"

"Only Senites can do that," she said with confusion. "Why go there? The Senites live very simply, and there's not much to see."

"We are very interested in architecture," replied Spock.

"Not now," insisted Kellen, grabbing Kirk's arm and dragging him toward the guesthouse. "Please, try to cheer her up. I want her to like it here."

"Why is that so important?" asked Kirk.

The question stopped Kellen in her tracks, and she gave him a quizzical stare. "Because this is where she has to live, and the Senites built all of this for our happiness."

Kirk looked pointedly at Spock and McCoy and said, "Why don't the two of you go ahead and arrange rooms for us. And see if you can find Renna."

His comrades nodded and moved quickly toward the sprawling white house, while Kirk took Kellen's hand in his. He chose his next words carefully, not wanting to offend an ally they desperately needed.

"Kellen," he began, motioning to the dusky sky, "there is a great deal out there that you don't know about. Renna has seen other worlds, other cities, and she probably has family and friends in places far away from here. Even if her father were not so badly injured, this would be a difficult adjustment for her, coming to Sanctuary. It's been difficult for all of us. Can you understand that a person might not be happy here?"

She bit her lip. "Maybe not right away, but in time . . ."

"Perhaps never," said Kirk. "If you want Renna to

be happy, you should think about the possibility of helping her—and us—leave Sanctuary."

"That's impossible!" exclaimed the blond woman, clearly shocked by the idea.

"I don't think it's impossible," answered Kirk. "I know the Senites have transporters, and they must have impounded thousands of spaceships over the years. I'm not asking you to betray anyone—I just want you to think about what I've said."

The young woman nodded, as if she would try to keep an open mind. She didn't pull her hand away, but instead gave his a tiny squeeze. "You are strange, Jim," she said, puzzled. "I don't have the feeling that you have been persecuted, as my parents and so many others have been. If you'd been persecuted, you might understand what Sanctuary is all about."

"I understand its purpose," Kirk replied. "But I also think people can make a mistake in coming here. This life, as beautiful and simple as it is, is not for everyone."

"No," Kellen answered sadly, "I have seen a few who were unhappy."

"What happens to them?"

She shrugged. "They go away."

The captain didn't press for details, but he doubted they had "gone away" into the stars. Instead, he gripped Kellen's hand warmly and began to walk with her among the profusion of orange-crested bladder plants.

"Let's just walk for a while," he said, smiling, "and you can tell me about your life here."

Even inside, Khyming's guesthouse bore a marked resemblance to a ranch, thought Dr. McCoy. Warm wood paneling and rustic furnishings graced its bright and airy rooms, and Spock and McCoy had no difficulty securing a sumptuous suite with a bedroom, a sitting room, and four large beds. The tight-lipped Senites who ran the place would not tell them who else was staying there, but they had seen a large party of dark-skinned humanoids, numbering about a dozen, in the dining room. They huddled together as if still under attack by some unseen force, and McCoy was tempted to tell them they didn't have anything to fear—except perhaps their Senite hosts. There was no sign of Renna, and the doctor assumed she must be in her room.

He sat in a plush chair on a wide veranda at the rear of the house, sipping a glass of olive-colored wine and watching darkness and fog consume the towering jungle. Spock was not exactly pacing, but he stood stiffly, watching the doorway to the dining room.

"Relax, Spock," urged the doctor. "Watching that door won't make anybody come through it."

Spock stiffened to attention and replied, "The captain said we should not relax too much."

"No"—McCoy yawned—"but relaxing too much is not something *you* have to worry about. You could at least sit down."

The Vulcan considered the idea for a moment, then took a seat in one of the plush chairs scattered about the veranda. He still didn't look relaxed.

"I wonder what they're doing on the *Enterprise?*" mused McCoy. "They're probably having a helluva time explaining all this to Starfleet. And Starfleet is probably having a helluva time making do without the *Enterprise.* All because we wanted to catch one lousy pirate, who is either dead or stuck here like we are." He craned his neck to peer into the gloomy sky. "Do you think they're still up there, Spock?"

"Unknown," answered the Vulcan. "It would be logical for them to remain in orbit for a period of time, but it has been five days. Starfleet regulations require a search period of forty-eight hours for a missing landing party, and we have exceeded that time."

"Yeah," muttered the doctor, "and they couldn't search for us even if they wanted to. It doesn't look good."

The Vulcan nodded in agreement. "Our situation would seem to be rather untenable."

A grim silence followed as darkness descended completely upon the whitewashed house at the edge of the jungle. Salmon-colored lights flickered on, giving the veranda a strange glow that matched the sky, which was lit from behind by Sanctuary's first moon. They heard the footsteps of a solitary figure approaching from the side of the house and turned with relief to see who it was.

"Hello," said Renna, slumping into one of the chairs. She glanced around. "Where's the third musketeer?"

"I don't know," McCoy lied. "What have you been doing?"

"Looking around." The slim brunette shrugged. "Interesting what stuff you can find in this village."

"You referred to *The Three Musketeers,*" Spock observed. "Are you familiar with Earth fiction?"

"Uh, well," stammered Renna, shifting uneasily in her chair, "it's just a phrase I picked up somewhere."

McCoy suggested knowingly, "From Federation computers, maybe?"

"Look," she said angrily, "as far as I can tell, we're all in the same fix. None of us wanted to be on Sanctuary, but here we are. You people don't represent anybody now, so stop pretending you do."

McCoy lowered his voice to ask, "Are you still interested in leaving this planet?"

"Not while my father's in the clinic," answered Renna. Then she sat forward conspiratorially. "If he were well, and we had the right plan . . ."

The door from the dining room opened, and Kellen and Kirk strolled onto the veranda. Upon seeing Renna, they let go of each other's hands.

Renna smiled archly at Kellen. "I see the welcoming committee is working overtime."

"Well, *you* haven't been much fun," the blond woman answered defensively. "At least Jim is interested in learning about our lives here. Khyming isn't really so bad."

"I bet he's interested, all right," said Renna, gazing pointedly at the captain.

He returned her gaze for a moment, then pulled up a chair. "So tell me," he asked cheerfully, "what do people do for amusement in the evenings?"

"We have tea dances!" Kellen said excitedly. Then she looked downcast. "But there's not one tonight. We also have a library where you can take out books. Mainly, we have dinner and talk." She smiled at Kirk. "And take walks."

Renna stood up and stretched her arms. "I think I'll take a walk—to the clinic to see my father."

"There is no need for that," came a lilting voice.

Everyone turned in unison to see a white-robed figure standing in the doorway of the guesthouse. It was Zicree.

"What do you mean by that?" Renna asked warily.

The Senite stepped onto the veranda, its hands folded politely in its long white sleeves and a look of care upon its ageless face. "Your father is dead, my dear. We are sorry."

"Dead!" she shrieked, stunned. "But you said you could keep him alive!"

"A decision was reached not to do so."

126

"What!" she shrieked again. "Nobody consulted *me* about that."

The slim Senite said nothing. It simply turned and padded back into the rambling guesthouse.

Kellen moved to comfort her friend. "The Senites wouldn't have done it unless it was for the best," she assured her earnestly.

"Oh, shut up, you little twerp!" snapped Renna, shoving the woman away. Fighting tears, she stormed into the house. Kellen looked pained and confused for a moment, then ran after her new friend.

"Hmm," said McCoy, "now there's somebody who likes the Senites even less than we do."

The three reluctant fugitives stood quietly on the veranda of Khyming's guesthouse, waiting to see if Renna, Kellen, or Zicree would return. When no one appeared, the captain finally motioned Spock and McCoy to follow him to the edge of the jungle and gather close.

Kirk whispered, "It took a lot of small talk for me to get it out of her, but Kellen told me that the Senites do indeed have a transporter room inside their seminary. She said the entrance to the place is through a cave and is heavily guarded, and there's no other way to get up to the ridge. But she says that people from the village are occasionally taken there for religious training. She went there often as a child."

"Yes," said McCoy, "but will she take *us* there?"

"I'm not sure," answered Kirk. "She's very loyal to the Senites."

"Did she go by herself?" asked Spock. "Or was she always accompanied by a Senite?"

Kirk replied glumly, "I gather she was always accompanied by a Senite."

The Vulcan concluded, "It will be very difficult to convince a Senite to help us."

"Maybe you don't need that," whispered a fourth voice.

With alarm, they swiveled in the direction of the voice and saw Renna crouching in the shadows of a bladder tree. She stood and made her way quietly toward them.

"How long have you been listening?" asked Kirk.

"Long enough," she answered. "Don't worry—I ditched Kellen. I made a discovery of my own today. I found a closet in this very building where a few Senite robes are stored. I suppose they have extras in case they get theirs dirty. None of you could pass as Senites, but I might be able to."

"I'm sorry about your father," said McCoy.

Renna turned away and dabbed at her eyes. "As far as I'm concerned, *they* killed him. You may not have noticed, but there aren't any people in wheelchairs around here. Nobody disabled or mentally diseased. I think the Senites like to keep things a little too perfect in Khyming. I bet if my father had been in your sickbay, McCoy, you would've managed to save him."

"That's kind of you to say," replied the doctor. "I certainly wouldn't have pulled the plug after only a few days."

"Renna," said Kirk in a businesslike tone, "you know who we are. And I think we know who *you* are. Why are you willing to help us?"

"It's not to help you," she answered. "I said I'm from Alloseng, and that's true. In fact, I'm a wealthy woman there, with an estate that makes their seminary look like a dump. As far as you knowing who I am, you don't really know, and it's going to stay that way. If we help each other escape, you have to pledge to me that you will let me go free. I will pledge to you that I will, uh, lead a simpler life than I used to. You came here looking for a pirate named Auk-rex, and you can safely put in your records that Auk-rex is dead."

"Agreed." Kirk nodded.

"Captain," Spock interrupted, "regulation 2477.3 prohibits us from—"

"Damn regulations!" McCoy cursed under his breath. "Regulations won't do anything to get us off this planet."

"Auk-rex is dead," Kirk told his first officer. "Let's leave it at that." He turned to Renna. "About this plan?"

"We need more information from Kellen," she replied, gazing at Kirk with intense black eyes. "You seem to be on better terms with her than I am, so I'll leave that to you. We need to know the hours and the types of classes they have in the seminary, so that if I come up there leading you three, it won't look suspicious. And we need to know where the transporter room is."

"All right," agreed the captain. "What about you?"

"I won't steal a robe until we're ready to go," she whispered. "They may count them. Don't worry about me—I have some experience in these matters."

Kirk smiled. "I'm glad you're on our side."

Renna shrugged. "Strange bedfellows, as they say. We can't do anything more tonight, so I'm going to bed. Good night."

"Good night," the men muttered in unison, and Renna marched swiftly back into the house.

"A remarkable woman," observed Spock.

"That she is," agreed Kirk. "I hope we can trust her."

Chapter Nine

SCOTTY STOOD at the science station on the bridge of the *Enterprise,* thinking about Mr. Spock, who usually stood there. He tried to keep his attention on the sensor readings that pranced across the screen, changing constantly with subtle shifts in wave patterns emanating from the planet, but thoughts of his missing comrades kept intruding. If Mr. Spock were here now, would *he* know what to do? The Scotsman was fresh out of ideas on how to respond to this predicament with any sort of reasonable action. He now viewed the loss of the captain, first officer, and doctor as a tragedy, perhaps irreversible. He could not guess what they were facing below, or how to help them.

Starfleet had understood the predicament and, for once, there seemed to be no immediate crises in star systems closer to home. The maneuvers would go on without them, and Starfleet had dispatched another ship to Sanctuary, the USS *Neptune* oceanic research ship.

Starfleet had decided to follow a backdoor policy to see if the gates to Sanctuary could be opened by an offer to exchange information on aquatic life and oceans. Scotty didn't want to dissuade them from this notion, although he doubted they would make much headway with the single-minded Senites. He was glad the *Neptune* was coming, because it would help to corroborate his reports, but the engineer also knew the smaller ship might be coming to keep vigil after the *Enterprise* was inevitably called away.

He turned to look at the planet on the viewscreen, filled with aqua seas and strafed by gleaming white clouds. It was strangely compelling, he had to admit, and he could see why there was an almost daily influx of new arrivals. But did they realize what they were giving up? There was no way of knowing what they were getting in exchange for their freedom.

He heard Uhura speaking into her mouthpiece. She was so skilled that she could conduct her business without interrupting anyone else on the bridge, but Scotty was attuned to everything that happened around him. In fact, so little had happened in the endless hours of waiting that he'd turned into an eavesdropper, and he was waiting for Uhura when she looked up.

"I don't suppose the Senites have called?" he asked with forced cheerfulness.

"No." She shook her head forlornly. "But Captain Garvak of the Klingon vessel wishes to speak with you. He says he only has a moment."

"Put him on the screen." Scotty strode to the captain's chair.

"Greetings," said the gray-haired Klingon. He was dressed incongruously in a formal green uniform plastered with insignias and decorations, instead of his usual short-sleeved leather tunic. "I come to bid you farewell."

"Indeed?" Scotty smiled broadly, knowing this was an occasion for rejoicing, for several reasons.

"Yes." The Klingon nodded smugly. "It seems my superiors finally read my dispatches. They have reached a conclusion I reached years ago: Sanctuary is the most effective prison in the galaxy. No one who goes there is ever seen or heard from again. Why in Kronos should we try to stop our enemies from reaching that pesthole?" He shrugged. "I am sorry if that appraisal does not sit well with you, but my days of futility are over. Henceforth, there will be no imperial Klingon vessel stationed at Sanctuary. We are well rid of most of those who flee there."

With a quick salute, he added, "Good-bye, Commander Scott. I hope we never meet under conditions of war, but I know that is possible."

"Perhaps not forever," answered Scotty. "I have included in my dispatches a full report of all the aid and advice ye've given me. I wish I could've proven your assessment wrong, but ye've been correct and straightforward in every regard."

"Experience is a harsh teacher," declared Garvak. "I will die before I come back here. Farewell." The image of the hardened warrior was replaced by another view of the glimmering planet.

"I'll put the Klingon ship on the viewscreen," offered Sulu.

The bridge personnel of the *Enterprise* watched with a mixture of sadness and envy as the sleek Klingon warship eased out of orbit. As if in salute, it tilted a gull-like wing at them for a moment, then achieved warp speed with a flash of light, and was gone. At least someone had escaped Sanctuary, thought Scotty.

Hand in hand, the attractive fair-haired couple strolled among the shops and vendors of the picturesque cliffside village. People smiled as they passed them, because everyone knew Kellen, and her new beau seemed quite presentable, especially in the new clothes she had picked out for him that morning. Captain Kirk nodded pleasantly in response, even at the Senites. He looked like he was having a grand time, when all he could think of was how to steer the conversation in the direction he needed it to go. A light drizzle began to fall, and they ducked into a tearoom.

"So," he said, shaking raindrops off the sleeve of his new beige jacket, "tell me more about what it was like to grow up here. What kinds of classes do the Senites teach?"

"Philosophy, mainly," answered Kellen. "They are a very ancient order, and their teachings explain much of what they are doing for everyone in this part of the galaxy."

"If I wanted to take a class," asked Kirk, "what would I ask for?"

Kellen frowned in thought. "I suppose you could take a class in beginning philosophy."

"Is that class taught every day?"

"I don't know. I could find out."

"Would you please?" Kirk smiled at her.

Kellen nodded and walked to the back of the small restaurant to consult the Senite proprietor. Kirk peered out the window at the falling rain, wondering what time of day it was and how he could extricate himself from Kellen without making her upset, or suspicious.

She returned with a smile on her face. "Jancree says there is a beginning class this afternoon. But you must consult your adviser—that would be Zicree."

"Of course," said Kirk. "Shall we have a seat?"

Kellen beamed with delight, and Kirk steered her to a table by the window, far away from the Senite's

133

station in the rear of the room. He waited until the white-robed figure had served them steaming helpings of tea and biscuits to continue his interrogation.

"You know," he remarked, "it seems odd to me that you have never seen any more of Sanctuary than this island. Having done it myself, I wouldn't advise you to take a boat between here and the mainland, but you could transport over. The Senites would let you use their transporter, wouldn't they?"

Kellen looked shocked at the idea. "I don't think so," she replied. "I know they transport people when they first arrive on Sanctuary, but none of the refugees use it after that. No, I don't think the Senites would let us use their transporter."

"But I would like to explore this planet with you," said Kirk, reaching across the table to take her hand. "There's so much we could see and do. Then again, maybe the Senites' transporter isn't advanced enough to send us anywhere we want to go."

"Oh, I certainly think it is," she protested. "I've seen their transporter room inside the seminary—it's huge, large enough to send an army somewhere."

"I'd love to see it," Kirk declared. "Once you reach the seminary, it's right inside?"

"No, you have to go up to the second floor," answered Kellen. "The door is marked by a red circle. But you had better ask Zicree about all this."

"Oh, I plan to," he assured her, stroking her hand gently. "I want to learn the Senite way of doing things."

Renna, Spock, and McCoy sat as patiently as they could on the veranda of Khyming's guesthouse, waiting for the return of Captain Kirk. Renna rose to her feet and strolled with forced nonchalance into the warmly paneled library. She began scanning through the miscellaneous volumes available on the reading terminal. She had already determined that it was a stand-alone computer that contained nothing but stored texts, albeit of a very eclectic nature.

As she scanned various topics, she began to think that she and the Senites had much in common, because they were both robbers of technological information. If this small sample was any indication of the sorts of data they had gathered over the centuries, then they were in a league far above hers. Of course, there was a measure of sadism in the fact that space travel and the application of most of the knowledge in the data bank were forever denied to the inhabitants of Sanctuary.

At least, that's the way the Senites wanted to make it appear. Renna had her doubts, because she couldn't imagine that the Senites, or any race, could figure out every angle. They had missed something in their vaunted defense strategy, and she was pleased with her choice of cohorts to help her find it. True, Kirk and company had been her enemies until a few days ago, but she and they were natural allies at this stage, because they'd all jumped into the same dark pool with their eyes closed. Having been a thief and a pirate all her young life, Renna was quite certain that she recognized fellow travelers in the sterile Senites. They were bent, to use an old Earth phrase, in more ways than one.

Of course, she and her father were originally from Earth, and she didn't care anymore whether the Three Musketeers knew it or not. They had other problems, and she enjoyed seeing their discomfort at having been trapped in an even bigger web than the one they had spun for her. Renna had always known that she and her father would be caught one day, but she couldn't have foreseen the strange form of her punishment. Sanctuary had just enough freedom to be tempting, but she couldn't stand the fact that all her years of work—and her father's—had gone for nothing. If retirement was to be the fate of Auk-rex, let it at least be in the midst of the spoils.

But her father was gone, and she was alone. In the last few years, she had been the captain of their tiny but effective enterprise. He was the computer genius who had figured out how to tap, via microwaves, into almost any computer before its owners knew what was happening, often during negotiations. Once a ship's shields came down, the computer was theirs for the picking; they simply located the most valuable cargo and transported it to their own hold. Then it was good-bye, Charlie.

There had been imitators, of course, and the legend of Auk-rex had grown by leaps and bounds. That rigorous life was now over, and he was gone. The ending had come with a fierceness that made her feel like they were being punished. Well, the loss of her father, best friend, and partner was a hard enough blow, and Renna was determined to salvage what she could of the business.

She heard Kirk enter before his men heard him, and she watched him stride past the open doorway. He stopped, considering whether he should speak to her, but he finally kept marching through the dining room and out onto the veranda. She turned off the computer terminal and wandered after him. He fascinated her, but she was going to keep her hands off for the time being. She wanted to keep her wits about her, and she suspected Kirk did, too. Renna knew he was expending his energy on Kellen, and she was relieved that the woman had a new hobby.

Yes, she thought, these were good co-conspirators. They were honest and she wasn't, which gave her the advantage. It also made them predictable, which was what she wanted. Of course, the captain could renege on his promise to let her go—and the Vulcan certainly wouldn't mind—but she didn't think he would. If they ever got off this confounded planet, they would all be too grateful to complain.

She spotted her associates in their usual place, huddled at the edge of the patio, next to the looming bladder trees. They looked like conspirators, but she didn't care—boldness was their only weapon. No one expected them to escape from Sanctuary, so they had to try.

Upon joining the group, she whispered to Kirk, "So what did you find out?"

"There's a beginner's philosophy class this afternoon," he answered. "I told Kellen I was going to find Zicree to enroll in it. More important, the transporter room is on the second floor, and the door is marked with a red circle."

"Very good," approved Renna.

It was Spock's turn to report. "Dr. McCoy and I have located the entrance to the cave. There was one Senite guard on duty."

"Is there any reason why we should wait?" asked the captain.

"None," answered Renna. "There are two Senites in the guesthouse—the three of you do something to distract them, while I steal a robe. Let's meet at the first pavilion at the top of the spiral stairs."

"All right," said Kirk with a bemused smile. "If you need my advice in any of this planning, please ask."

"I will," she said casually, "but it's very simple. You have done your part, Captain Kirk, by getting the information, and I will do mine by getting us inside. Spock and McCoy will do their parts by figuring out the transporter controls. It's called teamwork, and if you can think of a better way . . ."

"Not at all," protested Kirk. "I only wonder if there's something we might have overlooked."

"I agree with Renna's plan," said Spock. "The

element of surprise is crucial. We can overpower the guard, if need be."

"That's what I like about you, Spock," remarked the slim brunette, "you're practical. You know we'll get one chance at this, and that's it."

Grumbled McCoy, "The worst they can do to us is make us take another boat ride."

Kirk nodded, then bellowed, "Wine! Can't we get a bottle of wine out here?"

Renna winked at them and scurried off around the side of the rambling house.

Kirk could see that both Senites who were in attendance that day were hovering around the large party in the dining room, so he turned to McCoy and screamed at the top of his lungs, *"How dare you call me that!"*

"But that's exactly what you are!" yelled McCoy. "And I'll call you that any time I like!"

"Oh, yeah!" thundered Kirk. "I'll make you eat those words!"

By now, the Senites had come running, and several of the new arrivals were peering out the curtained windows at the loudmouths on the veranda.

"Now, now," said Spock with reasoned assurance, "anger never solved a problem. Let us order some wine and have a toast."

"I can't drink with *him,*" snarled Kirk, pointing a finger at McCoy. "Did you hear what he called me?"

"No, I did not," Spock answered truthfully.

"He called me a . . . what was it?"

"A pompous windbag," the doctor replied.

"That was it!" shouted Kirk. "Those are fighting words."

"We can bring you some wine," one of the Senites offered.

"Very well," muttered the captain. "Do so at once!"

He winked at McCoy as the two Senites scrambled to do his bidding. Kirk motioned with his head, and the three troublemakers followed the Senites into the dining room. Kirk and McCoy continued to glare at each other, as one Senite returned to the large party and the other padded into the kitchen.

Kirk couldn't see Renna, but then he didn't know the location of the closet she was raiding. As long as the Senites were kept busy, that was all that mattered for the moment. When the Senite returned with a bottle of hazel wine, McCoy promptly spilled it.

"You're clumsy, too!" growled Kirk.

"I'm not going to drink with a pompous windbag," countered the doctor. "I'm leaving!"

McCoy marched out, and Kirk motioned imperiously. "Forget the wine. We'll get something in the village."

The Senite sighed with exasperation. "As you wish."

"We are sorry for the commotion," Spock assured him.

Kirk and Spock made their way slowly out the front door of the guesthouse, seeing nothing of either Renna or McCoy. Finally, they spied the doctor loitering near the bottom of the spiral staircase; it led up to a small white gazebo that connected several rope bridges to various parts of the village. He started to climb as Kirk and Spock meandered toward the small structure.

At the top, they found Renna and McCoy already occupied. The doctor held a white robe in one hand and was helping Renna strip off her jacket and pants with the other. She stood shivering in the drizzle in her unisex Senite underwear.

"Here!" she whispered, tossing a dish towel to Kirk. "Wrap this around my breasts. Got to strap them down if I want to look like a Senite."

He blinked in surprise for a moment, then drew the towel around her shivering torso. He pulled her roughly to him as he tied the towel in a strong knot. She paid him scant attention as she adjusted the towel to camouflage her feminine attributes.

"McCoy," she said, "here's some string. Tie my hair back. I have to wear the hood, but that will look normal in this rain."

Efficiently, they transformed the lithe young woman into a lithe young Senite. She looked too pretty to be a Senite, thought Kirk, until she began to practice a bland expression that would make the most blissed-out street sweeper proud.

He chuckled under his breath. "You know, Renna, in Dohama they do just the opposite—some of the Senites dress like women."

"I don't doubt it," replied Renna. "They make my skin crawl. But listen, while I'm a Senite, call me Rencree."

"Rencree," repeated Kirk, stepping back to admire their handiwork. She was small for a Senite, but she had selected a small robe. He thought he could still detect her breasts, but then again, he knew to look.

"I must talk like this," she said in a furry, nondescript voice. "Spock, lead the way to that cave."

The Vulcan nodded and strode onto a rope bridge that stretched upward two levels into the hierarchy of Khyming. Renna pulled her hood down over her face and folded her hands into the ample sleeves of her robe, looking every bit like one of the ubiquitous caretakers of Sanctuary. Kirk and McCoy fell in behind them and stepped carefully across the wet slats of the bridge. The rain made the swaying seem all the more treacherous, and they pulled on the handrails to climb the last few meters.

They found themselves standing in a honeycomb of

apartments carved into the cliffside. Or maybe they were caves, thought Kirk. The Senites might have begun their struggle on this planet in caves, hidden from the original persecutors, and now they refused to leave their hivelike domain. His idle theory was corroborated a few minutes later when they stood at the entrance to what appeared to be a labyrinth of cave tunnels. Most led to apartment entrances, but one stretched away into the distance, where a white-robed figure could be seen seated at a desk.

"Permit me," said Renna in her Senite voice, stepping in front of Spock and leading the way down the tunnel. Kirk, Spock, and McCoy fell in behind her, trying to look more curious than nervous. They were on their way to class to learn about their new world, Kirk reminded himself, and he planted an eager smile on his face.

Renna, or Rencree, stopped at the desk, where her counterpart looked up lazily. "Greetings," it said.

"Greetings," she replied, still waiting. Kirk admired her act—she wasn't going to volunteer any more information than was needed.

The Senite guard peered at her. It was one of those young, burly Senites who appeared to be used often for such duty. "You are not a resident here," it concluded. "What is the purpose of your visit with these fugitives?"

"Beginning philosophy class," she replied in a lilting but low-pitched voice.

"Ah, yes," said the guard, consulting a schedule frozen under plastic on its desk. "But that is not for one hour yet. Why are you so early?"

"Testing," the ersatz Senite replied.

"Testing?" The guard smiled, looking Kirk, Spock, and McCoy over. More and more, Kirk was beginning to feel like a prisoner.

"You may pass." The Senite slid its hand over a colored panel in a peculiar fashion. The metal door behind the Senite's desk slid open and allowed them passage to a turbolift.

Renna swallowed hard, trying not to look at Kirk and the others. When the door clanged shut and nothing happened, she said hoarsely, "Second floor."

"Thank you," responded a metallic voice.

With a barely discernible movement, the turbolift journeyed upward for several seconds before opening onto what looked like a vast bunker carved from a cave. Lines of various colors stretched along the floors and walls; Kirk decided they were indicators, and marched down the red-lined corridor. His bold decision was rewarded a few moments later when they spied a double door with a melon-sized red circle painted in its center.

The captain could hardly believe the ease of their entry, but this was no time to stop or reconsider. He scanned every corner and corridor about them while Renna pushed the door open and slipped inside. Spock and McCoy swiftly followed, but the captain waited to assure himself that no one had seen them enter before going inside.

It looked like a cargo transporter room, with huge chambers dozens of meters in height and width, gigantic lenses suspended from the ceiling, and rows and rows of controls and sensors. McCoy didn't know where to start, but Spock strode to the nearest control panel and began to study it. Motorized carts stood empty in a neat row, and cargo doors lined the farthest wall. This transporter looked capable of sending them all the way back to Earth, thought Kirk.

He rushed to Spock's side. "Can you locate the *Enterprise?*"

"Unknown, Captain," answered the Vulcan. "This

transporter room is designed to be run by a team of technicians. It is sufficiently complicated that I will need time to study it before I know its operations in detail."

"You haven't got any time," Kirk replied, more to himself than to Spock. Nervously, he prowled the row of alien computers and scanners, wondering which one would find the *Enterprise* and get them home.

McCoy hovered over what looked like a steering panel for the robot carts, but he was hesitant to touch any of the strange levers and dials. Renna started for the door to see if she could lock it, but she was a moment too late—the door swung open, and Zicree entered, followed by a triumphant Kellen.

"Do you see?" sneered the blond woman. "I told you we'd find them in the transporter room. Kirk did everything but ask for a map to this place."

The Senite shook its head with disappointment and drew a weapon that looked like a silver piccolo. "What are you doing here?"

"Isn't it obvious what they are doing?" Kellen asked. "They are trying to return to the persecutors! You were right to have me watch them. None of these fugitives can be trusted."

While Kirk glared at the young woman, Spock edged closer to Zicree.

"Why not let us go home?" asked McCoy. "It won't affect anything you're trying to accomplish."

"It is forbidden!" snapped Kellen. "That is what the persecutors want, to be able to come and go from Sanctuary."

"I gave you a second chance to redeem yourselves," said Zicree, "and you have repaid me with deceit. This is a very grave offense."

Kirk ducked behind the row of controls, distracting Zicree for a moment. That was all Spock needed to leap forward and apply a Vulcan nerve pinch to Zicree's neck, making the Senite slump to the ground in a white-robed heap. Kellen made a dash for the door, but Renna was all over her, wrestling the bigger woman back into the room. Captain Kirk slammed the door shut and threw a desk in front of it. Then a piercing alarm sounded so loudly that it seemed to vibrate the cave and everything in it. Spock rushed to Renna's side and applied a nerve pinch to the blond woman, who slumped into a stupor.

Kirk shouted over the wrenching alarm, "Spock! You've got to get that transporter working!"

"I believe," responded the Vulcan, "that I can beam us to the transporter's last setting. Without more time, I cannot beam us to the *Enterprise* or the destination of our choice."

"Where is the last setting?" asked Kirk.

"Unknown," answered Spock.

Angry fists pounded and shouts sounded behind the double doors, and a Senite tried to push his way in. Kirk threw himself against the door, smashing the Senite's arm and eliciting a howl of pain. McCoy piled a chair and more furniture against the doors, and both men leaned into the barricade to keep the Senites out.

"Get it working!" yelled Kirk.

Spock immediately began to manipulate one of several sets of controls. Lights danced in sequence between the lenses in the ceiling and the illuminated pads upon the floor, as he mastered the rudiments of the system.

"Everyone to the activated pads!" he called.

He didn't have to yell twice as Renna, McCoy, and Captain Kirk leaped upon the glowing transporter pads, and Spock eased the levers forward. Their molecules sparkled in columns of phosphorescent light before gradually fading away. With the doors deserted, the Senites smashed through the makeshift barricade. They came streaming into the room just as Spock dashed from behind the controls and onto the pad. A Senite fired a weapon that missed him by centimeters and bored a hole in the wall of the cave.

A second later, Spock was gone in the transporter beam, and the pack of Senites stood dumbfounded.

Chapter Ten

As the Senite transporter scrambled his molecules, Captain Kirk had no idea where he was headed, but he didn't expect to end up where he had already been. Nevertheless, he, McCoy, and Renna materialized on a main thoroughfare in the rowdy seaside village of Dohama. It was the middle of the afternoon, but there was not a single creature in sight in this town that two days earlier had been teeming with undesirables from all over the galaxy. The wind, which had so recently carried laughter and the smells of ale and grilled meat, was silent except for the dirty awnings it flapped. Dohama was completely deserted.

Before Kirk had time to mouth the obvious question, Spock materialized beside him. "We should run," suggested the Vulcan. "I tried to reset the transporter, but the Senites may find these coordinates and come after us."

Kirk nodded, and the small party set off at a determined jog down the center of the abandoned street. Without people to enliven them, the empty storefronts and gambling parlors looked fraudulent, like the scenery for a play that was over.

"This is Dohama, isn't it?" asked the captain, mystified.

"Yeah," answered McCoy. "That jewelry stand was where a Senite wanted to pierce my ears."

"Where did everyone go?" Kirk wondered aloud.

"Unknown," muttered Spock.

Kirk glanced over his shoulder, then led the runners around a corner. As soon as he felt they were out of the line of sight of the transporter coordinates, he slowed to a brisk walk.

"This is most peculiar," admitted the Vulcan, peering into a deserted tattoo parlor. "Two days ago, the residents seemed to have nowhere else to go."

McCoy pointed to a three-story building with several quaint balconies. "That's where the Senites were hanging out—the ones dressed as women. Where are they all?"

"I don't know." Kirk twisted around, trying to make sense out of it, when he discovered that someone else was missing. "Where's Renna?"

Like whirling dervishes, Kirk, Spock, and McCoy turned in every direction, trying to find the woman who had so recently joined their desperate quest. But they were back to three—Renna was gone, too.

McCoy stumbled into Kirk and muttered, "What's happening, Jim?"

"Calm yourself, Doctor," said Spock. "It is quite possible that Renna *chose* to desert us. Although not a very loyal decision, it could be considered a logical one. Disguised as a Senite, she may be safer traveling alone."

"Renna!" Kirk shouted angrily. "Renna!"

"Be quiet, you damn fools!" cursed another voice over their heads. They looked up to see the hulking, hirsute figure of Billiwog leaning over one of the railings of the Senite pleasure palace. "Get your big mouths up here," he whispered, "so you can see what's happening."

They quickly obeyed, entering the narrow three-story building and climbing the velvet-lined staircase to the top floor. There they found the shipbuilder waiting for them. He put his finger to his lips and motioned them toward a window with lacy curtains.

"Look out there," he whispered, "and you'll see what the Senites are up to. But don't let them see you."

Surreptitiously, Kirk, Spock, and McCoy took turns peering from the upper window, which commanded a view all the way to the beach, the one they had crawled up from when first arriving at Dohama. Although the town was deserted, the beach was not. A horde of Senites was busy piling what appeared to be bodies into several large conveyances. The motorized wagons had various gated compartments, each large enough to contain a sleeping, or dead, humanoid. The Senites were filling the slots as rapidly as they could, because a hundred more fugitives lay waiting, stretched out like dead fish along the sand.

"Good God!" breathed McCoy. "What are they doing?"

"Harvesting," said Billiwog. "I've been through several of these. You fellows were lucky you got out when you did."

"Fascinating," remarked Spock. "What is the purpose of this harvest?"

Billiwog shrugged. "I'll be damned if I know. It happens maybe once a year, as soon as the village fills up to the rafters with fugitives. The Senites must put something into the food and drink, because people start passing out in droves."

"How did *you* escape it?" Kirk asked suspiciously.

The burly humanoid winked. "Remember the other day—you asked me why I was cooking my own food? As soon as I see the village getting crowded, I start eating nothing but fish I catch myself. I'm sure the Senites know *I* know what they're up to, but I'm careful not to tell anyone and start a panic. I do what I can by telling people to get out of here, and I give them boats to do it."

"Why do you stay in this place?" asked McCoy with a shiver.

"I could ask you the same thing," Billiwog replied. "Why did you come back?"

The captain sighed. "That's a long story. There was a woman with us. Actually, she was dressed like a Senite. Did you see her?"

The humanoid scratched his beard and answered, "I didn't see any of you until you started bellowing." Then it dawned on him. "You brought a *woman* back with you?"

"Well, we thought we did." Kirk peered out the window again. "What's going to happen to all those people?"

Billiwog shook his furry head. "Can't say. But they don't ever come back, and Dohama is a lot more peaceful without them. Now, about this woman. You can have your pick of my boats—in fact, you can have *all* my boats—"

He was interrupted by a noise downstairs, like a door slamming shut. "Ssshh!" hissed the big man, motioning the others to be quiet. "Somebody's coming!"

Whoever they were they made no secret of their approach, as determined footsteps clamored up the staircase. Billiwog made for the open window, tried to climb out, and got stuck, preventing anyone else's escape. Kirk shoved a chest of drawers against the door, and Spock grabbed one end of the bed and began to drag it toward the door. McCoy made a futile attempt to free the giant from the window frame. Then he saw how pointless it was—another squad of Senites was gathering in the street below.

The door and the bureau suddenly glowed with a blinding light and vaporized, as Kirk and Spock scrambled to get out of the way. There was nowhere to hide in the gaudy bedroom, and Billiwog plugged the only escape route. All they could do was stand their ground and glare defiantly at the Senites who streamed through the blackened doorway. Each Senite stared grimly and leveled a silver weapon at them.

"Hey! Hey!" came a muffled shout from Billiwog, as he finally extricated himself from the window. "I'm your friend, Billiwog!"

He was instantly zapped by a blue beam, and his huge body spun in agony before it crashed to the floor, shaking the entire room. McCoy leaned over the body, preparing to check its pulse, but he was cut down before he could even reach it. Two more Senites aimed weapons at Kirk and Spock and discharged their beams.

Just before a jolt charged up his spine and blackness overtook his mind, Kirk had a horrible feeling he was going to find out what it meant to be harvested.

Renna was not sure why she had deserted her newfound comrades so quickly after reaching the strange, empty town. But her instinct for survival had seldom failed her, and their mad dash down the vacant street had given her ample opportunity to duck out of sight into an abandoned bar. She wasn't a moment too soon, as it turned out, because a squad of Senites quickly materialized on the same spot they'd arrived at moments earlier and started to search for the escapees.

Figuring the Senites would have portable sensors, Renna ran from the back of the bar and dashed across the empty street into another empty building. She kept going from one hiding place to another, always in a straight line, putting as much distance between herself and the white-robed troopers as she could. If they had portable sensors, as she figured, they would probably go after three life-forms instead of one. She felt a pang of guilt about saving her own skin, but she told herself that it was Spock's fault for sending them to a hideout in a ghost town.

After fleeing from the last row of buildings, Renna ducked into a small guard post beside an archway in a wall. She gulped several mouthfuls of air and tried to compose herself and her disguise. As she leveled her breasts with the towel, she heard far-off voices and the cawing of what sounded like a bird of some sort, and she made her way cautiously to a tiny window in the wall.

It was then that she saw something that terrified her into near panic, something so awful it was beyond anything she'd expected to see on Sanctuary: a whole army of Senites dragging bodies across the beach and tossing them into narrow cages on huge wagons. Her mouth felt as dry as the sand the bodies were lying on.

Among the carcasses were creatures of every description, of races she'd never known existed, all of them male, as far as she could tell. Occasionally, the Senites checked the bodies, holding meters to their mouths or jabbing them with hypos. They must be alive, she thought—most of them, at least—and the Senites seemed intent upon keeping them in a comatose state.

Suddenly, four more carcasses were dumped upon the beach in the sparkling aurora of a transporter beam. Renna swallowed hard, recognizing the young

151

captain, the doctor, and the Vulcan, but she'd never seen the great hairy being who accompanied them. She took no pleasure in the fact that she had evidently done the right thing by deserting them, and she shivered under the knowledge that she would have to save them from whatever fate the Senites had in mind. By now, Renna found herself thinking of Kirk, Spock, and McCoy as her men, her crew. Though they would be horrified to hear that, they weren't in any position to contradict her, she thought grimly.

Unfortunately, she couldn't walk into the midst of the Senites, sling three grown men over her shoulders, and carry them off. She would have to stick with her men until they woke up, helping to rouse them, if possible. In her favor, there were at least sixty or seventy Senites, working in a disorganized fashion to drag bodies to the conveyances. More Senites were coming and going, and more than a few had their hoods up to protect their bald pates from the sun. Without giving it a great deal of thought, Renna drew her hood over her head, making sure her hair was hidden, and stepped out of the guardhouse. Folding her hands into the sleeves of her robe, she strode briskly across the sand and into the midst of the Senite work party.

They paid her scant attention, and Renna saw a Senite of about her size struggling with the hairy creature who'd been beamed over with Kirk, Spock, and McCoy. She proceeded to grab a leg and begin hauling. In that way, without speaking a single word, she made one friend and kept close enough to make sure that her men were handled with reasonable care. After the wagons were loaded, she gathered in a single file with the other Senites and began to march behind the automated body carts. She had no idea where they were going, except away from the beach and deserted town and toward the impressive mountain range to the north.

Scotty got up from the captain's chair and stretched his arms, suppressing a yawn. Tedium and waiting made him more tired than the most demanding crisis, and he almost longed to be flat on his back in the fusion reactor, nothing but a wrench between him and the destruction of the ship. If that were the case, at least Captain Kirk would be on the bridge, barking orders and impossible timetables. Spock would be beside him, completely unruffled although the ship was going to explode in thirty seconds, and Dr. McCoy would be glowering and pacing. That was the way Mr. Scott wanted things, back to what passed for normal aboard the USS *Enterprise*.

The ship was in fine fettle—after all, the crew had nothing to do but the equivalent of swabbing the deck four times a day. Their ship wasn't the only one that had benefited from all the free time, thought Scotty; the *Gezary* was also in better shape than it had been in years. That thought reminded him of the bounty huntress, Pilenna, and the fact that he had an open invitation for some rest and recreation aboard the *Gezary*. Probably more recreation than rest, he thought with a smile. But he couldn't enjoy it, not knowing what was happening below to his captain and mates.

Blast that bloody planet, he cursed to himself, staring at the inscrutable turquoise sphere on his viewscreen. What was it, a haven or a trap? Were the Senites the greatest humanitarians of the galaxy, or misguided jailers? More important, were his friends alive and well and enjoying the creature comforts the Senites talked about, or were they sick and injured, perhaps even dead?

Scott knew the risks of transporting to the planet now—knew them all too well—but the temptation was almost overwhelming to march into the transporter room, beam down there, and find them. Damn the consequences! At least *he* would know if they were alive and safe.

If only there were some sort of lifeline he could hold on to, a way to be dragged back to the *Enterprise.* Without such a lifeline, he was not going to the surface of Sanctuary, and neither was anybody else. Failing that, if only there were some way to get the Senites' attention, some way to twist their arms a little bit.

"Commander Scott?" said Uhura, breaking into his angry reverie.

"Yes, Lieutenant?"

"The *Neptune* is close enough for ship-to-ship communications," answered Uhura, "and Captain Mora wishes to speak with you."

"Ahead of schedule, aren't they?" observed Scotty. "Put Captain Mora on the screen."

He was not surprised to see the wizened features of Donald Mora, one of the oldest captains in Starfleet. He was also one of the Federation's foremost experts on oceanography, and the two careers had dovetailed nicely with his assignment to the *Neptune.* He was a good choice to send on this mission, decided Scotty, because his maturity might give him patience. And he would need plenty of patience to deal with the Senites.

"Hello, Commander Scott," Mora greeted him with a smile. "Good to see you again. It's been many years."

Scotty couldn't help his own scowl. "I wish it were under better circumstances."

"I've been reading your reports," said Captain Mora with concern, "and I can appreciate your frustration. Is it really your assessment that the Senites will refuse all contact with the Federation?"

"You may be able to contact them," replied Scotty. "I was, but only through the graces of another ship in orbit. As far as communicating with them, their entire society is based on one directive: Come to Sanctuary if you want, but expect a one-way trip."

Donald Mora frowned. "That attitude doesn't seem possible from a race that sounds so advanced."

"They're advanced enough," said Scotty. "They have a shield around that planet that withstood a full-scale Klingon attack. It cuts off communications, sensors, everything that's within thirty kilometers of the surface. And they have long-range deflectors to protect incoming fugitives, as they call them. I must admit, their refusal to let anyone leave the planet is the only thing that discourages a pack of bounty hunters from going down there."

"Let me think about all this," said Captain Mora. "At warp six, I should be there in about four hours."

"Captain," added Scotty, mustering a smile, "if you can find a way to get through to the Senites, I'll buy you a fish dinner."

"I don't eat fish," replied Captain Mora, "too many of them are my friends. But I'll think about your problem. Out."

When the gleaming curve of the planet reclaimed the viewscreen, Scotty turned away. Looking at it only made him feel sad and helpless.

The motorized body carts rumbled up a mountain pass, followed by a single line of Senites that stretched for a hundred meters behind them. No one spoke to Renna during the long march into the mountains—in fact, no one spoke at all, even during the brief periods when they stopped to attend to bodily functions and sip a bitter tealike substance. Occasionally, there would be a groan or shout from one of the wagons, and a Senite would shoot a blue beam into the cage to silence the prisoner. Darkness was falling swiftly, casting eerie shadows from the spindly peaks, and Renna wondered if they would march all night.

She tried to console herself with the thought that, even if she couldn't rescue Kirk and his men, she might reach another transporter room or otherwise learn how to circumvent the Senites' security shield. But where could she go without them? she wondered. Her whole plan for escape depended upon that big ship of theirs riding in orbit. No, she decided, she had to find a way to save them, no matter what the risk. The only alternatives were to continue impersonating a Senite, which was doubtful for any length of time, or to escape into the mountains and live like an animal, as Kirk had said people were doing. Both prospects were equally unattractive.

As she watched the Senites marching stoically all around her, Renna decided they were pathologically insane. They had extensive transporter technology, yet they marched all night through treacherous mountains instead of using the transporter. At least the sedated prisoners got to ride to wherever they were going. Even considering the amount of energy that would be required to move hundreds of people, such sacrifice bordered on masochism.

Of course, she thought, the Senites reveled in their sexlessness, conformity, and sacrifice. They even found a way to impose it upon their guests by separating the sexes into villages like Khyming and Dohama. They professed sympathy for the fugitives, yet treated them like recalcitrant children, spying on them and monitoring their actions. They also raised snakes like Kellen. And what kind of beings coddled their guests one day, then knocked them out and threw them into cages the next? Crazy beings, that's what kind.

Renna was so lost in psychoanalysis and trying not to trip that she wasn't aware of the searchlight beaming through the thick fog ahead of them. Finally, she lifted her head and saw it, and she picked up her painful feet and walked a little more quickly, as did every Senite in the meandering line. Finally, they rounded a bend in the trail, and she saw the source of the light—a gaping passageway in the base of the highest peak. It loomed before them like a sheer tower of light, large enough to pass a hundred wagons, bearing a million sedated fugitives. Renna gulped, fearful and relieved at the same time.

"Isn't it beautiful?" she heard someone whisper.

She turned to see her small friend, the one she'd helped in carrying the hairy giant to the wagon. "Yes," she whispered in agreement.

"The Reborning is so beautiful," the small Senite added.

"Yes," Renna agreed, staring ahead at the column of light. She guessed she would soon find out what a Reborning was.

The gigantic doorway swallowed the wagons one by one, and the Senites marched reverently after them. Renna craned her neck to get a better look at what appeared to be an immense cavern, but the golden lights that rimmed the doorway were all but blinding. She had to close her eyes as she passed under them, and she felt a queer tingling and warming sensation. The tiny hairs on the back of her neck twitched unpleasantly, and she hurried under the lights as fast as she could without bumping into the Senite ahead of her. Renna had read enough medical journals stolen from various ships to guess that the lights were some sort of sterilizing or antibiotic precaution. She could well imagine how dirty the marchers were from their long trek, but why did they need to be sterile?

Renna began to fear that they would be required to strip and change into clean robes, but that minor fear was erased as soon as her eyes cleared and she got a

157

good look at her surroundings. The cavern was as mammoth as she had imagined from the outside, with a ceiling that was a dozen stories high. She could count at least that many levels of tiny rooms, or cells, lining the walls of the cavern.

On the main floor of the cavern, she saw hundreds of shining metal beds in row upon uniform row. But they weren't just beds, she noted—they were operating tables!

Around each table was a compact cluster of monitors, life-support equipment, and what appeared to be laser operating instruments. She shivered, and the hairs on her neck stood by themselves this time. Only the most disastrous war could demand this sort of massive medical facility, assumed Renna. Before she could give it any more thought, the other Senites began to unlock the wagons and remove the comatose prisoners, and she quickly followed their lead.

Kirk, Spock, and McCoy were in the last wagon to arrive, and the other wagons were unloaded first. Renna marveled at the way the Senites, who must have been as tired as she was after their grueling hike, pitched in without complaint. A bit more carefully this time, they hauled the strange collection of humanoids to the operating tables and strapped each one down. It was loathsome work, but Renna had to assist. The straps were of a dark, spongy material that felt like it had the tensile strength of steel. Doctors, or at least Senites who were carrying monitoring devices and whose white robes were spotless, inspected each unconscious patient in turn.

"This one's dead," said a furry-voiced doctor, hovering over a Klingon. It motioned to the others to take him away, and the Klingon's bed was quickly cleared for a living specimen.

Another doctor peered curiously at a homely alien with red skin and arms that dangled from the operating table to the floor. The creature barely had any neck. "Not humanoid enough," pronounced the doctor. "Dump him somewhere out in the mountains."

Hmm, thought Renna, there were times when it paid not to be too humanoid. This scenario was repeated several times, as dead bodies were discovered among the living and several of the stranger races were reprieved. Renna kept her eye on Kirk, Spock, and McCoy, because it was obvious that the operating tables were going to be filled before their wagon was unloaded. She longed to ask someone what all the preparation was about, but she didn't dare. Were they going to be revived, then imprisoned? If so, what was the point of the operating tables?

Finally, Kirk's wagon was unloaded, and he and his men were carried to turbolifts and taken to the cells that overlooked the immense operating arena. Renna was about to follow them up when a voice sounded on a loudspeaker. It echoed throughout the vast cavern:

"We thank you all for your participation in the Reborning," intoned the voice. "This is a glorious day for those assembled here. Each of you was reborn in the same hallowed manner that has been employed by our order for centuries. We regret that you have no memory of this unique experience, and so we will take a few moments to review the Six Holy Steps of Reborning:

"First, the ritual washing and shaving of the initiates. Second, the brain operation, in which harmful past memories are erased. Third, the sexual organs are removed forever. Fourth, hormone treatments to remove any residual trace of gender. Fifth, electrolysis and cosmetic surgery are used to ensure a uniformly pleasing appearance. Sixth, recovery and training. In approximately seventy days, the initiates will return to our community as loyal members of the order, devoted to the mission of Sanctuary."

There was a murmur of appreciation, and the speaker continued, "We realize how weary you must be, and you are not required to perform any further services. But if you wish to take part in the ritual washing and shaving, please report to level three for clean robes. The rest of you are relieved of duty and may report to the transporter room on level two. Praise be to the holy order of Senites."

"Praise be," echoed dozens of lilting voices.

Renna felt herself reeling, as if she was about to faint, and it took a major effort of will to stay on her feet. Her friend caught her by the elbow and smiled beatifically at her.

"You are weary," said the Senite. "I am staying for the ritual, but I will escort you to the transporter."

Renna shook her head and composed herself. "I am staying, too," she answered in a firm voice. "It is my duty."

The small Senite nodded appreciatively and joined an exodus of fellow Senites to the turbolift. Renna followed them, wishing she could take a torch to this whole lousy planet. Maybe she couldn't do that, but she would do everything in her power to see that Captain Kirk, Dr. McCoy, and Mr. Spock were spared from being lobotomized and castrated.

Chapter Eleven

SCOTTY PERSONALLY operated the transporter controls that brought Captain Donald Mora aboard the *Enterprise*. He was a trim man with energy that belied his eighty-some years, although his face looked every minute of it, thanks to a good portion of a life spent working outdoors and underwater.

"Hello, Commander Scott." He beamed, stepping down from the transporter platform and shaking Scotty's hand.

He managed a smile. "Good to see you, Captain Mora. I trust ye had no difficulty with the other ships in orbit?"

"My, no," he answered. "In fact, they're a friendly lot. As I was coming out of warp, an Orion contacted me to see if I wanted to trade any criminals for slave girls."

"Aye," replied Scotty, "salt o' the earth. Ye missed meeting the Klingon who was in orbit. He was finally recalled after his superiors decided that Sanctuary was the most effective prison in the galaxy."

Mora nodded glumly. "From your reports, I gather they are not far from wrong. May I speak frankly, Mr. Scott?"

Scotty motioned around the empty transporter room. "We are alone here."

"Very well," began Captain Mora. "You are no doubt aware that we have been sent here to replace you. The *Enterprise*, I mean."

"Aye. It was not likely we'd be left here indefinitely."

"But you'd like to stay indefinitely?" asked Mora.

"Indefinitely, no," answered Scotty, "just until we rescue the captain, Mr. Spock, and Dr. McCoy."

"But there's the problem. You see, you have no real plan to rescue them, and Starfleet knows that."

"May I speak frankly, too?"

The captain nodded. "Please do. This is a private conversation."

Scotty paced as he spoke. "Starfleet doesna know those three men as I know them. Although there is little we can do at the moment, I feel—somehow—they will be able to make an escape attempt. I don't know how. I don't know when. But I know we must be ready to help them when that time comes."

"Spoken as a loyal friend," Captain Mora said sympathetically. "But without a concrete plan, Starfleet will not let the *Enterprise* be tied up here. If I could just report to them the slightest bit of progress, the beginning of a plan . . ."

Scotty grinned slyly. "Indeed, Captain, I have the beginning of a plan. I think we ought to invade the planet."

"Invade the planet?" Captain Mora frowned. "I thought you said it was dangerous to go down there."

"Not necessarily dangerous," replied Scotty, "sim-

162

ply one-way. I'm sure you or I could beam down there safely this very moment. Inorganic matter by itself is destroyed—we've already seen that with the numerous probes we've tried to send down. But organic creatures are accepted without reservation. If we could assemble the correct invasion force, one that could intimidate the Senites without firing a shot, they might be forced to negotiate with us."

Now it was Donald Mora's turn to smile. "You're a very devious man, Commander Scott."

"I am," he replied grimly, "when the lives of my shipmates are at stake."

Quite on purpose, Renna stood at the end of a long line, waiting to receive a fresh robe. From the third floor of the mammoth cave, she looked down upon the hundreds of creatures strapped to gleaming metal tables and tried to imagine the horror of what was about to happen. To be stripped of one's identity and memories—and sex—it was too much to fathom. Maybe most of them weren't the best specimens of whatever stock they came from, but they didn't deserve to end up as Senites.

Her mind somersaulted over every possibility and escape route. Each of the dozen or so levels that ringed the operating arena seemed to consist of a catwalk and a combination of cells, offices, recovery rooms, and the like. On level three, she had passed a small theater and had seen a group of Senites sitting there, as if waiting for a show to begin. She well imagined there were many observers and specialists who wouldn't be called on until later in the process. The Reborning, as loathsome as it was, was a major medical achievement; it was mass-production surgery on perhaps a thousand patients at once.

The specialists, doctors, whatever they were, all appeared to be older Senites, as if it took many

Rebornings to learn the job fully. They prowled every level of the cave, inspecting patients in the private cells above and on the production floor below. After the drudge work of shaving and cleaning, thought Renna, the brain surgeons would go next. If she didn't rescue Kirk and his men by then, it would be too late. But how could she escape having to clean and shave the unfortunates below? The only answer was to kick herself up a notch and become one of the doctors.

Renna's surreptitious inspection ended when she found herself at the front of the line, eyeing a bulky Senite behind a counter. What had it been in its previous life, she couldn't help but wonder, an Elysian or a Saurian? Now it was a Senite in charge of robe distribution in the Cave of the Reborning.

"May I have two robes?" she found herself asking. She quickly added, "My friend is sleeping, and I will take one to it."

The round-faced Senite studied her closely with a rather stupid gaze, and Renna fought the temptation to squirm under her hood. Finally, it scolded, "Sleeping is prohibited. Your friend should come itself."

"It is weary," added Renna, "but it does not wish to miss the ritual."

"If it wishes to sleep, send it home," replied the Senite. "What sizes?"

"Small for me," answered Renna, "and large for my friend."

Renna grabbed the robes, trying to suppress a sense of triumph—she now had three robes, counting the dirty one she wore. That was one robe short, but a plan was percolating in her mind. From close up, none of her three comrades would pass muster as a Senite, but they might from a distance. First, she had to confront the hurdle of changing into her clean garment, and she peered along the catwalk to see where the other Senites were disrobing. To Renna's relief,

164

they were as modest as sexed beings—one by one, they entered the tiny cells that stretched along the curved corridor, drawing the curtains behind them.

Most of the cells she passed were occupied, which stood to reason considering that she had been among the last in line. Finally, a curtain parted in front of her, and she waited for its occupant to emerge. She and the gangly Senite smiled benignly at one another before she ducked inside and closed the white curtain behind her. It was a small but presentable hospital room for a single patient, with gleaming equipment that looked capable of sustaining life forever. There was a fountain in which to wash her face and hands, and she proceeded to do so. And then her eyes lit upon something else—another robe wadded up in the corner.

Renna removed her own soiled garment, much relieved that she could do so in privacy, and finished cleaning up. She rearranged her clothing, wondering grimly if the Senites ever practiced their conversions on women. She didn't see why they couldn't, but there were apparently so few women on the planet—most of them congregated in one place—that she didn't imagine they would be considered plentiful enough. She gulped when she remembered that the Senites thought they were doing the initiates a tremendous favor.

After tidying herself, Renna was stuck with the problem of hiding three large robes under her small one. She stole the sheets from the bed, wrapped them around the robes, and tied the bundle to her stomach. It made her into a rather portly Senite, but not all the Senites were slim, especially the older ones, likely a side effect of the loss of testosterone. Renna peered into the mirror and shaped her paunch for several moments before noticing that her face still looked too young. She needed makeup and some kind of instrument to carry that would make her look like a member of the medical team. As quietly as possible, Renna began to root through the drawers and equipment in the little room.

She found some brownish powder that she combined with her own saliva to create makeup. Luckily, she was getting more worry lines by the moment, and she applied the dark substance to the burgeoning lines in her face and turned them into age lines, she hoped. Renna knew she would have to be careful to avoid letting anybody gaze into her face for more than a second or two. By this time, the voice and mannerisms were the easy part.

No hand-held instruments were lying around, and she rifled through the drawers in a desperate search. Finally, she took a deep breath, stood, and gazed calmly around the cramped room. She would have to make an instrument, she decided—and then her eyes alighted on the silver handles of the water fountain. The faucet handles had the same sort of unsymmetrical kidney shape as the Senites' hand weapons. If they were waved around real fast, thought Renna, they might look like medical instruments.

She grabbed the closest handle, discovered which way it was supposed to turn, and twisted it the opposite way. Brute strength enabled the young woman to loosen the handle, as water started spouting into the air like a plumber's nightmare. Renna thanked the stars that she hadn't put on her clean robe yet as she spun the handle and fought the spraying water. One handle would be all she could get, and it would have to do.

Freeing the handle, she looked around for something to stuff into the geyser, then decided the raging leak might make a nice diversion. Renna adjusted her paunch and her makeup one more time, then slipped into a robe that fit tightly but still covered her fake stomach. Taking a deep breath, she plunged into the corridor and joined a steady exodus of Senites toward the turbolift.

As she walked, she stole a peek over the railing to see what was happening below. Several Senites were rapidly stripping the fugitives of their filthy clothing, while a handful had begun to bathe and shave them in a ritualistic fashion that started at their toes and worked its way up. She couldn't worry about those poor creatures now, Renna decided, and she tried to put them out of her mind.

The ersatz Senite hid her ersatz instrument in the sleeve of her robe and wondered how long it would take before somebody noticed a flood of water spewing onto the catwalk. She didn't have long to wait; shouts sounded almost immediately, and several Senites ahead of her stopped and turned. Renna, however, bolted through the packed crowd and entered the first empty turbolift she could find. Unfortunately, a younger Senite stepped in after her.

"Level six!" she blurted to the computer.

Renna looked up and found the younger Senite, who was quite handsome for an androgynous being, staring at her. It quickly looked away and muttered, "Level one."

"Is this the first Reborning you have seen?" she asked in a fatherly way.

"Yes," admitted the Senite, looking embarrassed. "Is it so obvious?"

"Tell me," whispered Renna in her huskiest voice, "do you ever have dreams of a previous life?"

"Yes," breathed the young Senite. "What does that mean?"

"It means they didn't get everything," Renna replied as the door snapped open. She stepped out on level six, and the door closed behind her on the stunned expression of the young Senite.

For the first time since reaching this horrid place, Renna had a chance to catch a normal breath. Level six was exactly what she wanted—a place where not much was going on. She strode along a catwalk that was about halfway up the beehive shape of the great cavern, and she could see considerably more activity on another floor higher up. The strange complex was not even close to its maximum capacity, and she didn't want to think about what that meant.

She continued down the empty corridor, which was lined with darkened rooms. From a level above came an inhuman howl, and it froze her in midbreath. The wretched creature yelped again but stopped abruptly, and she heard voices for a moment. All this action occurred about two floors above her, Renna estimated, and she wondered if that was where they had taken the other prisoners. She turned around and made her way back toward the turbolift.

On level eight, Renna was forced to keep her head down, because Senites were all around, dashing between various cells and sedating prisoners as they awoke. The initiates were strapped down in their beds, not as tightly as those on the operating floor, but not free to move. One would start groaning or tossing, and a medic would rush to sedate him. They used hypos exclusively, and Renna assumed it was because a number of stun blasts in a short period of time would probably prove dangerous, if not fatal. She gripped her faucet handle as if it was a hypo and started rushing from cell to cell, staying only long enough to see who was in each one.

Her determined checking of each patient in every cell was only slightly more frantic than what most of the other Senites were doing, and it finally paid off. In one cell, she spied the taciturn face of the Vulcan—his complexion more sallow than usual and his eyes closed serenely. Damn it, thought Renna, if only she had a real instrument that could revive him. She bent over his inert form to make sure he was still alive.

With heartthrobbing quickness, his hand shot up and gripped her around her neck. She couldn't even struggle, because his grip was immobilizing. "Spock," she croaked, "it's me—Renna!"

His hand loosened and fell limply to his side. His eyes were still closed serenely, but he spoke as Renna leaned over him. "I am sorry I did not recognize you, but feared you were a Senite. I have lain awake for some time. I am very relieved to see you under these circumstances."

"You don't know how relieved you should be," she whispered, pretending to examine him. Other medics continued to pass by outside the cell, and there were no curtains to shut. These were holding tanks.

"Where are we?"

"It's a Senite factory," she murmured. "They're lobotomizing and castrating people from that village in order to turn them into Senites."

"A somewhat radical method of reproduction," answered Spock. "Do you have an escape plan?"

"First," said Renna, "we've got to get you into one of these robes I brought." She lifted her robe, removed a wad of fabric from the bundle, and laid it on the Vulcan's chest. "I think that's the clean one."

"Go to the door," said Spock, "and distract their attention from the cell. I will be out in a moment."

Renna nodded and slipped outside onto the catwalk. A Senite was walking toward her, alertly peering into each cell it passed. Renna walked toward the specialist and pointed downward.

"What has happened?" she asked urgently, peering across the great chasm at cells and rooms on the other side, farther down. Because of the curvature of the cavern walls, she was able to find the minor commotion caused by the geyser she had set loose in the

169

changing room. She pointed it out to the approaching Senite. "There, do you see?"

Another Senite approached from behind them and paused to see what the fuss was about. Had this Senite turned to look behind it, it would have seen Spock slipping the robe over his Senite-issue shirt and pants. The Vulcan pulled the hood over his distinctive ears and stepped into the corridor to join the onlookers.

He caught Renna's eye, and she rocked back on her heels in relief. "It's under control," she announced, before scurrying down the corridor. A tall, thin Senite followed her, while the others were still trying to figure out what was going on.

Renna and Spock couldn't stop to search the adjoining cells, as they would have liked—they had to put some distance between themselves and the crowd Renna had attracted.

"The captain?" Spock asked. "And Dr. McCoy?"

"They must be in some of these cells," she whispered. "None of you were taken down there, thank your gods."

"We shall need some way to revive them," said Spock, "because they don't have my metabolism." He spotted another Senite making the rounds a few meters ahead of them, and tapped Renna's shoulder.

She nodded, and they slowed to allow the Senite to walk ahead of them, until it entered one of the cells. Then they sped up.

"Praise be to the holy order," intoned Renna as she and Spock entered the tiny chamber.

The Senite blinked at her with surprise, which gave Spock ample time to reach out and grip its neck. The Senite dropped into a well of unconsciousness. Renna caught the falling figure and helped Spock lay it on the bed, next to an unconscious fugitive with scaly, checkered skin.

"That nerve pinch thing is a handy talent," remarked Renna as she aided Spock in searching the body. "Can you teach it to me?"

"No," the Vulcan answered. He took a small medikit from the billows of the Senite's sleeve and opened the silver case. There was a single hypo and perhaps twenty colored vials for it, most of them blue and a handful red. Several of the blue ones had evidently been used.

"I surmise," said Spock, "that the blue vials are a sedative and the red ones, of which there are fewer, are a counteractive stimulant. Let us hope that these hyposprays are not encoded to the Senites like their weapons. I suspect the reason we cannot operate their weapons is that the Senites may have implants and transmitters inserted into their bodies during the surgery."

"If you say so." Renna shivered. "There are a lot worse parts to the surgery than that."

The scaly fugitive on the bed began to twitch slightly, and Spock quickly loaded a red vial into the hypo and delivered it into the alien's arm. The Vulcan motioned Renna to step back, while he loosened the fugitive's bonds and took a position behind the bed. Groggily, the scaly being came to his senses and sat up. He looked first at the unconscious Senite beside him, then gazed at Renna; it didn't take long before he growled angrily and lurched toward the woman. Luckily, Spock was behind him and applied the nerve pinch with such strength and precision that the fugitive toppled back into unconsciousness.

"Whew!" breathed Renna as she helped Spock return him to the bed. "At least we know it revives them."

"Yes," said Spock, "we can revive the captain and the doctor when we find them, but how do we escape?"

"There are transporters," offered Renna, "but we

may be faced with the same problem we had before—not enough time to learn how to control them."

"I feel confident I can disable the transporters," answered the Vulcan. "Then we could escape by other means without being followed."

"The door is wide open," said Renna, indicating the blaze of golden lights around the entrance to the vast cavern.

"Very well," said Spock, loading another red vial into the Senite hypo. "Let us search the cells closest to where you found me."

Activity was still intense on the catwalk of level eight, with numerous Senite doctors rushing to and fro, keeping the waiting fugitives sedated. A strange sort of chanting issued from below, as the young Senites ritualistically bathed and shaved the comatose initiates. Renna tried to ignore what was happening down there as she followed Spock from cell to cell.

The Vulcan had adopted a stooped posture and slow manner of walking that made him look ancient, but that was preferable to revealing his unshaven chin. There was too much activity and too many Senites on urgent missions for them to pay much attention to the odd pair, and it wasn't long before they found a cell where a handsome young human lay strapped to the bed.

"Watch the door," Spock ordered.

Renna did just that as the Vulcan bent over the sleeping figure and injected him. He left Kirk's bindings fastened for the moment, even when the captain began to awaken and strain against them.

"Jim," cautioned Spock, "be still. Renna and I have come to free you, but we are in grave danger. This is a place where fugitives are surgically altered to become Senites. You cannot simply jump out of bed, do you understand?"

"Yes," muttered the captain, ceasing his movements and closing his eyes once more. "Where's McCoy?"

"We have not located him yet, but we will return when we find him. I am loosening the straps, but you must appear unconscious or you will be sedated again."

"Understood," breathed Kirk.

Another Senite walked by the door and peered inside, and Spock pretended to reinject Kirk.

"Is everything under control?" asked the Senite.

"Yes," answered Renna, turning away and leaning over Kirk, so that all the Senite had to address were the backs of two white robes.

"Sadly," remarked the Senite, "two initiates have died, and we have two tables open below. Is this initiate healthy?"

"No," Renna answered immediately, "he is having trouble breathing."

"Make him comfortable," replied the Senite doctor. It turned and addressed someone in the adjacent cell. "Take that one below."

When the Senite moved to direct operations in the other cell, Renna poked her head out and saw—to her shock—two white-robed figures carrying the unconscious body of Dr. McCoy to the turbolift. The Senite who was apparently in charge followed them.

She rushed back to Spock and Kirk. "It's McCoy!" she gasped. "They're taking him down to the operating table."

Kirk snapped off his restraints, swung his legs over the side of the bed, and leaped to his feet. "Let's get him."

Renna yanked the pair of dirty robes from around her waist and tossed one to Kirk. "At least put this on," she insisted.

He complied, quickly pulling the robe over his clothes and covering his head with the hood. Then he stepped into the corridor and followed the retreating Senites with their limp cargo. By moving swiftly, the trio was able to catch up with the three real Senites just as they carried McCoy into a turbolift. Staring at the floor, they took up uneasy positions in the crowded conveyance.

The door shut, and the Senite in charge ordered, "Level one." He then peered curiously at Kirk and asked, "Why aren't you wearing a clean robe?"

Kirk lowered his head farther and tried to ignore the query, hoping the turbolift would come to a quick stop. But his inquisitor persisted, "I asked you a question. Look at me!"

The Senite gripped Kirk's chin and gazed into his face—wishing immediately it hadn't. "You—you're not of the order!" it sputtered. "Guards!"

The captain smashed the Senite in the face with his fist, sending the being careening into another Senite, who dropped McCoy to the floor. As the third Senite lunged for the captain, Spock intercepted him and slammed him against the wall.

Renna kicked another in its kneecap, then delivered an uppercut that sent it tumbling into Kirk. In the tight quarters of the turbolift, it was sickening thuds, elbows smashing into midsections, heads butting heads, and a wild free-for-all that rocked the turbolift on its descent. A Senite tried to draw a weapon, and Spock wrestled it from its hand and applied a nerve pinch. Soon the floor was littered with white-robed bodies, and Kirk and Spock bent to extricate the unconscious McCoy from the pile.

"Correction!" Renna gasped to the turbolift computer. "Level six!"

The turbolift, which was already shaking from the turbulent battle, reversed itself with a groan and ascended to level six. Fortunately, that level was still quiet, and Kirk, Spock, and Renna were able to carry the four unconscious figures off the lift before it was summoned elsewhere. Renna located a darkened classroom, and they dragged the Senites and McCoy inside. While Renna stripped a robe off one of the Senites for McCoy, Spock deftly operated the hypospray. First he injected a red vial of stimulant into McCoy, then blue vials of sedative into the three Senites.

"Bones," said Kirk, leaning over his friend. "Bones, can you hear me?"

The doctor was gradually coming to. "Oh, my head," he moaned, struggling to sit up. "What's going on? Where the hell are we?"

Kirk grinned. "We just saved you from becoming a Senite."

"Good," moaned McCoy. "I don't look good in white."

"We have inadvertently learned how the Senites perpetuate their species," said Spock. "By castrating and lobotomizing a large number of fugitives."

"Ugh!" gulped McCoy.

"You're not out of here yet," warned Renna, handing McCoy the robe she'd just pilfered. "You might all still become eunuchs if we don't figure out how to escape. They're not likely to let anyone go from this place voluntarily, to spread the word."

"My suggestion," said Spock, "is that we disable their transporters, so they cannot immediately come after us, as they did last time."

"Where are the transporters?" asked Kirk. "Are they at all secluded?"

"They're on level two," answered Renna, "and behind curtains. But Senites are coming and going constantly. Spock would get only a few seconds, and he might need a diversion for that. The only entrance to this place I know of is not guarded, but it's in plain sight."

Kirk opened his mouth to say something, but a scream erupted over their heads and a muffled explosion sounded. They rushed out of the classroom to peer over the railing, along with hundreds of other white-robed figures on other levels, and saw a fugitive wildly thrashing a Senite two floors over their heads. Several Senites on the main floor were aiming weapons, but they were reluctant to shoot for fear of hitting their fellow Senite. Plus, an errant shot had apparently caused a small explosion in a room behind the escapee. Spock could make out checkered skin on the rampaging fugitive.

"That's the first one we injected," he told Renna.

"Your nerve pinch didn't last too long," she answered. "Must've been the stimulant."

The Senite's howls increased as the fugitive picked him up over his head and tossed him over the rail and eight stories down onto a row of monitors that clattered with a racket that echoed throughout the cavern. Senites started to converge on the renegade with hypos, but he pummeled them one by one in the narrow corridor and sent two more hurtling to their deaths. A trigger-happy Senite on the bottom cut loose with a brilliant blue laser beam, which crumpled a piece of the catwalk and turned it into molten metal but missed the maniac entirely.

"This is our chance," said Kirk. "Renna, lead us to the transporter."

She nodded, knowing there was no point arguing over who was giving the orders. They were a team, and it was time to act like one. They moved swiftly toward the turbolift and waited only seconds for one to appear, as most of the Senites were preoccupied with the ungrateful initiate on the eighth floor. Renna gave the destination as level two, and everyone adjusted their hoods as they made the swift descent.

Renna emerged first from the turbolift followed by three extremely hunched Senites, who walked a bit too much like aged monks for her taste. Luckily, every Senite in the crowded corridor was standing at the railing, craning its neck to view the drama on deck eight.

"Look! There's another one!" yelled a Senite, pointing upward.

Kirk paused briefly to look and saw a hirsute humanoid crash into the railing with a Senite under each arm. He dangled one of them over the edge, screaming, and the other he gripped in a choke hold and held in front of him as a shield. The Senites on the production floor twitched their weapons nervously but did not shoot.

"Don't fire at me!" he bellowed. "You dirty blighters! I'll kill them! I swear I will!"

"That's Billiwog!" whispered a startled McCoy, gripping Kirk's arm. "More of them are starting to wake up, and the Senites aren't paying attention."

Reminded about paying attention, the captain looked around but couldn't locate Renna and Spock. Finally, he saw a slim Senite waving to him from a bank of red curtains at the rear of the anteroom. She disappeared as soon as she got his attention. The captain tapped the doctor's arm, hunched his shoulders, and strode toward the spot. McCoy trailed behind, but they could still hear Billiwog ranting: "Free them! Free them! You dirty blighters!"

They slipped behind the thick curtains and found a second cavern with an immense array of transporter pads spread across the floor and giant crystal coils hanging from the ceiling. Lining the walls was a bewildering collection of instruments and replicators.

Spock stood working at one of the many consoles, and Renna was bent over an unconscious Senite, rifling through the folds of its robe.

She held up a medikit and remarked to Kirk, "This is all the creeps ever carry."

The captain managed a tight smile but didn't stay to chat. He still felt confused and disoriented by coming to in this elaborate cave, strapped to a bed, surrounded by creatures who wanted to alter his mind and body. But there wasn't time to analyze the situation, or to decide whether the Senites were more deserving of hatred or pity. After all, each of them had been a victim strapped to the same metal table. All he knew was that escape from Sanctuary was more urgent than ever.

He strode to Spock's side. "How is it going?"

"As well as can be expected," answered the Vulcan. "I will need more time to operate the scanners, but I have located the emergency override that shuts down power to the transporter. There will be a lengthy delay before they can use it again."

"What about finding the *Enterprise?*"

"Given enough time—"

And just then, time got shorter, as a squad of armed Senites began to materialize on the transporter platform. As the half dozen Senites solidified on the platform, one took aim at Kirk and looked like it was about to squeeze off a laser shot, but Spock's slim fingers danced on the controls. Instantly, the Senites began to dematerialize once again. Their confused images wavered in and out for a few seconds, then finally vanished.

"Where did you send them?" asked Kirk.

"Back to wherever they came from," replied the Vulcan. "I believe now· would be a good time to disable the transporter."

"Do it," said Kirk.

A pulsating siren suddenly pierced the relative quiet of the transporter room, and there were renewed shouts outside. Renna glanced at McCoy, and the two of them dragged the unconscious Senite out of sight. A second later, the glowing energy coils went dark, the machines blinked off, and the transporter room was immersed in darkness.

Chapter Twelve

THE SCREAMING SIRENS from the main cavern and the cool darkness of the transporter room seemed at odds, but they combined to give Kirk, Spock, McCoy, and Renna enough time to duck behind equipment and squirm into corners. By the time a Senite pulled open the curtain, sending a streak of light lunging across the floor, the transporter room looked to be useless and deserted.

Another Senite appeared in the doorway, making two silhouettes. "Who shut this down?" it shouted over the siren.

"Must have been the overseer," answered the first. "At least none of them can escape this way. We don't need a guard here, but let's get some guards to the main door."

The curtain shut, and the streak of light retreated across the floor. Still huddling in the darkness, Kirk called out, "Renna! How else can we get out of here?"

"The main door is all I know about," she answered. "But I was thinking—there are the wagons that brought you here. They're parked just inside the door."

"Captain," Spock interjected, "some Senite equipment we can operate, and some we cannot, such as their weapons. I believe the Senites implant transmitters during their surgery, and this enables them to encode certain equipment against unauthorized use."

"So the trucks may or may not work," concluded the captain. "Has anyone else got a better idea?"

There was no response. Kirk stood and pulled his hood around his face. "Lead the way, Renna."

The four fugitives stepped through the red curtains into sheer bedlam. Senites were running in every direction, most of them fumbling with weapons. There were screams and piercing sirens, and a full-scale uprising was in progress on level eight as more fugitives regained consciousness. Several unfortunates strapped onto tables on the operating floor were also howling in confusion, especially whenever a Senite was tossed over the railing to come crashing down amongst them.

Renna led her small party to the turbolifts, but there were already dozens of Senites waiting to board, even pushing and shoving against those who were trying to get off. She turned to the hooded figure of Kirk. "We're only on the second floor," she explained. "We can jump."

"We'll follow you," said the captain decisively.

They bolted through the chaos, away from the turbolifts, past the transporter room, and around the curvature of the catwalk, making their way steadily toward the aurora of golden lights at the exit. Kirk could see where the natural archway opened on the floor beneath them, and the idea that they were so close to freedom made him run all the harder. But Renna was slowing down, taking time to peer over the railing at the anarchy below.

She stopped Kirk and pointed down. "There it is—one of the trucks."

He followed her eyes to a contraption parked directly beneath them. The thing looked like a flatbed railroad car full of coffin-sized cages. It didn't look like much of a drop, but Kirk couldn't tell how sturdy the wooden slats were that covered the top of the crude vehicle. He could see Senites taking up positions around it, and he knew there wasn't time for drawn-out thought processes. The sirens blared urgently, and a major brawl was taking place outside the turbolifts on level eight. The armed Senites didn't know who to shoot.

He gathered Spock and McCoy around them. "We're jumping down onto that wagon below us and driving it out the door. Spock, you and Renna find the controls—she's seen this thing operating. We're liable to attract some attention, and McCoy and I will keep them at bay. Ready?"

"Lead on," declared Renna, grinning.

Kirk gripped the railing and swung himself over, landing with a loud crash on top of the wagon. One of the Senites looked up, and Kirk rolled out of sight. Several shouts distracted the Senite guard, and Renna and Spock leaped upon the roof and rolled in the same direction as Kirk. The Senite started to climb up the wagon to investigate at the same moment that McCoy got enough courage to leap.

"What are you doing?" it shouted at the startled doctor as he landed.

Spock and Kirk reached over the side of the wagon, grabbed the Senite under its arms, and hauled it to the roof. Kirk covered its mouth while Spock delivered a nerve pinch that silenced its struggles. They looked around, expecting an onslaught of Senites, but each of the white-robed guards had its attention directed to noisier scenes. Had they glanced at the truck, they might have seen what looked like two Senites pulling a third one aboard.

Crouching low on the rickety slats, Kirk nodded to Spock and Renna, and they crawled toward the robotic cab, where the directional equipment was housed. As they got closer, they saw they weren't the only ones with that idea: Two Senites were climbing from the other direction.

Renna kept her head down and moved faster, and she swung into the narrow cab before Spock got there. She began to study the instruments, having used plenty of equipment without the benefit of a manual. She heard angry voices, and the Vulcan swung down beside her, leaving the two Senites to Kirk and McCoy, who were converging quickly. She and Spock eyed different sections of the machinery as a thumping fistfight commenced over their heads. She hoped Kirk and McCoy were winning, because if they weren't, it was too bad—she and Spock were pulling out of here.

Renna flipped a switch, the vehicle shuddered, and instruments lit up inside the cabin. Spock nodded approvingly. "We have power. I can see no steering mechanism, so I presume the vehicle has photoelectric sensors and an automatic guidance system. But which control is forward?"

"Take a guess," offered Renna, "like I did."

They heard a scream overhead that continued down the side of the truck, and they knew somebody had fallen off. A laser blast jarred the roof over their heads, shearing off several centimeters of wood and metal, and there wasn't time for more than a guess.

Spock waved his hand over a prominent sensor panel, and the vehicle lurched backward, knocking both of them off their feet. The Vulcan tried to brace himself, while helping Renna get her footing.

Above, Kirk and McCoy had no sooner ducked from the laser blast than they were surprised by the sudden movement. They ignored the remaining Senite to grab anything they could to keep from falling. McCoy slipped off the roof of the wagon and clung precariously to the iron grating of one of the cages, while Kirk smashed his fist through the wooden slats in an attempt to grab the metal frame underneath. The Senite floundered for a few seconds, then got his arms around a post that separated two sections of cages. He might have hung on all day had Kirk not belted him in the face with the heel of his boot. The Senite flopped off the vehicle as it thundered toward the cave wall, and McCoy closed his eyes and cringed, anticipating the crash. But the wagon sensed the impending obstruction, reversed course, and rumbled toward the glowing lights of the entrance.

They were the center of attention now, and both the anxious Senites and the crazed fugitives converged upon them. From nowhere, a hairy figure swung from the tattered remains of a curtain, swooped to a spread-eagle position over their heads, and dropped with a banshee yell. The roof didn't begin to hold him, and he ended up trapped in the mangled wreckage of several cages, bellowing like a moose.

There was nothing, in fact, that Kirk and McCoy could do to prevent picking up passengers as the giant body cart rumbled toward the gleaming lights of the exit. They had all they could handle just to hang on, and it didn't help that Senite laser blasts were tearing holes in the vehicle, reducing it to a twisted skeleton.

Kirk's skin felt oddly warm and prickly as the

golden lights washed over him, and that was followed by the cool sensation of night air, a welcome taste of freedom from a very unpleasant place.

The bumpy ride and sudden darkness were disorienting, and Kirk wasn't sure what to do next, except hang on. The jarring reminded him of hayrides he had taken as a kid, when somebody had kicked the tractor into high gear.

"Help! You filthy blighters! I'll kill you! Help me!" yelled their loudest passenger.

"Quiet, Billiwog!" ordered Kirk. "We can't free you now. We're all along for the ride. Everyone—don't make any false moves. McCoy, are you all right?"

"I *can't* move!" yelled the doctor. "I'm barely hanging on!"

"I'll try to locate you all," promised Kirk. Before he could move, he was startled by a hand that alighted firmly on his shoulder. It was Spock.

"Good timing," breathed Kirk. "Can you see how many people we're carrying?"

Despite the jarring ride, the Vulcan used his uncommon sense of balance to get on his hands and knees and crawl along the twisted spine of the wagon. Kirk heard him assuring their unseen passengers that he wasn't a Senite and that they would be stopping soon.

"We damn well better!" growled a voice that could only be Billiwog's.

Kirk peered into the hazy darkness off the rear of the wagon and could make out nothing but the faintest glow of golden lights. Within a few seconds, even that weak glimmer was gone, leaving the captain with no sign as to their direction or whereabouts. Spock was creeping back over the top of the wagon.

"There are seven in total," he reported. "The four of us, Billiwog, and two other fugitives. Nobody seems to be following us from the Senite complex."

"They're probably running for the transporters," said Kirk with satisfaction. "I still can't believe what was going on in that place."

"What was going on," said Spock, "was procreation without sex. Very illogical."

"I'm glad you think so." The truck bounced on a deep furrow and sent Kirk's jaw pounding against the roof. "Ouch!" he cried. "Are we going to let this thing run rampant all night?"

"We can stop it to rearrange our seating," said Spock. "However, since we cannot survey the terrain in darkness, I suggest we continue to put distance between ourselves and the Senites."

"Just stop it for a moment," Kirk ordered.

The Vulcan maneuvered deftly along the blackened roof and disappeared down a narrow hatch. A few moments later, the conveyance lurched and shuddered to a stop. With McCoy leading the way, the bedraggled passengers let go of their hazardous perches and dropped to the ground. Kirk stopped to grab a hairy wrist and help Billiwog extricate himself from the mangled cages before he leaped to the ground. When he did, he found McCoy, a blue-skinned Andorian, and a snout-nosed Tellarite, all rubbing aching arms and shoulders. Renna and Spock remained in the tiny cab, evidently studying the controls.

"What an escape!" exclaimed the Tellarite, shaking his fist triumphantly. "We owe you our lives."

"Yes," said the tall Andorian, bowing regally. "How can we repay you?"

"Well," said McCoy, "we've been looking for our shuttlecraft . . ."

The Andorian cocked his antennae thoughtfully. "I believe I may be able to help you."

"Really?" Kirk turned sharply toward the alien. "What do you mean?"

"There is a place—north of here, I would figure—called the Graveyard of Lost Ships. It's where the Senites store all the spaceships and other debris they don't need."

"I think I've heard of it," mused Billiwog. "Have you really been there?"

"I *lived* there for two years," answered the Andorian. "I'm not much of a tinkerer, not like most of those people, but I shall be glad to go back there. Believe me, I will never go in search of a free meal again."

"Do they ever manage to get any vessels flying?" asked Kirk.

Perhaps it was the darkness, but the Andorian's face did not look encouraging. "Sometimes," he muttered. "Look, I will be happy to take you there, considering we can ride most of the way on this strange craft. What we should do is set our course due north and look for a river I know."

"All right," said Kirk, climbing back up the side of the wagon, "we'll trust you to lead us there. We can't stay here very long, so don't anybody wander off. And keep a lookout to the rear—the Senites might still come after us."

"The Graveyard of Lost Ships," muttered McCoy to no one in particular.

Scotty stood on the main deck of the *Neptune,* staring into a two-hundred-liter fish tank. The greenish water was teeming with a million tiny yellow larvae, each about three centimeters long. They twisted and curled over each other like worms in hot ash, both repelling and mesmerizing the visiting engineer. All of the other tanks were empty, awaiting the hoped-for wealth of aquatic life-forms from the seas of Sanctuary, life-forms that Scotty doubted were ever going to arrive. His doubts were verified a few moments later when a dour Captain Mora joined him in the aquarium section.

"Well," he said glumly, "I tried again to contact the Senites. I've tried on every channel with a request that was entirely scientific and nonthreatening. No response whatsoever. No acknowledgment of our presence. What kind of society won't even acknowledge a scientific vessel that is orbiting its planet?"

"That's the Senites," remarked Scotty. "We can orbit all we want, but that's all we can do."

Mora shook his gray-cropped head. "I did something else," he said. "I contacted Starfleet about our invasion plans."

"Very good." Scotty beamed. "And who—or what —do we intend to send down there to get their attention?"

"You were looking at them a second ago," answered Captain Mora, staring past him at the teeming larvae in the green tank.

"What?" The Scotsman followed his gaze. "Aren't they a tad small to make much of an impact?"

"They're small now," explained the captain, "but those tiny larvae will grow into one million Regulan locusts, each about as long as your index finger."

He gazed fondly at the mad activity in the tank. "We keep a huge supply of them for food. Small animals can eat the larvae or the eggs, and larger creatures find the locusts themselves quite tasty."

"A plague of locusts," remarked Scotty with an approving glint in his eye. "That seems appropriate for the Senites." Then he cautioned, "But we can't do anything that would actually damage their ecology."

"I've thought of that," answered Captain Mora, "and this batch has already been irradiated—they're sterile. If we time it correctly, in a couple of days we can transport the entire tank down just as they're about to emerge from the larval state into adulthood.

188

A few will get eaten by fish or whatever's down there, but the rest will become a swarm that is bound to make life miserable for whoever they encounter." He glanced at Scotty and added, "That is, if you can guarantee they will pass through the Senites' shield."

"Aye, they will," answered the engineer. "Their shield must have some sort of filter that detects living matter and allows it to pass through. Our sensors dunna work within their shield, but we've located a few population centers with our telescopes. And we'll make damn sure ta let the Senites know it was *us* who sent them this little plague."

Captain Mora smiled. "The locusts will be gone entirely in a week to ten days, but I doubt if they'll be forgotten."

Scotty surveyed the writhing life-forms with new respect. "Aye, ye're wee buggers," he told them, "but you have a big job to do. Ye've got to get those bloody Senites mad enough to give us back our captain and officers."

"They'll be mad," Donald Mora assured him. "Anybody who's ever been attacked by a swarm of Regulan locusts remembers it."

It was almost noon on Sanctuary before the morning sun finally climbed over the immense mountain range that surrounded the narrow canyon. The flying creatures that swooped from the crevices and the odd fish that strolled from pond to pond all kept their distance from the noisy machine that rumbled up the pass. Seven weary souls clung to the twisted metal carcass as it rolled deeper into the wilderness. Captain Kirk was beginning to have his doubts that the tall Andorian knew what he was talking about. This land looked wilder than the place where they had first landed, as if no one had ever set foot here, not even crazy survivalists. It was depressing to think they were back where they had started, lost in the rugged mountains of Sanctuary. Only now they were worse off, because they were fleeing for their lives. Into what? The captain tried not to think too hard about it.

At least, he thought grumpily as he tried to fashion a seat amid the mangled bars of one of the cages, they were making good time. The Andorian had led them to a river, but that was hardly unusual in a land where it rained at least part of every day. Following his instructions, they had found a shallow place that allowed them to ford the river with little difficulty. But again, what did that prove? Since then, they had proceeded due north into a canyon that was growing progressively narrower and more difficult to navigate. The giant conveyance ran on solar power and apparently stored enough energy during the day to keep it going all night, but it couldn't keep climbing up a steep grade full of boulders and rutted streams forever. Already, the treads were spinning on the loose gravel, and Spock had taken over manual steering because the automatic guidance system had refused to allow the wagon to go any farther.

Water was no problem, but the captain was getting hungry, as he assumed everyone was. To their credit, none of them—Spock, McCoy, Renna, Billiwog, the chubby Tellarite, the well-mannered Andorian—had complained about hunger. But Kirk couldn't see how they could keep up this pace without stopping to hunt for food. Only fear of the Senites kept them moving, but the memory of those gleaming rows of operating tables was a powerful incentive. The captain finally decided they could go on for several more hours before getting desperate enough to stop.

The decision was suddenly made for them. With deadly accuracy, a fusillade of rocks came crashing down from the canyon walls, striking the cab where Spock and Renna were ensconced. The wagon careened off the streambed and up the slope of the arroyo. There were screams and shouts from almost everyone on board, and they scrambled across the top of the wagon to keep from being crushed. Another wave of boulders came thundering down, and Kirk saw the Tellarite get struck by one and vanish under the gnashing treads. McCoy lost his handhold in the mad scramble and tumbled off the rear of the vehicle.

"Bones!" shouted Kirk. He reached instinctively for his friend, but he was too late.

"You scummy blighters!" yelled Billiwog, shaking a fist at the unseen attackers. "Show yourselves!" He never stopped shouting as the vehicle teetered up the embankment.

Kirk saw Renna trying to claw her way out of the cab, and he crept forward to help her. She looked at him in sheer terror and barely managed to duck out of sight before another hail of stones pummeled the bouncing wagon. Kirk covered his head and felt the thunderous vibrations all around him.

Abruptly, the truck came to a complete stop, and its treads spun uselessly on bare rock. Its momentum gone, the giant vehicle listed like a sinking ship and began a slow collapse. With a frightening roar, it flopped onto its side and spewed a cloud of dust many meters into the air. Kirk hung on with all his might, but he was still flung from the vehicle into the dry riverbed. He tucked into a ball and rolled until he could regain his feet, then dashed for the safety of the boulders on the other side of the arroyo.

The captain wanted desperately to help his comrades, but as long as the rock attack continued, he was helpless.

Chapter Thirteen

WHEN MCCOY was tossed off the back of the runaway wagon, he grazed the canyon wall and rolled several meters down an incline until he sprawled face forward in a rain-soaked rut of mud. He groaned and felt himself lapsing into unconsciousness. What brought him back to his senses was a monstrous grinding sound, followed by a crash that shook the ground and spewed gravel onto his head. He coughed and spit out dirt, then looked up to see the giant vehicle lying on its side, like some kind of fallen prehistoric beast.

When nothing moved after a few seconds, there came a strange trilling sound from on high, like a dozen youthful voices shrieking an off-key la-la-la. The eerie cry, echoing through the canyon, was frightening enough to make McCoy want to run for cover. Then he thought better of it, knowing that he was still within range of their deadly missiles. He waited and watched, wondering if the assault would continue. But all he heard was the strange victory sound.

Their attackers were apparently content at the moment to have stopped the advance of the wagon, so McCoy rose stiffly to his feet and brushed himself off. It was then that he saw the body lying in the bladder plants a few meters away.

Inside the dusty cab, Spock shifted under Renna's weight. The woman was dazed but not unconscious, despite the warm trickle of blood coming from above her left ear. Upon losing control of the vehicle, Spock had braced himself inside the cramped cabin, anticipating the inevitable crash, and he had suffered no ill effects. He had also managed to catch Renna before she could be seriously injured.

"Oh," she groaned, "are we still alive?"

"Quiet, please," answered the Vulcan. He was listening to the victory trilling from atop the bluff, and he wondered what sort of creatures had attacked them. Knowing what he knew about the Senites, he could hardly blame anyone for attacking one of their body carts, and he hoped the victorious attackers could be reasoned with. As suddenly as it began, the strange cry stopped. Spock then heard shuffling outside the vehicle.

"Yo, in there. You all right?" called a gruff voice. It was Billiwog.

"Relatively speaking, yes," answered Spock. "Can you see who attacked us?"

"No," snapped the big humanoid, "but if I do, I'll wring their necks!"

"Help us out," said Renna, reaching for the big man's hirsute arms.

Spock moved her gently across his chest and over his head, until Billiwog could grip her under the arms and pull her out. Then the Vulcan crawled out after her.

The hairy humanoid stood admiring the petite

193

white-robed figure. "Is this the woman you brought back for me?" he asked, grinning. "I am grateful."

"Hardly," spat Renna. "You *should* be grateful— without me, you'd be on your way to becoming a Senite. Although it might've taken them a week to shave you."

Billiwog snarled, "The dirty blighters!" He craned his neck and surveyed the ridge. "Speaking of dirty blighters, where are they? Why don't they finish us off?"

"Unknown," answered Spock. He looked down the arroyo to see a slight figure jogging toward them. "Dr. McCoy," Spock hailed him. "Have you seen the captain?"

"No." McCoy scowled. "But I've seen the Tellarite, and he's dead. Crushed under the wheels."

McCoy started to examine Renna's head wound, but she brushed his hand away. "I'm all right. Where's the captain and the Andorian?"

They didn't have to look far for Captain Kirk, who came jogging toward them from the other side of the wrecked vehicle. "The Andorian took off . . . at a dead run," he panted, "and I chased him for a while. . . . So much for our guide. Let's get to those rocks on the other side of the canyon."

As soon as they were well away from the deadly ridge, they stopped and took stock of their situation.

"The Senites could be after us," Kirk said. He pointed to the far ridge. "Or whoever attacked us."

"Then we'll make our last stand right here," McCoy replied. "It's as good a place as any."

Spock cocked an eyebrow and remarked, "We cannot be certain, but it would seem that the Senites could have found us by now, if they were so inclined. And whoever attacked us from the ridge was apparently content to stop the Senite wagon, and our advance."

Kirk slumped down onto the dirt and sighed. "Yeah, I guess we sort of made a mess of the Senites' operation. They must be busy cleaning up. So everyone's accounted for, though the Tellarite is dead and the Andorian has run off."

"Who cares about them?" growled Billiwog. "We're alive, and I'm hungry. Anybody want to help me look for food?"

That night, the odd party of two human males, one human female, a Vulcan, and a giant of indeterminate species dined quite sumptuously on a large number of ambulatory fish, a herd of which was located by Billiwog. The brawny humanoid also knew which rocks could be struck to start a fire and which vines were fibrous enough to burn. They roasted the fish on spits over an open flame and ate their fill of the oily but tasty flesh.

Once the shadows started to race across the canyon, darkness was not far behind, and they were soon joined by Sanctuary's two moons—the small pink one and the giant white one. Due to the mysterious attack, Kirk insisted upon posting a guard for the entire night. He also insisted upon taking the first watch.

While the others slept peacefully for the first time in days, Kirk watched the parade of stars and moons across the narrow swath of sky that was visible between the towering peaks. All was still as the hours passed, and Kirk gradually relaxed—until something touched his shoulder from behind. Kirk gasped and leaped to his feet, snatching up a length of vine to use as a club.

"It's only me," breathed Renna. Her head was wrapped in a makeshift bandage made from the hem of her white garment.

"Sorry," he sighed, sitting back down on the ground. "You're supposed to be sleeping."

"I know, but I've been sleeping for hours already, and McCoy will never know. Mind if I join you?"

"Not at all." Kirk smiled at her. "You would be welcome company at any time."

"Oh," she said, alighting beside him, "that's not entirely true. If I were really the pirate you thought I was, you certainly wouldn't introduce me to Starfleet High Command. Or to your mother."

Kirk grinned. "I would introduce you to my mother. But I wouldn't tell her what you did for a living."

Renna watched the young captain as the merriment faded from his lips and his eyes drifted back to the gleaming beltway of stars. They watched the stars together for a long time.

"Do you think we'll ever get back up there?" she asked, swallowing hard.

"Yes," Kirk said solemnly, "I do. Don't ask me how. I just know that I'll never stop trying to get back."

Renna took the bandage off, freeing her lustrous black hair, and smiled wistfully. "Space was my playground, even when I was a baby. My father and I have houses and property, but they aren't really home. They never were." She pointed upward. *"That's* home. And now it's gone."

Kirk's voice was hoarse when he replied, "To be separated from the things you used to take for granted —isn't that the real definition of a prison?"

Renna tried to say something, but her voice caught in a sob. Kirk moved closer to her and put his arm around her trembling shoulders. They gazed fondly, affectionately—not at each other, but at a million sparkling diamonds scattered through the black web called space.

* * *

In the morning, they all gnawed on a few leftover fish and doused the smoldering embers of their fire. The Andorian had not returned during the night, and Kirk was growing increasingly skeptical. Was there such a thing as the Graveyard of Lost Ships? Or was it just a myth that the inmates of Sanctuary took some small comfort in telling one another? Unfortunately, there were only two courses available in the deep canyon: back to the Senite stronghold, or straight ahead into the unknown.

Kirk chose the unknown, but he also chose not to go unprotected. They stripped a few metal plates off the wrecked wagon and wrapped vines around them for handholds. Armed with these lightweight rectangular shields, they prepared to march northward up the narrow wash.

"All right," said Kirk, "spread out—at least ten paces apart, so we don't make too good a target. And keep your eyes on the top of the ridge. At the first sign of rocks, shields up."

McCoy hefted the piece of sheet metal in his hands and muttered, "I wish they were *real* shields."

"They are real shields, Doctor," said Spock. "Unfortunately, they're from the wrong millennium. They would have been considered quite adequate in your Bronze Age."

McCoy shrugged. "I guess they fit in with rocks as weapons."

Captain Kirk took the lead and motioned everyone to follow him. "Let's go. Keep your eyes open."

Despite Kirk's admonition about traveling ten paces apart, Renna walked directly behind Kirk, and McCoy bumped into Billiwog a few times. Spock brought up the rear, keeping his shield at chest level. They had traveled a few kilometers, climbing into ever more rugged terrain, when the first rock came sailing off the ledge above them. Kirk jumped back, and it landed at his feet.

"Shields up!" he called.

Everyone lifted their sheets of metal and waited for the onslaught. It came quickly as dozens of melon-sized and fist-sized rocks came arcing over the cliff a hundred meters above them. There were thundering sounds when the rocks hit the shields, and dull thuds when they struck the ground. Renna took a direct hit and dropped to her knees, and Kirk rushed to protect her.

"Form a phalanx!" he ordered, motioning to the others to draw closer.

The party of five pressed together and lifted their shields to make an armored canopy. This gave their unseen attackers a better target, but it also allowed them to bolster each other and absorb harder blows. Billiwog stood like a tree trunk in the middle of the group, purposely warding off the biggest rocks.

"The sneaky blighters can't stop us!" he growled. "Let's keep going."

They did exactly that and were soon stumbling forward through the assault like a ten-legged turtle. But they made progress, and the ferocity of the attack began to lessen.

"They are running out of ammunition," Spock observed.

He was right, thought Kirk, as the attack trickled off to an occasional dirt clod. A few moments later, they were walking as before, completely unmolested, but with shields held at the ready. Ahead of them, the creekbed narrowed to a small fissure in a rock wall. This was probably the source of the stream when it was running, thought the captain, but they would have to climb ten meters or so to reach it. That would leave them vulnerable to attack. Past that hole in the wall was—who knew what?

They had come to the end of the trail, such as it was. The Andorian who had led them here was gone, and they couldn't turn back. Kirk stopped and handed his shield to Billiwog.

"Cover me," he said. "I'm climbing up there to see what there is to see."

"No!" cried Renna. "It's too dangerous. They could pick you off with one well-thrown rock."

Spock nodded. "I would have to agree, Captain. Our attackers could be waiting in ambush."

"What do you want us to do?" asked Kirk. "Stay here the rest of our lives? Besides, I'm willing to bet that we've made faster progress than they have—we've been walking on relatively level ground, and they've had to scamper along that ridge. Besides, anybody can throw a rock. Pick some up and cover me."

Billiwog grabbed a rock that was as big as a watermelon. "Go, Kirk," he said. "I'll bash the dirty scum."

"Thanks." The captain smiled. "But keep your eyes open, too."

Kirk pulled up the sleeves of his jacket, dug his fingers into the porous stone, and began to climb. Where there weren't toeholds and handholds, he dug them, and he was soon scaling the rock wall like a gecko. All eyes scanned the horizon for signs of attack, but none came. The sky was a peaceful if overcast gray.

Grunting the last meter, Kirk finally threw his arm into the fissure and lifted himself up to see what lay beyond. Through the hole in the rock, he could see thick greenery and a path so wide it looked like a road. He pulled himself up until his stomach pushed against the ledge and he leaned forward to hoist himself up—then suddenly a claw gripped his arm, and a fearsome gargoyle with red eyes, wild hair, and sharp teeth loomed in his face.

Kirk recoiled, almost screaming, and he struggled to keep from falling. The snarling visage snapped at him and lifted a claw to rake his face. He teetered there, helpless, trying to maintain his balance. Then a missile whistled over his shoulder and struck the creature in the center of its frightful face. The thing howled and stumbled backward, and Kirk quickly lifted himself through the hole.

Kirk scrambled to his feet, prepared to fight, when he saw that his assailant was less than half his height, and almost childlike. It scampered away, making a few trilling sounds.

Kirk hastily surveyed the outcrop of rocks and determined that he had been attacked by a lone specimen of whatever it was. He called back through the hole, "Come on! Hurry!"

One by one, the rest of the party climbed the rock wall, using the toeholds and handholds Kirk had chiseled in the soft stone. Before the last one, Billiwog, started to climb, he passed up the metal shields. Kirk and the others struggled to pull the giant humanoid through the crevice, and he barely squeezed through.

"Who threw that rock?" asked Kirk. "That was a great throw."

"It was I," said Spock, "although several of us threw at the same time."

"A lucky shot." McCoy scowled.

"Lucky for me." Kirk glanced around. "I don't know exactly what that creature was, but it seemed childlike."

Billiwog shrugged his hairy shoulders. "There are lots of creatures who grew up in these mountains. They crash-landed or were abandoned by adults worried about survival. They are no better than animals."

"I don't know," said McCoy, "they put up a pretty spirited defense of this mountain pass. They obviously consider it to be theirs."

Renna shivered, but not from the cold. "What would any of us be like, if we'd lived all our lives in this place? Can't we go on?"

"Yes," agreed Kirk. He turned to survey the plateau they had reached. Unlike the rain-carved gully they had traversed below, the plateau opened into a rolling valley full of bladder trees, dense vines, and hanging moss. The cliffs were far enough away that ambush was out of the question, and beneath their feet lay a well-worn footpath. Kirk really couldn't blame the creatures for fighting to keep strangers out of their lush valley.

"Let's go," he said, "and show them we are only passing through."

Once again, the ragged party embarked on a journey into the unknown. As they walked, Kirk pulled his beat-up communicator from his back pocket.

"Kirk to *Enterprise,*" he said plaintively. "Come in, *Enterprise.*"

Renna smiled. "You *are* a dreamer, Kirk."

"You never know." He repeated his request, then listened for several seconds. But there was no response, and Kirk snapped the communicator shut. "But not today."

McCoy glanced up at the sky, where there was nothing but thick gray clouds that threatened rain. "I wonder what the heck *they're* doing to get hold of us?"

"Unknown," said Spock. "They have probably exhausted all of the logical courses of action. They may be resorting to somewhat desperate measures by now."

"Or they've given up," suggested McCoy, frowning.

Kirk shook his head. "If I know Scotty and the rest of our crew, I don't think that's likely."

There was an ominous crack of thunder, and the clouds dribbled raindrops upon them that felt as big as the stones thrown by their unseen attackers. One by one, they lifted their sheet-metal umbrellas and trudged forward in silence.

Some distance away, it was sunny on the island of Khyming. At the rear of the magnificent seminary, there was a special outdoor café reserved for high-ranking Senites and trusted refugees. It was there that the slim Senite Zicree was enjoying a leisurely lunch of healthful salad with his companion, Kellen. Zicree had just returned from an emergency on the mainland, but the Senite didn't want to burden the young woman with details, except to say that the same gang of persecutors had been causing trouble again. It took comfort from the familiar mist swirling around the central mountain, the white bungalows clinging to the cliffs, and the swaying network of rope bridges.

Kellen's pretty face sported a pout. "I can't believe that persecutors would actually come to Sanctuary to pursue their hateful goals. It's bad enough that they hunt innocent refugees—why can't they stay where they belong?"

The Senite shook its head and replied, "I misjudged them. Even though I knew they were persecutors, I thought they had the intelligence to adapt and learn to live in peace."

"What did they do now?" asked Kellen.

Zicree narrowed its eyes at the thought of the havoc they had caused in the Reborning facility, but it didn't say anything to the impressionable young woman. The pampered refugees of Khyming were ignorant of the Reborning, as well they should be. Recent events had proven again the need for secrecy.

"I don't wish to speak of their crimes," said Zicree. "We can only hope that we are rid of them."

The Senite was about to take a bite from its salad when something fell into the bowl. Zicree jerked back in revulsion as its salad began to twitch with a life of its own. Something long and green, with numerous crooked legs and flapping wings, struggled to extricate itself from the sticky salad dressing. On a planet where insects were mostly microscopic, such a thing was unheard of. The Senite stared in awe at the hideous creature.

"What is this?" it shrieked.

An ominous humming sounded. Another flying thing struck Zicree's cheek, and soon the Senite was bombarded by buzzing, whirring beasts. Kellen leaped to her feet with a mass of giant locusts clinging to her chest and her hair. Her screams of horror rent the air, as did a horde of winged invertebrates. The swarm of Regulan locusts engulfed the outdoor café, sending both servants and patrons fleeing in panic.

Waving its arms frantically, blinded by a million wings and deafened by the buzzing, Zicree staggered into the building. A Senite tried to hold the door shut against the horrible attack, but other screaming patrons forced it open, seeking refuge. Locusts poured into the seminary, and everywhere there was bedlam. Outside, Kellen lay curled in a ball beside her table, sobbing, although no harm had befallen her. The swarm lurched from one part of the village to another, causing terror and panic, but no real damage.

Zicree swatted a few remaining insects off its clothes and demanded of no one in particular, "What is the cause of this?"

To its surprise, someone answered, "The persecutors! The new ones in orbit. They have sent word that they are responsible."

That chilled the slim Senite to the very core of its altered body. The persecutors! It hardly needed to be told which ones. The recent arrivals had caused more

203

problems in the few days since they had appeared than all the other persecutors and scavengers had caused in three centuries! For a split second, Zicree almost wished that it had returned the three strangers to their mother ship. But no! That would be appeasing the persecutors—the one thing no Senite would ever do.

Through clenched teeth, Zicree vowed, "I will speak with them."

"That is forbidden," the other Senite cautioned.

Zicree grabbed its associate by the robe and forced it to look out the door at the havoc caused by the locust attack. "Do you wish to let this continue?" asked Zicree. "Do you wish to invite them to do worse? The programming of the shield will not stop living creatures from entering our atmosphere. We must *force* them to stop!"

"But how?"

Zicree considered for a moment, then let go of the Senite's robe. "Get me the Observation Unit."

Commander Scott and Captain Mora stood expectantly on the bridge of the *Enterprise,* waiting to see if their little messengers to Sanctuary would be acknowledged. Scotty had spent several hours reading scientific texts on the sterilization process, assuring himself that no damage could occur to Sanctuary's environment from releasing the locusts. At this point, Scotty hated the Senites, but that wouldn't allow him to disobey the Prime Directive. If they wanted to behave like pigheaded heathen savages, that was their right—as long as they understood they had to return his captain, doctor, and first officer.

Uhura swiveled around in her chair. "We are being hailed from the planet," she announced. Sulu and Chekov glanced over their shoulders at the acting captain.

Scotty stiffened to attention. Then he turned to the officer beside him. "Captain Mora," he asked, "do you wish to conduct this negotiation?"

"No, Commander," he said, "you're doing just fine. Good luck."

Scotty nodded. "Put it on the screen, Lieutenant."

"Aye, sir," Uhura answered.

A second later, the ageless face of Zicree appeared on the viewscreen. The Senite's normally bland expression was contorted with anger. "We wish to protest this unprovoked attack. This is biological warfare of the worst sort!"

"What attack?" said Scotty benevolently. "As my esteemed colleague Captain Mora said when he tried to contact you, we wish to exchange information on various species. We have sent you a few Regulan locusts for you to study. By the way, we have millions more, when those run out."

"That will not be necessary," the Senite replied. "We consider this a most barbaric act."

Scotty continued, more grimly, "In return, we wish you to send us Captain James T. Kirk, First Officer Spock, and Dr. McCoy. We have repeatedly sent you visual likenesses of these men, and we can do so again, if need be."

Zicree managed a tight-lipped smile. "There is no need for that—we know quite well what they look like. Apparently, you do not believe us when we say that your crew members—who came here of their own free will—are living lives of peace and contentment. To prove to you that such is the case, we are furnishing a visual record that was taken only a few hours ago. I direct your attention to your viewscreen."

The Senite's face blinked off, to be replaced by a perfectly tranquil scene in a pleasant outdoor café. There was no audio, but the image on the screen was stunning in its clarity: Sitting at a table, apparently

205

enjoying a hearty meal, were the captain, Spock, and McCoy! Everyone on the bridge leaned forward to stare at the screen, and they watched with amazement as a white-robed waiter came by to serve the trio more delicious-looking food.

"Blimey," Scotty murmured. "Uhura, close the audio."

"Audio closed," she said, troubled. "We can talk freely."

"Those are the missing men, aren't they?" asked Captain Mora.

"Or their spittin' images," answered Scotty, stepping closer to the tranquil scene. "Chekov, run a scan of that visual. Make sure it's not computer-generated, or they're not imposters."

"They don't look like they're suffering," said Uhura.

Chekov shook his head and reported, "Computer positeevely identifies that as the keptin, Mr. Spock, and Dr. McCoy. It is an unretouched visual record." His face was puzzled as he looked up at the unmistakable likenesses on the screen. "Could they have been brainwashed?"

"Just because they're eating doesn't mean they like it there," suggested Sulu. But no matter how hard they stared at the civilized setting, it was hard to find anything about it that a person would not like.

The visual faded away, to be replaced by the Senite, who looked much calmer. At Scotty's command, Uhura restored audio.

"So you have seen with your own eyes," said Zicree, "that your former officers are well treated, happy, and fulfilled."

"If that's the case," replied Scotty, "can we talk to them?"

"I'm afraid not," said the Senite. "Because no one ever leaves Sanctuary, all of our refugees must become

206

acclimated to their new lives. For them to talk to you now would only be upsetting and unproductive—for both of you. Why don't you admit that your attempts to 'rescue' them are misguided? We would all be better off if you would simply accept what cannot be changed."

Scotty slammed his fist into his palm, because words eluded him.

"Please," admonished the Senite, smiling for the first time, "no more childish pranks. They are beneath you. We recognize the Federation as a great power that is usually a force for good in the galaxy. We ask that you recognize our sovereignty and our mission. That is all."

The screen went blank, as black and final as the expression on Scotty's face.

"At least we know they're alive," said Uhura softly.

Captain Mora shrugged and walked toward the turbolift. "I must return to my ship," he said. "I'm afraid, Commander Scott, I must also put this in my report to Starfleet."

"Aye," Scotty acknowledged, "as will I."

The door swished open, and the officer left the bridge.

"This doesn't look good, does it?" asked Sulu.

Scotty slumped into the captain's chair. "Do ye mean," he sighed, "do I think we'll ever see those three again? In person, and not on some flippin' video? I don't know. But I won't give up till they tell me with their own lips that they want to stay on that blasted planet. And I dunna believe that mealy-mouthed Senite for a single minute."

For several moments after Scotty's declaration, there was no part of space as silent as the bridge of the USS *Enterprise*.

Chapter Fourteen

LONG SHADOWS were stretching across the valley, which was arguably the prettiest part of Sanctuary that they had yet seen in their reluctant travels, thought Kirk. Fed by numerous streams, ponds, and underground rivers, the bladder trees grew as high as those on the island of Khyming and sprouted orange flowers as large as a man's head. Lush moss several centimeters thick covered the ground, and thick vines snaked everywhere like a network of veins on a human heart.

The party of five had seen impressive herds of both the lungfish, as they'd dubbed them, and scrawny rodentlike mammals, and neither species showed much fear of the intruders. The sky was dotted with a flock of batlike creatures that swooped from one cliff to another, chasing the herds of fish. Even a constant drizzle could not dampen the beauty of this wild place.

Kirk and Renna found themselves walking together, swiveling their heads in unison at each new sight. They often glanced at one another, and Kirk felt uncomfortably like the male half of Adam and Eve.

"There are uglier places to live," said Renna offhandedly.

"I suppose so." Kirk shrugged. "You wouldn't have to worry about the neighbors getting on your nerves."

"It's going to be dark in another hour," Renna remarked. "We should keep our eyes open for a place to camp."

"Food and water are no problem," added Kirk, feeling like he was making small talk.

"If we have to stay here . . ." Renna began. But she didn't finish.

"Yeah." Kirk nodded, managing a smile. "If we have kids, Spock can be our baby-sitter."

"Pardon me, Captain?" asked the Vulcan, who was striding along a few meters away.

"Nothing," answered the captain. "We were just admiring the view."

"Captain," said the Vulcan, "I cannot be certain, but I believe we are being followed."

Kirk turned to look behind him, but he didn't stop walking. "How do you know?"

"That flock of flying creatures was startled by something about eighty meters behind us," answered Spock. "We cannot see them, but the animals know they are there."

Kirk stroked his chin thoughtfully and said, "The big group that attacked us before has had time to catch up. They can't ambush us, but they could certainly rush us. What do you think we should do?"

The captain's hushed voice attracted the attention of Billiwog and McCoy. "What's going on, Jim?" the doctor asked.

"Spock thinks our attackers are following us."

Billiwog whirled around with hairy fists clenched. "Where are the blighters? Bring 'em on!"

"Not so fast," said Kirk. "Just keep walking. Judging by the number of rocks they hurled at us, there could be thirty or forty of them."

"Well," said McCoy, "maybe they're just following us to make sure we get out of their territory."

"What *is* their territory?" asked Spock. "And how will we know when we have left it?"

"I don't know," muttered McCoy. "Why don't you go back and ask them?"

Spock raised an eyebrow. "Doctor, either you are being facetious, or you are not very concerned about my welfare."

"More likely," said Renna, "they're going to wait until we fall asleep, then jump us."

Billiwog smashed his fist into his palm and growled, "I say we hit them before they hit us."

The captain's jaw clenched with the weight of decision making. "We can't allow them to follow us," he said firmly, "and we have to find out for sure if they're there. So McCoy is right—let's ask them."

Kirk stopped suddenly, turned, and shouted, "Is anybody back there? Are you following us?"

"Show yourselves!" bellowed Billiwog.

Slowly, like the cry of a flying creature coasting toward them, a strange trilling sound began with one voice, was joined by others, and increased in volume until it was a chilling clamor. Then, like a horde of apes, a huge pack of creatures broke from the underbrush and loped toward them, screaming their frightful war cry.

"Do you have any more ideas, Doctor?" asked Spock.

"Yes," shrieked McCoy, *"run!"*

This was a popular notion, even with Billiwog, and

the fivesome took off at a full dash. Kirk figured they had a lead of about fifty meters, but the horrible cries made it seem more like fifty centimeters. They still clutched their sheet-metal shields, but those only served to slow them down. Kirk and Spock soon outdistanced the others, with Renna in the middle and McCoy and Billiwog falling behind. The lumbering giant was in real danger of being overtaken by at least forty smaller and swifter pursuers, and Kirk realized that only he and Spock stood any chance of outrunning them.

Kirk stopped and yelled, "Form ranks! Use your shields!"

He and Spock planted their feet and formed the first line of defense, and Renna and McCoy darted behind them. Huffing and puffing, Billiwog staggered into their midst with several of the scrawny gargoyles clutching at his heels. Kirk waded into them, swinging his shield like a club and bashing them onto their haunches. Spock did likewise, and McCoy and Renna tried to protect their flanks.

From the corner of his eye, Kirk saw Billiwog recover and hurl his shield like a discus into the oncoming throng, cutting several of them down in a gruesome pile. Then the humanoid charged the attackers, bellowing like an elephant and pummeling them with his fists. Despite the number he left crippled, they were soon clawing all over him, like dogs attacking a bear.

Kirk and Spock tried to drive off Billiwog's attackers, which left Renna and McCoy alone, fighting their own battles. Renna's screams joined the horrible sounds, and Kirk whirled around to see her tackled by two howling savages. A creature leaped onto McCoy's shield, while three more wrestled him to the ground. The captain ran to help Renna, kicking one of the creatures in the midsection and sending it flying.

Spock fought his way to the doctor and gripped two attackers by their necks, dropping them into unconsciousness. Despite their heroics, Kirk realized they were fighting a defensive battle against overwhelming odds. Three snarling gargoyles jumped on him, and he tumbled to the ground with one creature in each hand and another at his throat.

Like a lightning bolt hurled by Zeus, a terrific explosion shattered the air and rocked the ground. Another explosion thundered even closer, and the fierce child-sized creatures scrambled off the captain. Kirk sat up as a third explosion shook the ground, and he was relieved to see that the strange beings were in full flight, dragging their wounded with them.

He and Spock staggered to their feet and went to help Renna and McCoy, both of whom were dazed and battered. Billiwog remained on his knees, his thick fur red with blood. Nevertheless, they all turned to look northward, in the direction they'd been heading before the attack. On the darkening horizon, they saw the silhouettes of a new band of creatures, who appeared to be headed toward them.

"Now what?" panted McCoy.

"Unknown, Doctor," answered Spock. "If these are savages, they are armed with explosives."

"Senites?" asked Kirk with alarm. "They're the only ones who have weapons."

"We will know soon," Spock concluded.

Despite their injuries and weariness, McCoy, Renna, and Billiwog all managed to stagger to their feet to greet the new arrivals. There was no run and very little fight left in them, but they would not meet the unknown lying down.

"Ho, Kirk!" a voice called to them.

Spock glanced at the captain and raised an eyebrow. Kirk grinned in amazement and began to lead his bedraggled band toward the strangers. As they got closer, they saw the tall Andorian in the lead, his antennae standing at attention and his blue face beaming. He was followed by a motley collection of aliens, humanoids, and near-humans—a typical crowd for the planet of Sanctuary. Unlike the denizens of Dohama or Khyming, however, this group was distinguished by the fact that they carried crude weapons, binoculars, and hand-held sensors.

Kirk and his party nearly ran the last few meters, despite their exhaustion. "Are we glad to see you!" exclaimed Kirk. "We thought you'd deserted us!"

The Andorian looked slightly hurt. "Never," he said solemnly. "When the rocks hit the wagon, I knew that we had been attacked by the Lost Ones, and that we would need help. So I ran ahead while they were occupied with you. Unfortunately, we were farther from the Graveyard than I remembered, and it has taken me some time to return."

"That's okay," declared McCoy, beaming. "We're delighted to see you!"

"Your timing was quite excellent," said Spock. He studied a tubular weapon that was strapped to the back of one of the rescuers. "May I ask how you produced those timely explosions?"

"This old thing?" asked an albino humanoid, tapping the pipe. "It operates on a very simple mixture of potassium nitrate, sulfur, and charcoal."

"Gunpowder." Spock nodded.

McCoy glanced at the tube and its folding stand and said, "On Earth, they would call that weapon a mortar."

"Crude but effective," commented the albino. "It works very well against the Lost Ones. We could eliminate them, I suppose, but we like to keep them on this perimeter. They act as a deterrent to Senites and others who get too curious."

"I can imagine," said Kirk. "We have a million

213

questions, but most of all we want to see this Graveyard of Lost Ships."

"We are many hours away," the Andorian replied. "We made a forced march to get here, and you look as if you could use some rest, too. Perhaps we would be better off to make camp here and proceed in the morning."

"I agree," put in McCoy. "I want to take a look at some of these cuts and bruises. You don't happen to have a first-aid kit, do you?"

"Of course." The Andorian took a pouch off his shoulder. "At the Graveyard, we have something else that might interest you."

"What's that?" asked Kirk.

A snaggletoothed female stepped forward and peered at them. "Is your shuttlecraft called the *Ericksen?*" she asked.

Kirk nodded eagerly. "Yes!"

She smiled a truly gruesome smile. "Then we have it."

Kirk was awake before dawn, anxious to get to his shuttlecraft. He felt like they had been away from the *Enterprise* for a year, when it had actually been less than two weeks, about as long as a good overhaul in spacedock. Intellectually, he reasoned that it would not be such a simple matter as firing up the *Ericksen* and flying back to the *Enterprise,* but the fact that they were so close brought back all the old optimism. He was quite relieved when his own party and the dozen or so residents of the Graveyard gradually arose and started to break camp.

On the brisk walk to the north end of the valley, Kirk, Spock, and McCoy got to know several of their rescuers, and they soon knew why the Andorian had referred to them as "tinkerers." They loved gadgets and technology. The old snaggletoothed woman,

Sherfa, knew their shuttlecraft nearly as well as they did, and she described the controls, the engine, and the fuel capacity and made good guesses as to its range and speed.

"Will you help us get it flying again?" asked McCoy good-naturedly.

At that remark, the old woman's face darkened. "I don't know about that." She scowled. "As you'll find out, it's not entirely intact. The Senites are a peculiar variety of sadists. They dump all this stuff in our Graveyard, but they always remove a few crucial parts. High-end weaponry is always missing, and I doubt if the *Ericksen* has its stabilizers or fuel. Despite that, we occasionally cobble something together that will fly. In fact, you're just in time to see the latest flight—it's due tomorrow."

"Can they take three more passengers?" asked Kirk, quite seriously.

The woman frowned. "I think you'll be better off watching."

Her attitude reminded Kirk of the Andorian's response when he had first suggested they could get their shuttlecraft flying. What was it they were afraid of?

Billiwog spent his time on the long walk relating the horrors of the Senite Reborning factory, as well as their extraordinary escape—with himself cast as the hero. Then he regaled them with stories of Dohama, such as monumental drinking tournaments and fistfights. But he was quick to add that he would never frequent that hell-trap again, a vow with which the Andorian heartily agreed.

Renna described to them the genteel island of Khyming and their dramatic escape from that place. By the time the noonday sun was overhead, it was apparent that all five of them would be warmly welcomed into this new community. But Kirk preferred to think of the Graveyard of Lost Ships as a way

215

station en route to their real destination—the *Enter-prise*.

At the end of the valley, they climbed crudely cut steps in a rock wall to yet another plateau. This one sloped downward to the center of what appeared to be a very large and very dead volcano that had been filled over centuries with fertile soil. Belkot, the albino, climbed to the top of the ridge, removed his broad-rimmed straw hat, and swept it across the panoramic view.

"Welcome to the Graveyard!" he crowed.

The entire crater was choked with lush shrubs and undergrowth, and speckled among the trees at intervals of thirty meters or so were the hulks of countless spaceships. Some of them were as large as houses and were, in fact, serving as houses, with children playing out front and clothes strung on lines. Others were junkyard wrecks, rusting and picked apart, reduced to technological carrion. A few were escape pods and other vehicles too small to become anything but shiny and peculiar works of art.

The majority were shuttlecraft of one sort or another, and they sat interspersed among the trees like the camping vehicles Kirk had observed in pictures of old campgrounds on Earth. He felt like running into the valley and grabbing the first thing that would fly.

"Spock," he said with awe, "it's all there, all the accumulated spacecraft of centuries. We *can* get out of here!"

"Captain," Spock replied, "the fact that they are still *here* would indicate that most or more likely all are unable to fly."

"Yeah." Kirk frowned with dawning realization. He turned to Sherfa. "Can you take us to our shuttlecraft?"

The older female nodded glumly. "I can, but you must be realistic, Kirk. The *Ericksen* is now your home on Sanctuary, nothing more. Our evaluation is that it cannot fly."

Kirk jutted his chin defiantly. "We'll see. I have great faith in Mr. Spock and Dr. McCoy."

"Don't put your faith in me," grumped McCoy. "I can fix people, but not machines. I do understand, though, that some of their medical equipment is working, and they have geothermal electricity. So if you don't mind, Captain, I'll go and investigate that while you and Mr. Spock tune up the shuttlecraft."

Billiwog and some members of the rescue party were waving good-bye and starting down the hill. "They're taking me home for a meal," called Billiwog. "I'm going to talk to them about building sailing ships. Catch you at high tide!"

Sherfa stayed with the newcomers, along with Errico, the Andorian, and the albino, Belkot. Renna was unusually quiet as she stood on the lip of the crater, staring into the green valley dotted with silver spacecraft.

The captain turned to the subdued dark-haired woman and asked, "What are you going to do, Renna?"

"Make a home, make a life." She shrugged. "I'm going to follow Sherfa's advice. I'm going to be realistic."

"Let me take the young one with me," said Sherfa, wrapping a withered arm around Renna's shoulders. "Errico can show you to your shuttlecraft."

"I would be honored," the Andorian said, and bowed.

"And I will take Dr. McCoy to the infirmary," said Belkot, tipping his large hat.

The Andorian held up a long blue finger. "Do not forget, the launch of the *Lujexer* is tomorrow at sunrise. I expect you will all be very interested, as I am. This is the best opportunity yet for someone to escape the atmosphere. We have the shields operating on that one, don't we, Sherfa?"

She said disgruntledly, "We'll see. I think they're damn fools myself."

"Are you sure there's no room?" asked Kirk.

"You come and watch the launch," she advised, smiling malevolently. "Maybe you'll learn something."

McCoy and Belkot jogged down the hill, and the doctor called back to say, "I'll find you—as soon as I check out the infirmary!"

"Don't be too long," Kirk called after him. He bowed stiffly to Renna. "I guess we'll see you later."

"I imagine you will," she answered with a bemused smile. "It doesn't look like a very big town."

Renna waved briefly as she accompanied the older woman down into the vast crater. Errico set off in a slightly different direction, and Kirk and Spock followed.

"Fascinating," said Spock as the trio strolled among the space hulks and the families who lived inside them. "You realize, Captain, that the Senites cannot fail to know about this community. Therefore, we must consider that they approve of it, as they do Dohama, Khyming, the survivalists' camp, and perhaps hundreds of diverse communities."

"A place to put the techies," remarked Kirk, glancing around. "Errico, have you ever had a 'harvesting' here, like they had in Dohama?"

"Never," said the Andorian. "Generations have lived here without problems. In fact, there are some members of the community who wish to strengthen our ties with the Senites. We shall be more cautious of them, however, now that we know how the Senites reproduce themselves."

"How do the spacecraft get here?" asked Spock.

Errico shrugged his bony shoulders. "They just

appear—transported from wherever they land. Large ships are sometimes sent in pieces, which we put back together. Tinkerers study every vessel to see what the Senites have removed and what they have left. If the bona fide owners ever show up, as you have, they are granted ownership. Otherwise, the town council grants ownership to the neediest domestic unit."

"Logical," commented Spock.

The Andorian continued, "For the immediate future, the three of you are considered a domestic unit. I hope that is acceptable?"

"Most of the time," Kirk said with a grin.

They were startled by an eruption of water a few meters behind them, and they whirled to see a geyser shooting twenty meters into the air. Kirk and Spock approached the natural fountain, until they reached a clearing that had been roped off. From the ground around the geyser issued a number of coils and pipes that led to a small turbine, which powered a simple generator, from which wires snaked into the trees and supplied electricity to about a dozen households. The geyser roared for a few seconds more, then sputtered to a stop, but the generator kept clattering softly.

"That is the pride of the community," said Errico, "one of about fifty steam turbines that produce geothermal energy."

"Are there any dilithium crystals?" asked Kirk.

The Andorian shook his head. "Forget about dilithium or any complex fuel. We have been left some machinery and tools, but all energy sources must be indigenous."

Spock cocked an eyebrow. "With such pressure and heat in the magma, how can you be sure that the volcano is not potentially active?"

"We can't be sure," answered Errico. "But the geologists among us say it has been at least a thousand years since the last eruption, and they monitor it closely. We try to control the seepage of water into the magma, so there isn't a buildup of steam. Besides, this is where the Senites put the ships, so this is where we are. Come, your shuttlecraft is near."

They passed what looked like the remains of a Romulan warbird, picked over like the giant skeleton of some real avian species. Only twisted chunks of metal and infrastructure remained, and there were gaping holes where viewscreens and instrument panels had been plucked out. They passed a family of albino children playing in the yard of a troop transport, and saw parachutes that had been converted into greenhouses. All in all, the Graveyard of Lost Ships was a testament to the ingenuity, spirit, and cooperation of intelligent species from all over the galaxy. It also had its eerie quality, thought Kirk, like a junkyard or a failed amusement park, which the denizens of the Graveyard seemed reluctant to disturb.

The captain saw the streamlined bread-loaf shape of the *Ericksen* before Errico even had time to point it out. He jogged toward it, closely followed by Spock. They ducked through the open doorway and walked reverently through the small craft, stunned by the feeling of recognition and familiarity. Kirk thought Spock would go to the instrument panel, but instead the Vulcan rushed to check the ship's stores and rummage through the cabinets.

"They have left us a tricorder," he announced. "And our emergency provisions appear to be intact."

Kirk ran to the radio and flipped it on. "Kirk to *Enterprise*," he called. "Come in, *Enterprise!*"

The tall Andorian stood crouched in the doorway. "I am sorry," he said, "but your ship has been drained of power and fuel. That is typical, I'm afraid."

Kirk flipped every switch on the console, but no lights or sweet little chirps responded. It was a dead ship, as dead as the skeleton ship a few doors down.

"We can arrange electricity," said Errico. "In fact, I will go do that now, if I may be allowed to take my leave."

Captain Kirk turned to the regal Andorian, slightly ashamed that he hadn't been more grateful for their remarkable deliverance. "Errico, I never properly thanked you for saving our lives. You have been a true comrade."

Errico's blue skin turned slightly purplish. "It has been my honor." He bowed. "After all, it was *you* who saved *me* from that terrible Senite stronghold."

"Actually, it was Renna who did that." Kirk frowned. "She's another one I haven't thanked properly. But I will."

"Thank you, Errico," put in Spock. "An electrical hookup in the range of nine to fifteen volts would be quite satisfactory."

"I will attend to it," said the Andorian, and he bowed himself out of the doorway.

Spock turned on the tricorder and lifted an eyebrow appreciatively at the comforting beep and display of lighted indicators. "Captain," he said, "apparently the forcefield which the Senites use to disable alien technology does not extend to this location. We will no longer be operating in the dark. Even with no instruments on the conn working, I can give you a detailed report on the status of this vessel."

"Do it," said Kirk, a feeling of dread creeping up his spine.

For a few seconds, the Vulcan's slim fingers deftly twisted dials and punched in commands. Then he began his report: "Impulse engines intact but drained; thrusters drained; fuel tanks empty; storage cells missing; phasers missing; stabilizers missing—"

"That's enough," said Kirk, holding up his hand. He heaved a sigh of disappointment and paced around the cramped enclosure. "Anything that could generate enough power to get this thing off the ground is gone. The Graveyard people are right, aren't they? It's not going to fly."

"Not in its present condition," answered Spock. "Nothing is damaged, but the Senites are very thorough. Without fuel or stabilizers, this shuttlecraft will not move."

"Unless we put it on wheels and strap a horse to it," muttered Kirk. He pounded his fist in frustration. "We were so close!"

"Captain," said Spock, "the tinkerers must be capable of developing their own rocket fuel, or they would not be capable of the launch they plan tomorrow."

Kirk took a deep breath and tried to think positively. Through the open doorway, he could see long shadows stretching across the network of paths. He had learned that, on Sanctuary, nightfall strode swiftly behind those long shadows.

"Yes." He yawned. "We don't want to miss that launch tomorrow. Maybe getting some food and a little rest wouldn't be such a bad idea."

"Precisely," agreed Spock, searching through a plastic carton of food rations.

The infirmary was one of the few buildings that had been constructed of thatch, pumice, and other native materials, not cobbled together from old spaceships. McCoy arrived in time to see a young boy have his broken arm set by a skilled doctor with seven fingers on one hand and eight on his dominant hand. Dr. Muta claimed to practice holistic medicine, both as a personal preference and because what drugs had been scavenged from the ships had to be closely rationed. Two nurses assisted the doctor, and they all prescribed from the stock of homemade sulfa, quinine, and various herbal medications.

Several homes in the community apparently had sickbays that could be used for emergencies, but the infirmary was more roomy and comfortable. McCoy could understand how patients might like the rambling building after living in grounded spaceships most of the time. He was certain that Muta could set a broken bone, deliver a baby, or tie a tourniquet as well as anyone, which was a great relief to McCoy. If the thriving community had not had a good doctor, he might have been tempted to stay there to lend a hand. But they had one, and McCoy could focus his energies on returning to a community that didn't have a chief surgeon at the moment—the *Enterprise.*

He bade good-bye to Dr. Muta and the staff of the infirmary, and found himself standing outside in the center of a maze of dark paths. The only landmarks were the silhouettes of strange spacecraft looming over the trees and the occasional porch light swinging in the breeze. Then McCoy noticed another beacon— good-natured laughter—and he followed the pleasant sound.

He soon found himself at a yard party, in front of a copper-colored shuttlecraft; its living space had been doubled by the ingenious use of reflective tarpaulins and tent poles. A diverse collection of mostly two-legged creatures stood limb to limb with one another, holding every manner of beverage receptacle aloft, as a young bearded humanoid addressed them. He held his glass higher than anyone's.

"To all my friends," he said, "keepers of the Graveyard! Juuxa and I will be leaving you tomorrow, but don't grieve for us. We must see if the *Lujexer* can fly, after these many years of work on her. Thanks to Sherfa"—he nodded to the older woman, who tearfully hid her face—"the shields are forty percent of what they once were."

The young pilot swallowed hard. "No matter what

happens, if we break the Senite shield, or bounty hunters get us, or we become a star in the dawn sky, we will remember all of you fondly. The Graveyard is not a perfect place to live, but we know from the stories of the newcomers that there are far worse places on Sanctuary. We have been privileged to live here among you, and we treasure your friendship and collaboration."

The young humanoid looked as if he wanted to continue talking, but he was too choked with tears. A female of his own species rushed to the tree stump and hugged him, while the others applauded. Most of them were laughing, crying, or a little of both. Someone grabbed McCoy's arm and stuck a hollow geode in his hand. The rock goblet was brimming with dark and pungent-smelling ale that glittered within the blood-red crystal lining.

Belkot smiled at McCoy through deeply reddened eyes and cheeks that were glistening with tears. "It is the way of the tinkerer and inventor," he said, "to build, then to claim the right to test. Do not judge us too harshly."

"I don't judge you at all," said McCoy. He took a deep sip of the amber liquid. "You want off this planet, and you know there is a way. I hope you find it. We're looking for it, too." He took an even deeper gulp. "Gosh, this stuff is good. If your fuel is half as potent as this, those kids will make it!"

"I hope so," answered Belkot. "Please, come join us. Renna is here, and there are others you know."

The night was bright from the second moon by the time they walked Dr. McCoy home. That meant it was very late, and Kirk and Spock were awakened in their hammocks. McCoy was guided through the door by two residents, who swiftly said good-night and left.

"Bones?" asked Kirk, leaning out of his hammock. "I would ask you where you've been, but you're over twenty-one."

"I've been to a going-away party," drawled McCoy, sitting in the pilot's chair. "I'm a little tipsy, though."

"Evidently," observed Spock. "Who is going away, may I ask?"

"Nice young couple. Going up in that spaceship tomorrow." McCoy looked bleary-eyed at his captain and rasped, "Jim, they're going to die. And everyone knows it."

Kirk swung his legs over the edge of his hammock but remained seated. "Yeah," he said, "Spock and I were beginning to reach the same conclusion."

"What about this thing?" asked McCoy, motioning around the shuttlecraft. "Can we get it up?"

"There are a lot of things missing," the captain replied curtly. "Like stabilizers, fuel, and storage cells."

"However," Spock added, "we have a small gift from the Senites—a working tricorder."

"A tricorder," murmured the doctor. "I don't see how *that* will get us very far."

"We shall see," replied the Vulcan. "By my calculations, sunrise will occur in one hundred fifty-seven point two minutes, so I suggest that we continue sleeping."

"Wake me up for the sacrifice," groaned McCoy. He stretched out in the pilot's chair, crossed his arms, and began to snore.

The friendly face of Captain Mora appeared on the *Enterprise*'s viewscreen. He tried to look tough, but concern and sadness were etched on his sun-browned wrinkles.

"Commander Scott," he reported, "we are leaving

immediately. You will soon be receiving orders from Starfleet by subspace. I'm afraid I already know what those orders are, and I deeply regret that more time cannot be extended to the rescue mission. There is, however, profound relief at the highest levels that Captain Kirk and the others are still alive. I have suggested that a station be docked in deep orbit, perhaps around the large moon, to observe and maintain contact with Sanctuary. But that is not a job for the *Enterprise*. Good-bye, Commander Scott."

"Good-bye, Captain Mora," Scotty replied stiffly.

The solemn face blinked off, to be replaced by a long-range view of various ships in orbit around the turquoise sphere. Scotty had guessed that the *Neptune* would be leaving soon, because she had shifted to a roomier section of the orbital belt, three thousand kilometers from the *Enterprise*. Slowly, one of the blips pulled out of line and disappeared, and she was gone.

Scotty let the breath out of his lungs and dropped the shoulders he had been holding so stiffly. He strolled behind Chekov and Sulu and slumped into the captain's chair. Maybe they weren't beaten yet, but they were surely on the ropes.

Uhura swiveled in her chair, and her voice was barely audible. "Commander Scott," she said, "I have just received a message from Starfleet. It's very short."

Scotty nodded. "Short and to the point. Let's have it, Lieutenant."

"We are to report to Starbase 64 in forty-eight hours."

Everyone on the bridge held their collective breath, waiting for the acting captain to give the orders that would take them away from Sanctuary, and Captain Kirk, Mr. Spock, and Dr. McCoy. Perhaps forever.

Scotty cocked his head thoughtfully and scratched his chin. "That is a short message," he agreed. "The question is, do they want us to *be* at Starbase 64 in forty-eight hours? Or do they want us to *leave* in forty-eight hours?"

"I vould say," offered Chekov, "they vant us to *leave* in forty-eight hours."

"It's certainly open to interpretation," agreed Sulu.

Uhura smiled. "I will acknowledge the message."

"When you're done with that," said Scotty, "hail Captain Pilenna on the *Gezary.*"

"Aye, sir," answered Uhura.

Scotty let the green-skinned Orion's fingers probe the tense muscles of his shoulders. He hadn't come over to the *Gezary* for a back rub, but it seemed to relax Pilenna as much as himself. The exotic scent of her perfume, her lustrous red hair brushing his cheek, her strong fingers—they were all welcome distractions. He was in her private quarters, seated in the chair at her vanity table, and she leaned seductively over him. Luckily, she had been wearing clothes upon greeting him this time, or he wasn't sure what he would have done.

"Feeling better?" asked the bounty huntress.

"Aye," sighed the Scotsman, letting his head loll back. "You wouldna consider a commission in Starfleet, would you? We've got a therapeutic masseur, but he's not half as skilled as you."

Pilenna spun her chair around and slipped into his lap. "And you don't even know half my skills," she purred, stroking his dark bangs back from his forehead. "Actually, I was going to ask you the same thing. I'm tired of running this ship all by myself, and now that you've gotten it all fixed up, I thought you might like to join up."

Scotty chuckled. "And be a bounty hunter? That may be what we're doing here, but that's not our normal line of work."

The former slave shrugged. "We could do anything you want, Scotty. Carry passengers, run dilithium crystals—you name it. Lately, bounty hunting hasn't been paying all that well. This damn planet is putting us all out of business."

"I'd like to put *it* out of business." The engineer scowled. "But I've only got forty-eight hours."

"Then let's make the most of it," breathed Pilenna. She melted into him, her radiant hair caressing his cheeks a millisecond before her luscious mouth found his. Scotty responded with a zeal that surprised both of them, and they were locked in a passionate kiss when the comm panel on her vanity table intruded with an irritating buzz.

"Damn," she said, reaching over to slap the panel. "What is it?"

"Incoming ship," said a voice from the *Gezary*'s bridge. "From the gamma ray activity, it must be a big one."

Pilenna frowned. "I'll be right there." Very reluctantly, she extricated herself from Scotty's arms. "Business calls, my sweet. But, please, stay here and wait for me."

"I can't," said Scotty hoarsely. He stood and straightened his uniform. "We've only got forty-eight hours to find them. Pilenna, if you get a sign of a ship leaving the planet's surface, will you let me know?"

She patted his shoulder fondly. "Of course, my dear. You'll be the first to know. If you're leaving, go now, because we're pulling out of orbit to see what this is."

He took her hand and kissed it like the old-world

gentleman he was. "I'll consider your offer," he said, smiling, "when I leave Starfleet."

She winked. "Get out of here before I throw you in irons."

As the bounty huntress rushed out of the room, Scotty took out his communicator with a sigh. "Transporter room, beam me over."

Chapter Fifteen

CAPTAIN KIRK STOOD waiting at the launch site with a sparse number of early birds, it being far from sunrise. Despite Spock's suggestion, he hadn't been able to go back to sleep after McCoy's belated arrival. No sooner had he wandered out of their shuttlehome than he had hooked up with a crowd of early risers who were headed to the site. They talked reverently, in whispers, of the upcoming flight, assessing the merits of the liquid hydrogen fuel, the resurrection of the ship's shield, and the overall design of the *Lujexer*.

In the bright moonlight, Kirk followed them to a level expanse of sheer rock that had been scorched black by various earlier attempts to escape. The scaffolding held a slim, needle-nosed craft that looked hardly big enough for one person, let alone two. How much fuel could it possibly hold? How far could they go? wondered Kirk. The answers that came to mind weren't encouraging.

"Hello, stranger," said a voice.

Kirk turned to see a smiling Renna, looking freshly scrubbed and dressed in a frayed but form-hugging flight suit. "I'm glad you found your way here," she remarked. "Where are McCoy and Spock?"

"I hope McCoy is sleeping," said the captain with a chuckle. "Someone introduced him to the local intoxicant last night."

"Well, I gather that was a rather special party," answered Renna thoughtfully. She turned her attention to the scaffolding that held the rocketship. "We are here because we love spaceships. You, at least, got yours back. I wish I had *my* ship back."

"What ship was that?" Kirk asked innocently.

Renna grinned. "Just some old piece of tin I smashed up some time ago. You know, Kirk, you might as well plan on staying here and making the best of it. I've been told this is all going to end rather badly."

"I heard they got the shields working on this ship," said Kirk cockily. "And I've always believed that if there's a will, there's a way."

"The shields, they were saying last night, are forty percent or so," pointed out Renna. "Even if that's enough to break through, what are they going to do about the bounty hunters?"

"Nobody said it would be easy," Kirk replied stoically.

"It's cold," breathed Renna, snuggling into his chest. Kirk's arms wrapped around her instinctively. "You know," she went on, "we've gotten to know this part of the planet pretty well, but there's still lots to discover. What's out there on some of those islands? What's to the west of here? Don't you want to find out?"

"Yes, I do," the captain murmured into her ear.

"And I'll be able to find that out when I get back to the *Enterprise.*"

Renna twisted out of his grasp. "What about defeating the Senites," she demanded, "and taking over this jewel of a planet? It could be done."

Kirk chuckled. "Yes, I believe *you* probably could do it if you put your mind to it. But not me. I don't want one world—I want hundreds and thousands of worlds."

"I know." Renna nodded sadly, settling back into his arms. "That's why we were all condemned here."

Simultaneously, it seemed to Kirk, the area filled with the first rays of salmon-colored sun and a diverse selection of people. Kirk saw McCoy and Spock standing discreetly on the other side of the blackened launchpad, and he realized he still had his arms tightly around Renna. They were unable to talk about any of the issues that burdened their minds, but they were able to hold each other; and Kirk wasn't anxious to let go. He saw Spock fiddling with his tricorder, and he knew he would receive a detailed analysis of what they were about to witness. The whole crowd was strangely quiet and expectant, as if this were a solemn religious occasion rather than the launch of a homemade rocket.

The pilots finally made their entrance, accompanied by well-wishers and explosive applause. The young male and female who were making the flight seemed an excellent choice to Kirk, and he realized that the whole community must have sacrificed and collaborated to make their dream come true. It had to have been a huge team effort to assemble the raw materials, scrap, and skill needed to transform one of these crippled hulks into a worthwhile spacecraft again.

Kirk also felt the melancholy of the occasion, as if a

terrible knowledge was not being spoken. Although hope was rampant in the assembled throng, so were fear, fatalism, and a sort of morbid curiosity. The best they could see was two people triumphing over impossible odds, but the least they would see was two people dying.

Those two people strapped on pressure suits and helmets and waved to their friends as they climbed a rope ladder to the cockpit of the needle-nosed craft. Kirk wondered if it had once been an unmanned probe, it was so sleek and streamlined. The male wriggled in first, followed by the female, until they lay end to end, completely invisible except for the woman's arms. She snapped the canopy shut.

"What do you think?" asked Belkot, sidling up to Kirk and Renna.

"Ask me when it's over," Renna said, and shivered.

Kirk wondered, "How many flights like these have you had?"

"Too many." The albino frowned. "But we're hoping this one will be different. We have the shield partly working."

"Is Sherfa here?" asked Renna, craning her neck to look around.

Belkot shook his head. "No. She never comes to one of these, although she has done more work than anyone."

A few meters away, an impossibly gangly creature with several arms was talking on a crude walkie-talkie. "All systems check," he said, his limbs gesturing around like a spider's. "Begin countdown." The being waved a long appendage at someone closer to the ship and shouted, "Clear launchpad!"

"Clear launchpad!" rang out several voices, and the crowd began to push back from the scaffolding.

"Prepare for launch!"

233

"One hundred, ninety-nine, ninety-eight, ninety-seven . . ." someone began counting down. Other voices took up the chant.

Kirk could feel Renna's compact body tensing in his arms, and his own fingers dug deeper into her flesh. They were standing well back and were soon surrounded by observers, pressed limb to limb. Thrusters sputtered on the rocket's undercarriage, and it began to shake perceptibly on the rickety launcher.

As the air filled with heat, smoke, and noise, people pressed forward as if to feel the power of the burning fuel. The countdown was drowned out, but everyone could tell when zero was reached. The nozzles roared with an inferno of flame, filling the area with choking smoke. It hardly mattered, because nobody was breathing.

They held their breath until the rocket began to rise, shaking off the feeble ropes and belts that held it. The cheering mounted with every meter that the ship lifted into the air and rose into a crescendo that sounded louder than the engines. People were shrieking and laughing and pounding each other on the back as the rocket made a swift ascent, rising until it became little more than a spark in the rose-hued sky.

Many observers had binoculars, small telescopes, and hand-held instruments such as Spock's tricorder. As the blip got smaller, they shouted reports like, "There she is!" "Still climbing!" "Looks good!"

But suddenly, it didn't look so good. Suddenly, the shining light disappeared. "She's gone," someone said with shock.

"Where is it?" a woman wailed. *"Where is it?"*

"That's about where they always go," muttered a veteran. "The Senites got her."

"Lujexer, come in!" the gangly creature shouted into his radio. *"Lujexer!* Come in! Come in!"

But there was nothing on the other end.

Kirk felt Renna turn her head and look away, but there hadn't been any terrible explosion or flaming debris—just nothing. That almost made it worse on the crowd, because the sobs and shocked expressions came slower, leavened by disbelief and denial.

"Usual place," someone agreed. "Their shield didn't hold."

Belkot patted Kirk on the shoulder. "Do you see why we tell you to accept it?" he asked.

"But you don't accept it," Kirk argued. "You keep trying."

"We're fools," the albino said bitterly. He bowed his head and walked down the hill.

Renna pried herself away from Kirk's arms and turned to face him. "You only get one try," she cautioned. "I'd give it a lot of thought, if I were you."

The young woman joined the sorrowful exodus from the launchpad, leaving only Kirk, Spock, McCoy, and a handful of others too curious or stunned to move.

"Commander Scott!" called Sulu from the operations console. "I have just detected an explosion in the atmosphere over the planet." He turned around to look intently at the acting captain. "From my estimates, I would say the craft was trying to *escape* the atmosphere."

Scotty leaned forward in the captain's chair. "Are ye sure it wasn't a ship going in, maybe an unmanned probe or torpedo?"

"No," answered Sulu, "this was definitely a missile fired *from* the planet. It vanished approximately thirty kilometers above the surface, exactly where our sensors stop functioning and our own probes disappear."

"Sir," Chekov interrupted, "whatever it was, it did

not go unnoticed by the other ships in orbit. The Orion ship and the *Gezary* both changed course to intercept. Now they are returning to their orbits."

"Hmm," mused Scotty. "Maybe the inmates *do* try to escape from the asylum every now and then."

"I hope that wasn't the captain," said Sulu. "That ship is gone—vaporized."

"Maybe it was unmanned," suggested Uhura, "like a test flight."

Scotty nodded decisively and strode to Sulu's station. "Lieutenant, I want you to ignore the rest of the planet and track that missile back to its point of origin. I know you canna tell exactly without sensors, but maybe you can use telescopes and photographs to get an idea where the launchpad is. Change our orbit if you have to."

"Aye, sir," answered Sulu.

"Keep your eyes open," Scotty told everyone.

"I swear, Spock, you are absolutely ghoulish," said McCoy on the walk back to their shuttlehome. "You're the only one who enjoyed that tragedy back there. You're still replaying it on your tricorder."

"Precisely, Doctor," Spock agreed, without looking up from his hand-held instrument. "I have simulated the launch several times, and the result is always a successful flight. However, the flight we witnessed was not successful."

McCoy turned with exasperation to Kirk. "How can you argue with logic like that?"

"Maybe there's method to his madness," said Kirk. "What are you looking for, Spock?"

The Vulcan answered, "There can be no mistake—the flight was progressing successfully until it reached an altitude of thirty kilometers. At that point, it destructed without apparent reason. A failure for no reason is illogical; therefore, we can conclude that the

Senite shield is found at thirty kilometers and is programmed to repel driven flight."

"And what does that mean?" asked McCoy.

Spock turned off his tricorder and put it back into its case. "It means, Doctor, that we could not escape from the planet in the shuttlecraft, even if we had fuel and stabilizers."

"What you're saying," said the captain, scowling, "is that there is no escape for us? No point in trying?"

"Not necessarily," said the Vulcan. "I said the shield repels driven flight. It may not repel all types of aircraft. I have an experiment to perform."

With that, the Vulcan charged down the path, and Kirk and McCoy had to run to keep up with him. He dashed into the shuttlecraft and stayed there for several moments, while Kirk and McCoy stared at one another.

"Do you know what that devious Vulcan mind is up to?" asked the doctor.

"Not a clue," admitted Kirk. "But we could use some devious thinking at this point."

Spock emerged holding an expandable weather balloon and a small canister of helium, both of which were standard issue in the shuttle's survival kit. He began to fill the balloon.

"Oh, great," muttered McCoy, "we're going to find out what the weather is."

"Actually," said Spock, "we are going to learn very little about the weather, because I have removed most of the sensors. I have, however, left the transmitter and altimeter intact. Gentlemen, will you please help to hold the balloon—I am filling it to its maximum pressure."

Kirk and McCoy struggled with the attached line as Spock filled the balloon with helium until it was four meters in diameter and as large as the three of them put together. Their feet were beginning to lift off the ground by the time Spock tied off the balloon's nozzle. He pulled out his tricorder and pressed some buttons.

"Release it, please," he ordered.

It was with great relief that Kirk and McCoy did so, and the giant balloon launched into the sky like a bubble blasting out of the ocean. Spock followed its course on the tricorder, but the balloon was visible to the naked eye for a considerable length of time, and a curious crowd gathered to see what the second launch of the day was about.

"What do you three think you're up to?" asked the old woman Sherfa.

"I'm not sure," answered Kirk. "Spock is trying an experiment."

"I'll ask him later," Sherfa decided. "He looks too preoccupied to talk at the moment. You don't mind if I watch, do you?"

"Of course not," said Kirk. "I'm sorry about what happened at the launch this morning."

She sighed. "They were like children to me. I'm getting too old for that sort of thing. I may not help the next bunch of idiots who are fool enough to try that."

"Meaning us?" asked McCoy.

"I don't know." The woman shrugged. "What you are doing here looks quite different."

The weather balloon was now out of sight, although several people continued to follow it with binoculars and telescopes, and Spock never took his eyes off his tricorder. After a while, Sherfa and some of the others looked more than merely curious.

"How high is it?" asked the old woman.

"Thirty-five kilometers and rising," answered Spock.

"Wait a minute," said Sherfa excitedly, "that means it's past the shield!"

"By my calculations, yes," Spock replied. "At about

fifty kilometers, it will probably start to lose altitude, but it is past the Senite shield."

"Wait a minute," said Kirk, reaching into his back pocket and pulling out his beat-up communicator. "If we ride a balloon thirty-five kilometers into the stratosphere, will we be able to contact the *Enterprise?* Will they be able to beam us off?"

"Those are matters of conjecture," said Spock, "but I see no reason why not. All of this confirms what I noticed when we first entered the atmosphere in the shuttlecraft—the instruments stopped working at about thirty kilometers. Then today, the rocket vanished at thirty kilometers. That is where the Senite shield is the strongest. The shield is obviously programmed to stop driven flight trying to escape the stratosphere, but not gases drifting leisurely upward."

McCoy peered into the sky and remarked, "We finally know how high the walls of this prison are."

"Are you sure there's still somebody up there to rescue you?" asked a doubting voice. They turned to see Renna elbowing her way closer through what was now a considerable crowd. "Because if there's not, you're either going to suffocate in the thin air, or fall fifty kilometers to your deaths. Or the bounty hunters will get you," she added with a mocking grin. "In fact, I can think of a few people who would pay dearly for James T. Kirk delivered in chains."

The captain smiled. "You have some valid points, but all of this is purely conjecture. I presume, Spock, we haven't got a balloon in the shuttlecraft that's big enough to carry the three of us aloft?"

"No, Captain," answered the Vulcan. "Nor do we have enough helium."

McCoy waved his hands and proclaimed, "We don't need helium—we can use hot air! I've flown hot-air balloons before. It's easy."

"No, no," said Sherfa, "if Spock is right, the large burners you would need to heat the air would set off the Senite shield. And hot-air balloons are huge. The craft you want would have to be low-mass, almost entirely gas. And you would have to wear pressurized suits."

"That was my thinking," Spock agreed. "The only electronic device we could risk carrying would be one communicator."

"Okay," said McCoy, "how much helium do you have?"

"About as much as you do," answered Sherfa. "Helium does not occur naturally around here, but we have a great deal of hydrogen. Free hydrogen is a natural component of the gases we collect from deep in the volcano, and we can also extract it from water. That's why we use it for our rocket fuel. After all, hydrogen is the most abundant element in the universe."

"And one of the most flammable." Renna appealed to Kirk and McCoy: "Why don't you just set yourselves on fire right now? If you know anything about Earth history, you must remember the *Hindenburg.*"

"The famous zeppelin." McCoy nodded reverently. "It struck a tower in the United States and blew up. That was the end of the great dirigibles of the 1930s."

Spock cocked an eyebrow and said, "I am impressed, Doctor. I should have known you would be an expert on early-twentieth-century transportation."

McCoy squinted at the Vulcan, not sure if that was a compliment or not. By this time, the discussion had spread, and everyone within earshot was debating the merits of helium, hydrogen, and hot air. Many of them were computing how large the balloon would have to be to lift the trio thirty-five kilometers, and whether it should be super-pressurized or zero-pressurized. Dr. McCoy was actively contributing his opinions.

"I think you started something," Kirk whispered to Spock. "Can we really do this?"

"We can," said the Vulcan, "if we have the materials to build the basket and the balloon, the gas to fill it, and three pressure suits. However, all of the reservations brought forth by Renna are still valid."

"I know," muttered Kirk. He turned to look for the pert, dark-haired woman, but she had disappeared. "I don't suppose we could take her with us?"

"No, Captain," Spock replied. "In all probability, she is Auk-rex, but Starfleet regulation 927.9 prohibits willfully endangering a prisoner's life."

"But it's okay to willfully endanger our own lives?"

"In this case," said Spock, "we must endanger our lives. I see no other possibility for escape. We must also act as soon as possible, because every second's delay increases the probability that the *Enterprise* will be summoned elsewhere."

"Yes." The captain frowned. "We're supposing that Scotty has found a way to stay up there for two weeks, despite those ships he mentioned before we lost contact, and Starfleet."

"I believe, Captain," said Spock, "that unless Commander Scott has relinquished command, the *Enterprise* is still in orbit."

"A leap of faith, Spock?"

Spock cocked his head. "A prediction based upon observation of past behavior. Of course, if my prediction is wrong, there will be disastrous consequences."

"We either take your balloon ride," summed up the captain, "or we accept the fact that we have to spend the rest of our lives here."

"That is the decision," agreed the Vulcan.

"How high up is thirty kilometers?"

"High enough to be interesting," replied Spock. "On Earth, which has a similar atmosphere, the record for a manned balloon flight is thirty-four point seven kilometers, and there have been several flights in the thirty-kilometer range. Of course, we have an advantage in that we do not have to design the craft to return to the ground."

"Yeah, some advantage. How much gas would we need? What kind of pressure?"

Spock held up his hand. "I suggest we answer one question first: Are we going to do this?"

"Yes," Kirk answered decisively. He wondered if he had just joined the Graveyard suicide club.

After the freewheeling discussions had died down, Kirk, Spock, and McCoy met privately with Sherfa, Belkot, Errico, and several other leaders of the Graveyard of Lost Ships. They met in the community's courthouse, a large freighter with a blackened hull, the result of a none-too-careful entry into Sanctuary's atmosphere. Nevertheless, its hold offered a spacious private room with a white board, upon which the participants freely drew diagrams and flowcharts to illustrate their points.

Belkot had just drawn what looked uncomfortably like a giant coffin, suspended from a small, spherical balloon by a cord that was, in scale, perhaps sixty meters long. The entire contraption was longer than the freighter in which the meeting was taking place. He pounded the diagram with a pale finger.

"The long rigging," explained Belkot, "looks dangerous but will give the balloon more stability, especially on takeoff. This won't be a leisurely ride—that much hydrogen will make you ballistic when you take off. And I don't know if you can carry enough ballast to make a difference. But if we install some vents at the top of the balloon, and run lines into the cabin, you can control your ascent, and even return to the ground."

Dr. McCoy squinted at the diagram. "I don't mind all that hydrogen being as far away from me as possible," he remarked, "but how big is that cabin? Is it going to be pressurized?"

"That all depends on time," answered Sherfa. "How soon do you want to go?"

Every eye in the empty hold turned to Captain Kirk. "Tomorrow," he snapped.

There were murmurs and comments about how it couldn't be done. Sherfa only smiled in her gap-toothed way. "We have known you a short time, Captain," she said, "but we recognize a headstrong man of action. We've had many in our midst like you—some are gone, of course. If you can be per-suaded to take your time with this endeavor, I believe your chances of success will be greater."

Kirk leaned forward across the table and stared every man, woman, and creature in the optical organ. "This escape has no chance of success if our ship is not up there. Let me remind you again—we only need to go *one way*. All the talk of vents and lifelines and escape hatches is beside the point. The balloon only has to go up, with us strapped to it."

He straightened up and smiled sheepishly. "I don't mean to lecture you, but if I were back on my ship, I'm sure I could rig this experiment in twenty-four hours. I don't have the resources here, so I have to depend upon you. And I don't think we need a fancy cabin—lightweight pressure suits like that couple wore this morning would be fine. If we have to hang around up there at fifty kilometers for a few days—well, something's gone wrong. All we need from you is a big balloon and enough hydrogen to fill it up."

Sherfa turned to Belkot and said, "If the Harrakas can do without their new greenhouse, I think they

243

have enough tripolymer sheeting to make the balloon. We can also use the insulation from the *Paragran,* and we have plenty of molecular bonding material."

"If I may make a suggestion," said Spock. "We should use a balloon that is zero-pressurized as opposed to super-pressurized." The Vulcan turned to his captain to explain. "A super-pressurized balloon has greater pressure inside than the outside air—it would lift quickly but continue to expand as it ascended. If we use a balloon that has less pressure than the outside air and only enough hydrogen to gain the desired altitude, it would expand in the thinning air until it and the air were at equal, or zero, pressure. Its ascent would stabilize for at least a few hours at that altitude. Zero pressure will not tax the seams of the balloon as much either."

Belkot nodded. "Ideally, you'd level off at about thirty-five kilometers, but we'd have to make sure you had enough hydrogen to get that far."

"I have made some preliminary calculations," said Spock. "Perhaps you would care to check my figures."

"This is great," proclaimed Kirk eagerly. "So you're going to help us?"

"Yes," grumbled Sherfa. "We suffer fools gladly." She rose to her feet and looked at everyone around her. "Spock and I will head up the committee to make the balloon and rigging. Belkot, you can collect the hydrogen. Hole number four gives off the most free hydrogen, and you can also check how much we have left in the *Mathulsa*'s fuel tanks. Mr. Spock, what do you think a good preliminary estimate would be?"

The Vulcan cocked his head and replied, "I would estimate two thousand cubic meters."

"Sounds about right," Belkot agreed.

The woman turned to Kirk and McCoy. "Gentlemen, I will leave it up to you to design your own basket. Or whatever you choose to hang yourselves from. Remember, low-mass, no metal."

"I have an idea about that," said McCoy, grinning.

"Errico," Sherfa said to the tall Andorian, "you beg, borrow, or steal three pressure suits. Ask politely, but check everyone's locker."

The regal blue-skinned being nodded solemnly. "I will not rest until my mission is accomplished."

"There's just one more thing," said the old woman, looking squarely at Captain Kirk. "I want you to send us a sign, shoot a rocket or something, if you are rescued. If we ever get anyone off this rock, we want to know about it."

"Agreed." Kirk smiled warmly. "Just keep watching the sky."

Chapter Sixteen

WHILE SPOCK SET about organizing the balloon construction team, Kirk and McCoy returned to their shuttlehome. The doctor promptly took down their nylon net hammocks and measured them. He found three more hammocks in the survival gear, a sewing kit, and some scissors; gathering them up, he began to work.

Kirk watched the seamster for several moments before he finally had to ask, "What are you doing, Bones? I'm not sure I want to sleep with you in one giant hammock."

"I doubt if we'll be getting very much sleep," answered McCoy. "We're going to be hanging from the balloon in this hammock."

"What?" exclaimed Kirk. "We're gonna hang in a hammock thirty-five kilometers in the air? Will it hold us?"

"These hammocks hold us all right now," argued McCoy. "There is a misconception that you are

246

buffeted about in a balloon. Even at high speed in high winds, a balloon ride is very smooth, because you are traveling the same speed and direction as the wind. I'll make the hammock stronger and bigger than it needs to be, in case we have to carry some ballast."

"I don't know," Kirk muttered doubtfully.

"It's low-mass and nonmetallic, too," replied McCoy. "As Spock says, I know a thing or two about twentieth-century transportation."

"All right." Kirk shrugged. "I'm going to test my communicator to make sure it's still working after all this time. They set us up with electricity, and you should be able to receive my signal at the instrument panel. If you hear me, answer."

"Okay," said McCoy, not skipping a beat in his sewing.

The captain stepped outside and walked about twenty meters from the shuttlecraft. Two green-skinned children stopped their play to watch him. Smiling at them, Kirk flipped open his communicator and heard the welcoming chirps. "Kirk to shuttlecraft," he said. "Come in, shuttlecraft."

"McCoy here," came the reply. "It's working fine. Let's hope Scotty hears it as clearly."

"That's a relief after carrying this thing around with me over all those rivers, mountains, and oceans. When we get the pressure suits, I'll mount the communicator inside my helmet and leave it operational."

"Good idea," replied the doctor. "I've got to get back to work on this hammock."

"Make it strong, Bones. I'll see how they're doing with the balloon and the hydrogen. Out."

Kirk folded up the communicator, put it in his pocket, and turned to see someone else watching him in addition to the children. Renna was wearing an attractive dress that flowed from her creamy shoulders, over a revealing neckline, and down her slim hips and legs. The brightly flowered pattern made her lustrous black hair look like night over the neon lights of Dohama. He swallowed dryly, wishing there were some way he could take her with him.

"You look lovely," he said with all honesty.

"Thank you," Renna replied with a charming curtsy. "Actually, this dress is all there was left after they took every stitch of clothing available to make your balloon."

"Speaking of which," Kirk said quickly, "I'd like to see how they're doing. Do you know where Spock and Sherfa are?"

"Yes." Renna took his arm. "I'll walk you there."

She felt warm and natural striding beside him, and Kirk found himself pulling her closer, despite his best intentions. He could not imagine any woman in the galaxy more suited to him in daring and determination than this young woman. At the moment, he couldn't imagine any woman more desirable either. But he was about to leave her, perhaps only to die. The nearness of her youthful body made Kirk wonder briefly whether escape was worth the risk of death— but, of course, that was precisely Renna's intention.

"I'm going to miss you, Kirk," she said simply. "But I guess you don't have that same problem with me."

"I'm usually partial to beautiful women who save my life," he joked. Then he grew serious. "But I can't take you with me."

She stepped angrily in front of him and gave his chest a push. "I don't want to go with you," she snapped. "I want you to stay *here,* you damned idiot! I'm trying to save your life again. Let Spock and McCoy go up there, if they want. You have more to live for—you have me."

"That's very tempting," he admitted. *"You're* very tempting. But even if I stayed, you would never have me. What I am is up there, in a ship that's been crippled and close to falling apart more times than I care to think about it. But that's where *I* am, even now."

Renna bowed her head, her dark eyes filling with tears, and Kirk wrapped his arms around her. They held each other in silent desperation for several seconds, until finally she looked up, forcing a smile through her tears.

"You can't leave me," she whispered. "I'm the reason you came down here. I'm Auk-rex."

"I know," Kirk said. "But even if you were the greatest mass murderer in history, Spock has informed me that we couldn't risk your life. And I don't think you're going to plunder many Federation ships with Sanctuary as a base."

"No," she sighed, "I suppose not. But you don't mind if I overthrow those pompous Senites and take over this planet, do you?"

The captain cleared his throat and looked slightly uncomfortable.

"Oh, I forgot," Renna said, smiling, "the Prime Directive. Well, who knows what laws I might break, if left here all by myself? You might have to come back someday and arrest me."

"With pleasure," answered Kirk.

She threw her arms around him and kissed him with an intensity and exuberance that took him by surprise. He had no sooner responded than she pulled away, wiping her eyes.

"I can't watch any of this preparation, or watch you take off," she said hoarsely. "Just keep on this path, and you'll find Sherfa and her crew. Please, don't die, Kirk."

"I won't," he promised with more certainty than he felt. "Good-bye."

Renna turned and walked swiftly away, a youthful

vision in a summer dress and the pirate scourge of the galaxy. For a brief moment, Kirk weakened and nearly ran after her; but then he reminded himself of the things he had told her. God, he hoped he was making the right decision.

The balloon construction crew was working at the blackened launch site, the only clearing in the overgrown crater that was large enough to accommodate giant sheets of clear material stretched end to end.

Kirk stood at the edge of the forest, watching with admiration as Sherfa directed the careful measuring and cutting of large ovoid strips. Spock hovered near her, holding a blueprint and furnishing advice that she passed on to her workers. Farther away, the gangly creature with several arms was measuring lengths of plastic cable for the rigging.

A fragile-looking older man was testing various molecular bonding compounds on the cast-off trimmings. He had just glued two pieces of material together and was trying to see if he could pull them apart, but he couldn't give it much of a test. Suddenly, a great hairy being strode toward him.

"Let me see that," growled Billiwog. "I'll tell you if it'll hold or not."

The giant humanoid grabbed a wad in each hand and pulled for all he was worth. Even grunting and straining, he was unable to loosen the bond.

"Well done!" Billiwog grinned, slapping the worker on the back and nearly knocking him over. "If you made it any stronger, it might carry *me!*"

"Billiwog!" called Kirk. "How are you?"

"Hello there, Captain," the humanoid cried, waving back. He was at Kirk's side in a couple of strides and leaned down to whisper in his ear, "Hey, you aren't really going up in this thing, are you? It's just

250

sort of an experiment to keep these folks busy, right? Make 'em forget what happened this morning."

"Well, it is sort of an experiment," Kirk agreed. "But, yes, we are going up in it. Tomorrow, by the looks of it."

Billiwog shook his furry head. "You're crazy, Kirk. Sanctuary isn't that bad that you've got to kill yourself."

"Killing ourselves is not part of the plan. It's just something we have to do, like you have to build boats."

"Yeah," grumbled Billiwog, looking downcast. "I guess those days are over if I decide to stay here. Not too many oceans around."

"But wait," said Kirk, grinning, "you've got a new ocean—the sky! Watch what they're doing here and learn how to build balloons. You can sail the air currents anywhere you want on this planet."

"Yeah," said the humanoid, his whole hairy face brightening. "I could explore mountains and deserts —go anywhere."

"Talk to McCoy," Kirk suggested. "He knows all about hot-air ballooning, and that's all you'd need. You don't need this high-altitude stuff we're doing."

"Thanks." Billiwog nodded. "I hope you make it, Captain." The giant patted him gently on the back and strode away.

Kirk thought about talking to Spock, but he decided that he should no more interrupt the first officer than he would interrupt Scotty in the middle of an urgent repair. Sherfa glanced at him, then quickly turned back to her busy crew. Never look at the condemned man, Kirk thought ruefully. He hoped she was wrong, but he welcomed the dedication and professionalism she brought to the task, even if her heart wasn't in it. He decided to leave rather than interrupt anyone's work.

The captain stopped someone and asked directions to the ship called the *Mathulsa*, where he knew Belkot was storing the hydrogen. It was a surprisingly small planet-jumper, but Belkot explained to him that its roomy fuel tanks had the most easily adaptable ducts for transferring gases from other vessels and sources. Plus, it was already half-full of hydrogen left over from the fuel for the late lamented *Lujexer*.

"Don't worry," Belkot assured him, "we're only about three hundred cubic meters short of the two thousand we need. The stuff we're getting out of hole number four is not pure, but it should get you up there. We've got mobile tanks we can transfer it to, when the time comes."

"I have every faith in you," said Kirk.

"And I in you," answered the albino, tipping his straw hat to the captain. "Before you came, we didn't have a clue how to get beyond that terrible shield. But now we do. We may never send anyone else up there again, but it's nice to know we can."

Captain Kirk bade Belkot and his crew good-bye and left them to their work. There was really nothing for him to do, which was beginning to make him nervous. Once they were launched, there wouldn't be anything at all for him to do, except hang under a balloon filled with highly combustible gas and try to contact the *Enterprise*. This balloon flight was beginning to remind him of tales he had read about the first manned spaceflights on Earth, when the astronauts and cosmonauts were little more than laboratory animals strapped inside giant Roman candles.

Kirk took a long walk through the Graveyard, and more than once he thought about Renna. He wandered among the rusting hulks of spaceships that would never fly again and thought about his life.

It grew dark in the Graveyard before Kirk resolved his doubts in his mind. He took some solace from thinking about those early astronauts and cosmonauts, not to mention pioneering aviators and sailors who'd journeyed blithely into the unknown with much less going for them technologically than he had. Plus, he had his companions, Spock and McCoy— and Scotty, Sulu, Chekov, Uhura, and the rest of the crew. Kirk stood in the center of the serene crater, gazing up at the night sky, with only a few dim lights to disturb his view of the stars. Somehow he knew they were still up there. He was betting his life on it.

Later, as he headed in what he hoped was the direction of the shuttlecraft, Kirk heard uproarious laughter, followed by off-key singing. His pace quickened, and he arrived at the *Ericksen* to find a party going full blast, with well-wishers spilling into the surrounding paths.

"Jim!" McCoy called to him jovially. "We were about to send out a search party for ya!"

"Hey, Captain!" Billiwog waved. "Come and drink some of this rocket fuel. You won't get nothin' but cold gas tomorrow!"

Before Kirk could step into their midst, he was accosted by Errico, who held a lightweight blue pressure suit in front of him. "That should fit well," said the Andorian, "and we can adjust the pressure for a human. I'm sorry to trouble you, Captain; enjoy your party."

"Thanks, Errico," Kirk replied. "Is it always like this before a launch?"

"Always," answered the dour blue-skinned being, as if the purpose of such festivities eluded him.

McCoy came over to Kirk and handed him a geode cup, this one filled with sparkling yellow gems that made the ale look like molten gold. Kirk stared into the cup for an instant, thinking how beautiful life was, then looked up to see a smiling but very emotional Dr. McCoy.

"What do you think, Jim?" he asked, grinning. "Are they up there?"

The captain nodded. "I think so. But I want you to understand, Bones, that this escape attempt is strictly voluntary. I won't mind at all if you show some good sense and choose to stay here."

"And miss the greatest balloon ride of my life?" scoffed McCoy. "You know, it's possible that we could survive this flight tomorrow even if there's no *Enterprise*. God knows where we would end up."

"I would say survival is possible," offered a third voice, "but not probable." Spock joined Kirk and McCoy and made a slight gesture with a glass goblet that contained water. "If we drift far, the chances are excellent that we will come down in the ocean, where we would likely be consumed by aquatic creatures."

"That's just like you, Spock," grumbled McCoy, "always looking on the bright side."

"I am merely stating the fact that we will have absolutely no control over this craft," responded Spock. "If we are not transported off by the *Enterprise* —or someone else—we will drift for several days without food or water, then probably come down in the ocean. On this planet, our probability of landing in the ocean is perhaps twenty-five to one."

McCoy snapped his fingers. "I think I've figured out what our ballast is going to be."

"What's that?" asked Kirk.

"Food and water! If, just if, we come down on land, we might need the food and water. Let me go talk to Belkot and line up some packaged food, roast loins, jugs of water, anything that's heavy."

The doctor scurried away, and Kirk said to his first officer, "I told Bones, and I'm telling you—this attempt is voluntary. If you would rather stay here, we'll do what we can to rescue you at a later date."

"Thank you, Captain," Spock said, "but I have little

doubt of our ability to reach the proper altitude. Therefore, the risk lies entirely in whether the *Enterprise* is still within transporter range. As you said, I suppose it is an act of faith, but I place faith in my shipmates every day. Is it illogical for me to do so now?"

"No, not at all." Kirk smiled and lifted his glass. "To your health."

Spock did the same. "Live long and prosper."

Chapter Seventeen

THE PARTY BROKE UP EARLY, even before the second
moon had appeared over the twisted spires of Sanctuary. Captain Kirk didn't deliver a speech, because
what could he say to a community he had known for
only a few hours? These were strangers, but strangers
committed to the same goal—recapturing the technology that was their heritage. There was no other
explanation for the fervor they threw themselves into
the next morning. Sherfa was everywhere, pulling
everything together, from mounting McCoy's net to
the rigging to driving pylons into the ground to secure
the balloon, which would soon be straining at its
leashes.

To check for leaks and to test the pumping and duct
systems, Spock asked Belkot to inflate the balloon to
its maximum pressure. They used ninety percent
forced air and ten percent hydrogen to give it a bit of
buoyancy. The balloon topped out at a bit over
twenty-four hundred cubic meters and showed no

signs of leaks in its molecular bonds. Barely bobbing off the ground, the transparent balloon looked like a giant soap bubble trapped in spiderwebs. The rigging seemed haphazard to Kirk, but the ropes had been laid in crisscross patterns on purpose. There would be two giant nets—one around the balloon and another one around the balloonists. Between them would stretch sixty meters of the toughest tripolymer rope that could be scrounged in the Graveyard.

Kirk stood at the edge of the launchpad, trying to recall Belkot's diagram, but he couldn't imagine the contraption stretched to its entire length.

"Did you ever read *The Wizard of Oz?*" asked McCoy, standing beside him.

"No," answered Kirk, "but I saw the visual. Is this going to be more like the wizard taking off at the end, or the tornado picking up the house?"

"At first, maybe a little like the tornado," said the doctor. "Then there won't be any sensation at all. Just like you were lying in a hammock."

"Well, don't let me go to sleep," Kirk joked. "I've got to contact the *Enterprise.*"

"I'd better go finish my job," said McCoy. "I've got Errico and Billiwog scavenging for food. Heavy food —no crepes suzette on this trip. We'll just hope we don't land on some godforsaken island and need it."

"Billiwog should be able to root out the food," the captain agreed.

After Dr. McCoy left, Kirk once again felt superfluous. But, he reminded himself, he was the captain of this strange vessel as well as of the *Enterprise*. He had given the order that had started all this frenzied activity, and now, as usual, it was up to him to stand back and let others do their jobs. There was nothing he had to learn, no skills he had to master in order to pilot this craft. They would be slaves of the wind.

Kirk had one task to accomplish. He took his

communicator, opened it so that it lay flat, and affixed it with bonding material to the inside of his high-impact helmet, the one that came with the pressure suit scrounged by Errico. Then he tried on the helmet to make sure it fit properly, and was relieved to find that the device was completely unnoticeable. Kirk set the communicator to voice activation, so that all he had to do before they took off was turn it on. Responses were likely to be quite loud, but he wouldn't mind hearing Uhura's voice loud and clear.

Spock approached him to say, "I am adjusting the air bladders in our suits to better protect our internal organs. I believe we should have a fitting in about an hour. We launch in late afternoon, an hour before sunset, when the air currents are the most stable."

Kirk nodded. "Will everything be ready?"

"'Ready' is a relative word," answered the Vulcan. "It is difficult to say when an experimental craft that has never flown before is ready."

"I guess the answer is, we're going anyway."

"Exactly." Spock nodded. "I will bring the pressure suits here when they are ready for fitting."

"I'll be here," said Kirk.

The captain remained at the launch site throughout the day, a conspicuous presence on the periphery, available for brief discussions and to offer opinions, but mostly watching. The tensest moment of the day occurred when the real hydrogen mixture was pumped into the balloon. First, ropes were thrown around a large hoop that secured the passenger net to the rigging, and then the ropes were tied to impressive steel pylons. These moorings had to last until lift-off, and Sherfa made sure they were done correctly. Then the balloon itself was lashed to the ground by moorings that would be released as soon as it was partially filled. Sherfa made certain those ropes were both driven into the ground and gripped by two or more volunteers, because they would be the first to feel the strain.

To avoid having a spark set off the hydrogen, the mobile gas pump and fuel tanks were stationed as far away as the length of hose would allow. In a short time, the balloon began to blossom with hydrogen, straining at its bindings. Kirk came closer, certain that another hand would be needed somewhere. Suddenly, one of the ropes slipped off its pylon and dragged two volunteers along the ground, as the amorphous half-filled balloon tried to ooze like a jellyfish out the opening it created. Kirk dove for the rope as it slithered by and wrapped it around his waist, digging in his heels. This held the line for the seconds needed for more workers to pile on and capture it. They unwrapped Kirk and lashed the rope to a pylon, while the balloon reluctantly resumed a globular shape.

The next tense moment came when they let the balloon go, after filling it with eighteen hundred cubic meters of hydrogen. The only thing they needed on the ground was the passenger net, so there was no reason not to let the balloon fly semifree. Despite its undulating, bloblike appearance, the balloon shot into the clouds like a ballistic missile as soon as the ropes were released. Now it was up to the second set of moorings to do their job. Some of them started to slip, but each rope had half a dozen volunteers hanging on it and a crew to repair the damage. There were no errant ropes this time.

Slowly, as the magnificent balloon unfurled sixty meters in the air, a cheer went up from the collected throng. It was echoed in the forest and on every front porch in the Graveyard, as all eyes watched the sphere and its thin rigging sticking straight up in the air. It looked more like some fantastic tower than a lighter-than-air craft. A lump caught in Kirk's throat as he looked at the magnificent sight. In all his years of flying, he had never thought he would fly in a conveyance that was so primitive yet so fanciful. The amount of work it represented was staggering, even if the physics involved had been well known for eight hundred years.

The rest of the afternoon passed almost in a daze. They tried on the pressure suits and swelled them up to their full pressure, which offered maximum protection for internal organs as well as ample breathing air. Kirk's fit so well that he took off the helmet and deflated the suit, but kept wearing it.

Under McCoy's watchful eye, they loaded the netting with two cases of suspect packaged food, a large frozen chunk of edible herbivore, three sacks of beans, and several nonmetallic jugs of water. The netting dragged on the ground, but the weight didn't seem to affect the balloon at all. The sinking sun was touching the rim of the crater, and the familiar long shadows sprawled across the Graveyard.

It was time, thought Kirk, and everyone else seemed to sense it at the same moment. People stopped what they were doing, which was mainly nervous pacing, and stared at the three newcomers. They hadn't spent very much time in this community, but they had fit in and been made welcome. And they were getting a royal send-off.

Among the crowd, Kirk saw Sherfa and, standing beside her, Renna. Both were trying to smile. He saw Billiwog manning one of the ropes, and Errico and Belkot on another; they were grinning, even the Andorian. Kirk looked at his comrades, Spock and McCoy, and a silent order went out: Inflate your pressure suits—we're going.

Kirk reached into his helmet and powered on the communicator. Before he put it on, he turned to

260

Sherfa and shouted, "Watch the sky! I'll give you a signal."

The old woman waved back, and the young, dark-haired woman gave him a mock salute. That was one prisoner he might come back for, thought Kirk, as he pulled the helmet over his head. Eager helpers adjusted their pressure suits until the oxygen was flowing and they were as safe as if they were in their mothers' arms.

McCoy went first into the large net and settled himself on the frozen carcass. Spock took a seat on the packaged goods, and Kirk sat on the sacks of beans. They were shoulder to shoulder in the constrictive net, but their pressure suits maintained a little cocoon around each of them, so it didn't seem so constrictive. Because the suits had been scrounged from different crafts and races, there was no way for them to communicate, except to look each other in the eyes. Since their heads nearly abutted, that wasn't difficult.

Belkot and some of the others checked the netting and as much of the rigging as they could reach. It all appeared secure—almost too secure, thought Kirk with a gulp, as there was no way to separate them from the balloon. They were sure as hell going wherever it went. He looked into McCoy's eyes and saw excitement blended uneasily with stark fear; in contrast, Spock looked like he was about to take a nap.

Kirk lifted his hand in a definitive wave. At once, a prerehearsed ritual began, as the teams began to untie their respective lines. On each rope, a handful of volunteers tensed their bodies to catch the pull of 1,800 cubic meters of hydrogen. By watching each other and working in unison, the crews were able to fling their lines into the wind at the same time. Then, like puppets being yanked offstage by the puppeteer, Kirk, Spock, and McCoy were hoisted into the air.

They felt a collective wrenching in their stomachs as they became airborne, but the pressure suits quickly compensated until the only feeling was a mild light-headedness. Kirk looked over the edge of the net to see the ground swirling away beneath him, and he quickly screwed his eyes shut.

The strangest sensation was no sensation. To know that he was traveling upward through free air at a speed of hundreds of kilometers an hour, yet feeling nothing, gave Kirk a dreamlike sensation, as if this weren't really happening. The balloon overhead was almost invisible, and the thick strand of connecting lines seemed to stretch into infinity, like Jack's bean-stalk. His only contact with reality was looking down, but that made him dizzy. Still, Kirk forced himself to look down to try to get some sort of bearing. He also saw McCoy desperately looking around.

Then they passed through a bank of clouds that obliterated their vision entirely. For an unknown distance, they inhabited a world of gray smoke in which they couldn't see their own hands in front of their helmets. This was the dreamiest part of the trip, and Kirk had to remind himself that he was awake and traveling unabated into the thin air of Sanctuary's stratosphere.

Finally, they broke from the high cloud bank, and Kirk could see Spock leaning down and studying the clouds intently. He soon figured out that the Vulcan was trying to gauge their speed, knowing that the slower they were going, the closer they were getting to their destination, as the hydrogen and the thin air equalized in density. Kirk looked up at the balloon and noticed that it had lost much of its flabbiness and had filled out into a respectable globe. They were still going up—that much was evident—which meant that they weren't at thirty-five kilometers yet.

Spock reached into the cartons he was sitting upon

and began to toss packaged goods over the top of the netting. The boxes plummeted like tiny bombs, piercing the clouds and disappearing. The Vulcan wasn't concerned about the boxes doing any damage, since the odds of them landing in wilderness or ocean on this planet were overwhelming. When McCoy started to get off his slab of meat, Spock motioned him to remain seated. For the time being, sacrificing the boxes would suffice to give them a little more speed.

A couple hundred kilometers overhead, on the bridge of the *Enterprise,* a voice sounded loudly over the intercom: "Photo imaging to Commander Scott."

"Scott here," answered the acting captain. "Have you got something?"

"Yes, sir," came the voice. "You know that crater you asked us to monitor? Long-range telephoto lenses reveal what looks like a balloon rising rapidly over that area."

"A balloon?" asked Scotty. "You mean, another weather balloon?"

"Oh, bigger than that," came the reply. "Big enough to be a manned flight, and a high-altitude one at that."

"It's still out of sensor range," responded Sulu, "but I can take us directly over the crater."

"Yes," said Scotty, "get us close." There was a momentary drone as the impulse engines worked to adjust their orbit.

"Thank you, Ensign," Scotty told the imaging technician, "keep us posted."

"Yes, sir."

Chekov bolted upright in his seat and announced, "Sir, both the *Gezary* and the Orion ship are changing course to match ours. They are approaching at full impulse."

Scotty peered at the viewscreen, where two tiny blips were swiftly converging upon them. Those blips would be warships in a matter of moments. "Yellow alert," said Scotty. "Do not take your eyes off 'em, Ensign."

"Yes, sir," answered Chekov.

The bounty hunters came to a stop a respectable distance from the *Enterprise,* although less than fifty kilometers away. The *Gezary* was a sleek vessel with three nacelles in close proximity, like a trimaran sailing ship. The Orion ship was bulky, greenish-brown, and pitted with odd designs; it reminded Scotty of a World War II hand grenade he had once seen in a museum. That they were working in tandem was painfully obvious.

"Shields up," said Scotty.

"Yes, sir," Chekov answered with obvious agreement.

"Hail the *Gezary,*" said the Scotsman, striding to the captain's seat. "Make it voice only, because I want to keep their ships on the screen."

A few seconds later, Uhura responded, "Captain Pilenna on audio."

Scotty flicked a switch on the arm of his chair and said sternly, "Captain Pilenna, this is Commander Scott. I have reason to believe that our people are trying to make an escape from the planet in a balloon. I ask you and the Orion ship to withdraw, so that we may rescue them."

"Darling," responded a husky voice, "that's not how we operate around here. You have no proof it's your people on that balloon. You can't just tell us to go away and forfeit whatever bounty there might be. Something is floating our way, and nobody knows what it is."

"I warn you," said Scotty, "our friendship willna last if you hamper our rescue operations."

The voice that responded was suddenly cold and

unfriendly. "You wouldn't join forces with me. I owe you nothing." There was an audible pop.

"They've broken off contact," said Uhura.

Scotty muttered, "They've broken off more than that." He flicked the switch again and declared, "Transporter room, stand by."

Captain Kirk strained to lift the frozen loin over his head, unable to get a good footing in the spidery net. Spock finally reached up a hand and helped him hoist it over. The chunk of meat hurtled into the clouds beneath them, and Kirk could imagine McCoy making some kind of wisecrack. He glanced over at the doctor, who was grinning like a damn fool. He was actually enjoying this flight.

Kirk had no sensation at all of where they were, or at what altitude. He knew there would be no sirens or bells when they passed through the Senite shield— they wanted to be treated like just another ball of gas—but Spock was concerned enough about their slowing speed to start tossing out the ballast. From what little he could see, the balloon looked puffed to capacity, so Kirk had to assume they were getting close.

"Kirk to *Enterprise!*" he said into the hollowness of his helmet, knowing the communicator would activate automatically. "Kirk to *Enterprise*. Kirk to *Enterprise*. Kirk to *Enterprise.*" It became a chant that he never stopped for an instant as they rose into the stratosphere.

Uhura nearly jumped out of her seat, and she shrieked, "It's the captain!" She quickly recovered enough to say, *"Enterprise* here! I read you, sir! We'll beam you up."

"Gezary firing phasers!" Chekov proclaimed as the

viewscreen erupted in waves of energy beams that engulfed the *Enterprise* and jarred the bridge, knocking people off their feet.

Uhura shouted to be heard: "Transmitting coordinates to transporter room! Stand by. Commander Scott, they're on that balloon, but we have to beam them off."

"Orion ship firing disrupters!" announced Chekov. *"Gezary* firing phasers!"

Scotty gripped the arms of the captain's chair as the ship was rocked again and again, but he managed to punch his communicator switch and call out, "Transporter room! Have ye got those coordinates?"

"Yes, sir, we're locked on. We're waiting for you to lower the shields."

The pummeling from the two ships off the bow continued unabated, and the *Enterprise* rocked like a punch-drunk fighter.

"Shields at forty percent," called Sulu, "but holding. We can't drop them now!"

"We've got to!" growled Scotty. "They're only doing this to make us keep our shields up." As the ship rocked again, he sprawled across his chair and hit the communicator switch. "Transporter room, don't wait for my command. When I drop the shields, energize!"

"Acknowledged!" barked the voice, as the ship rattled and sparks burst from the science station.

"They're firing toward the planet!" shouted Sulu.

"That does it," snarled Scotty. "Chekov, give 'em a brace of torpedoes. Scatter pattern."

"Yes, sir!" declared the Russian with a grin. He let the computer launch seven photon torpedoes, but picked the last setting himself.

The scatter pattern was intended to blind and disorient the enemy, and the Enterprise crew watched as a chain of explosions sizzled across the bows of the

266

attacking ships. Chekov's missile, slipping in behind the others, struck the *Gezary* full-on in the engine compartment. The ship sputtered greenish flames from its wound and began to slip out of orbit toward the planet. The Orion vessel continued to fire.

The balloonists were blissfully ignorant of the battle taking place over their heads, until a phaser beam from the Orion ship struck their balloon. At once, Kirk's excitement turned to utter terror. The hydrogen explosion was like a supernova, turning the sky above into a flaming ball. Fingers of fire raced toward them across the thin air and would have consumed them, but they were already falling faster than the flames could travel.

Kirk tumbled as if he were weightless, in total free-fall. He saw two bodies spinning on either side of him, one of them wrapped in the shredded hammock. All that was left of their magnificent balloon was a glowing ember that floated far overhead like an iridescent butterfly. It had happened so quickly that it took him another moment to realize that if they dropped beneath the Senites' shield, they would just keep on dropping.

Kirk screamed, "Uhura! We're falling! *Beam us up!*"

"They're falling!" gasped Uhura.

Mr. Scott gulped but stuck calmly to the only chain of events that would work. "Lock phasers onto that Orion," he ordered.

"Phasers ready," called Chekov.

"Drop shields," said Scotty. "Fire phasers!"

Two blinding beams of phaser fire swarmed across the bow of the Orion vessel, lighting it like an incandescent bulb. The bow swelled with bluish light and exploded like a blood vessel. The rest of the ship glowed white-hot for a moment before it sputtered and cooled to a dead khaki color.

Lieutenant Kyle watched as three figures in alien pressure suits materialized in the transporter chamber. All of them floundered on the platform for a moment before they realized where they were. Then Kirk and McCoy leaped to their feet, tore off their helmets, and screamed with joy at their deliverance.

Spock strode to Kyle at the transporter controls and requested calmly, "Would you please inform the bridge that the landing party has returned."

"Yes, sir!" said Kyle, grinning broadly. "Transporter room to bridge—the landing party has returned!"

There was quiet jubilation on the bridge, but Scotty was busy trying to ascertain how much fight was left in his adversaries. After a few seconds, some lights appeared to sputter on in the Orion ship.

"The Orion captain wishes to break off hostilities," Uhura reported. "He says it was a misunderstanding."

"Not on *my* part," muttered Scotty. "But the captain, Dr. McCoy, and Mr. Spock are safe, and that's all that matters. Therefore, I'm in a forgivin' mood. Tell the Orion he can withdraw. But put our shields back up."

Seconds later, Uhura reported, "Captain Pilenna of the *Gezary* wishes to speak with you. On screen."

Scotty stiffened to attention and nodded. "On screen it is."

The voluptuous redhead appeared on the viewscreen with most of her beauty intact, but little of her confidence. Behind her, her normally reserved crew rushed around frantically.

"Commander Scott," she said, "I beseech you! Our

orbit is decaying, and we are headed toward the planet. We haven't got any engine power at all. Will you beam us aboard your ship?"

"It's not my ship anymore," Scotty replied coolly. "We have our captain back. I believe your ship will survive entry into the atmosphere, and the Senites will no doubt transport you off before there is any danger. Therefore, all I can say is, good luck on Sanctuary."

"You can't do that to us!" Pilenna shrieked. "What if they find out who we are? Listen, we only wanted to give you a little competition for whoever was in that balloon. We didn't know it was your captain! Won't you please save us from going down there?"

For a moment, Scotty almost relented. He was considering whether to beam them aboard when the image of the green-skinned woman suddenly grew faint.

"Transmission breaking up," said Uhura.

Pilenna's plaintive face and figure were rasterized into a million pieces, and her voice became low and unintelligible. Before the intent eyes of Scotty, Uhura, Chekov, and Sulu, the bounty huntress and her crew vanished from the bridge of the decaying vessel, just before it vanished from the *Enterprise*'s screen.

"The Senites got them," said Sulu with finality.

Scotty smiled wistfully. "Aye, and they got a handful."

The turbolift door opened and three familiar—if bearded—figures strode onto the bridge. They just stood staring around at the bridge crew for a moment, their broad grins doing all of the talking.

"Welcome back, Captain!" Scotty finally sputtered.

Kirk said, "Mr. Scott, I'm glad you're still here."

"Well," stammered Scotty, "Starfleet did request our presence elsewhere, but their orders were, uh, very confusing."

"Wery confusing," confirmed Chekov, grinning.

"We know the sidewalk cafés are nice," put in Uhura, "but what else do they have down there? What's it like?"

"Fascinating," answered Spock. "The marine life is quite diverse, and the giant mollusks are especially interesting."

McCoy remarked, "The Senites have some quaint customs, too."

"Quiet," said Kirk, waving everyone to silence and heading to the captain's chair. "Over a long dinner, we'll tell you all about it. Right now, Uhura, I want you to contact a Senite named Zicree on the planet."

"Captain," she replied, "we haven't had much luck communicating with the Senites."

"Tell him it's me. He—it—should respond."

They waited expectantly for Uhura to relay the request. Finally, she looked up from her console, clearly impressed, and reported, "Zicree will speak with you, Captain."

"He'd better," said Kirk grimly.

The slim Senite appeared on the screen, no longer looking ageless and aloof, but shaken and tired. "Captain Kirk," he began, "I wish to protest this breach of our security system, as well as the blatant discharge of weapons in our—"

"Shut up," snapped Kirk, "and listen to me. Our laws forbid me from coming down there and teaching you a lesson, but the other residents of Sanctuary may not feel any such restraint, now that they know what you do with fugitives."

"Captain," Zicree implored, "I plead for your understanding. We Senites have no other way to reproduce ourselves except for the Reborning. We take only the riffraff from Dohama, and they are better off—"

"Have you asked them that?" interrupted Kirk. "Maybe some of them would agree to the Reborning if you asked them. As it is now, it's nothing but forced torture and mutilation. There's not a damn thing I can do about it directly, but I can crank up the Universal Translator and make sure that every space-traveling culture in this sector knows what you're doing down there."

"Please, Captain," protested the Senite, "we are proud of our reputation as the last refuge of the persecuted."

Kirk vowed, "You'll have a new reputation when I'm done. You've got several thriving communities down there, yet you choose to treat most of the fugitives like animals or children. Or worse, as fodder for your torture mill. The secret is out, Zicree. Nobody will wander unsuspectingly into Dohama again."

The Senite sighed and slumped perceptibly in its chair. After a moment, it said slowly, "What you say is true. There is much resistance in our ranks, but we will have to change. Your escape and knowledge of the Reborning means that we will have to change—even if it could mean the death of our species."

"You are not a species," Kirk argued. "You are *hundreds* of species, most of which have been cosmetically altered. That's what Sanctuary is—hundreds of species, working together to build a new life. If you would just look around, you would see that you have something marvelous there, a fantastic opportunity."

"Yes." Zicree nodded. "I understand. I will try to convince the others. I may even succeed."

"Try," Kirk urged.

"Good-bye, Captain Kirk," Zicree said with a faint smile. "Your visit has been most illuminating."

The Senite's image faded away, leaving the captain to stare at the sparkling curve of the aquamarine planet and wonder how much impact they had really had. Would Starfleet ever be able to come back here and pay a normal visit to Khyming, Dohama, or the Graveyard of Lost Ships? Or would Sanctuary shrink deeper into isolationism?

The captain stood and stretched his arms. "Where are you supposed to take us, Scotty?" he asked, yawning.

"Starbase 64," answered the engineer. "But if ye don't mind, sir, I'd like to check on the engine room. Beaming you aboard was not quite as easy as it may have seemed."

"I can take the bridge, Captain," Spock offered. "I feel strangely exhilarated. I found the balloon ride fascinating, and look forward to repeating the experience at a later date."

"You do that," said the captain, starting for the turbolift. "I'm going to take a nap."

"Just a second," put in McCoy. "You're going to get a physical first. You lost a bet to me."

"What?" bellowed Kirk. "What bet?"

The doctor smiled smugly. "If you didn't capture Auk-rex, you said you would let me give you a physical. I don't see her here."

"Wait a minute," Kirk protested. "You've just seen me rowing, climbing, hiking, swimming, and fighting for two weeks straight, and you don't know if I'm in shape or not?"

"You look a little haggard," McCoy said sympathetically. "Besides, I need to check all of us for strange bugs we might've picked up down there. Might as well start with you."

"All right." Kirk sighed. He paused at the turbolift and turned back. "One moment. Ensign Chekov, I would like you to shoot a photon torpedo in the direction we came from, but ignite it thirty-five kilometers over the surface."

"Captain?" queried the helmsman. "Torpedo ready, but may I ask why?"

"Something some of the people down there will see," said Kirk, "and understand. Fire when ready."

"Torpedo away," said the confused helmsman.

To Captain Kirk, the exploding torpedo looked like the merest blip over the endless horizon of Sanctuary. But he knew that in the Graveyard of Lost Ships, it was a shooting star in the night sky, a perfect omen for making wishes come true.

STAR TREK®

DEATH COUNT

by L.A. Graf

The disappearance of Andorian scientific genius Muav Haslev fuels tensions between the Orions and Andorians - tensions that come dangerously close to full scale war. Captain Kirk and the crew of the U.S.S. *Enterprise* are called to Starbase Sigma 1, located on the edge of Andorian-Orion space, to patrol the sector as a deterrent to hostilities.

On arrival, the crew encounters an inexplicable series of events, beginning with missing equipment and shipboard malfunctions. After a deadly transporter accident, Kirk suspects sabotage - suspicions that are confirmed by the mysterious murders of three Federation officials. Now, Kirk and crew must put together the fragmented pieces of the puzzle, before the Starship *Enterprise* faces destruction and the galaxy faces interplanetary war.

WAR DRUMS

The planet Selva - a lush colony world settled by a hardy group of humans, who found the planet already inhabited by a small gang of young Klingons. When violence erupts between the two groups, Captain Picard and the U.S.S. *Enterprise* are sent to render assistance.

Worf leads a landing party to the planet while the Starship *Enterprise* is called away on another urgent mission. On Selva, Worf and his party find that the old hatreds and prejudices between humans and Klingons are revived, and the settlers are out for blood. Now, Worf must prevent a horrible massacre, before all of them fall prey to Selva's deadly secret ...and raging fury.

Also available by John Vornholt from Titan Books

MASKS

The *Enterprise* journeys to Lorca, a beautiful world where the inhabitants wear masks to show their rank and station. There, Captain Picard and an away team begin a quest for the planet's ruler and the great Wisdom Mask that their leader traditionally wears. Their mission: establish diplomatic relations.

But Picard and his party lose contact with the ship, and Commander Riker leads a search party down to the planet to find them.

Both men are unaware that their searches are part of a madman's plan. A madman who is setting a trap that will ensnare both landing parties, and leave him poised to seize control of the awesome Wisdom Mask.

And the planet Lorca itself.

For a complete list of Star Trek publications, T-shirts and badges please send a large SAE to Titan Books Mail Order, 19 Valentine Place, London, SE1 8QH. Please quote reference ST56.